RESCUE
MISSIONS

W. W. Norton & Company   New York • London

R E S C U E
M I S S I O N S

STORIES

Frederick Busch

Copyright © 2006 by the Estate of Frederick Busch

All rights reserved
Printed in the United States of America
First Edition

For information about permission to reproduce selections from this book,
write to Permissions, W. W. Norton & Company, Inc.
500 Fifth Avenue, New York, NY 10110

Manufacturing by The Haddon Craftsmen, Inc.
Book design by Chris Welch
Production manager: Anna Oler

Library of Congress Cataloging-in-Publication Data

Busch, Frederick, 1941–2006.
Rescue missions : stories / Frederick Busch.—1st ed.
p. cm.
ISBN-13: 978-0-393-06252-6
ISBN-10: 0-393-06252-X
1. Domestic fiction, American. I. Title.
PS3552.U814R47   2006
813'.54—dc22

2006013011

W. W. Norton & Company, Inc.
500 Fifth Avenue, New York, N.Y. 10110
www.wwnorton.com

W. W. Norton & Company Ltd.
Castle House, 75/76 Wells Street, London W1T 3QT

2 3 4 5 6 7 8 9 0

FOR JUDY

The author is grateful to the editors of these magazines in which the following stories appeared, sometimes in altered form: *Boulevard* ("Now That It's Spring"); *Daedalus* ("The Rescue Mission"); *Five Points* ("Manhattans" and "Patrols"); *The Georgia Review* ("One Last Time for Old Times' Sake" and "Metal Fatigue"); *Harper's* ("The Hay Behind the House"); *Idaho Review* ("Something Along Those Lines"); *Ploughshares* ("The Bottom of the Glass"); *The Threepenny Review* ("Good to Go"); *Tin House* ("I Am the News," originally published as "The Boys"); *Zoetrope: All-Story* ("Frost Line").

"Manhattans" was republished in *The Pushcart Prize XXX: Best of the Small Presses, 2006 Edition.*

CONTENTS

THE RESCUE MISSION

I worked hard, that year, at jobs that repaid me only in wages. I received no pleasure from what I did, and no one praised or honored me. But no one struck me, either, and I was forced to wake up in the early afternoon, to shave and bathe, to put on laundered clothing, and to leave the Polk Street apartment for what, in Syracuse, New York, could be called the world at large.

On the job at this time, I lined my desk with small clay figures I pinched and prodded from a moist, gray ball I carried in a plastic bag in my backpack, along with my sketchbook and pencils. I made misshapen dogs, deformed beasts of the barnyard, and creatures inspired by movies about outer-space wars. The desk was in the stubby trailer maintained by the Rescue Mission, and the trailer was in the giant parking lot of a supermarket famous for the quality and cost of its meat and produce. Very good cars circled the trailer in which I sat to mind the goods left off by high-class shoppers with a conscience, or those afflicted with slightly flawed microwave ovens, or good clothing into which they could no longer slide with ease. Whatever they dropped off, whether wearable, repairable, or edible and tinned, the Mission accepted. I spent my shift in fixing what I could, and people who really knew household machines worked on the rest; the Mission gave the food away and sold the appliances in its store downtown in the medical district. This was a gloomy neighborhood of low, boxy office buildings and wet, broad streets, with a psychiatric hospital, a medical center, and the office of the county medical examiner where people went to identify their dead. The Mission used its income to buy food for the homeless and for families in need. Can you name a family that is not in need?

I accepted the generosities of shoppers on their way from work, I wrote out the receipt and handed over the list of suggested tax credits they might claim. I smoked a lot of Lucky Strikes and tried to convince myself to read about Hans Hofmann in New York, I had just left New York, and I kept wishing I was there. As for Hofmann, I didn't want to read about him. I wanted to be him, or any artist that purposeful. So I smoked, I sketched, I made clay figures. I fought the tightness in my stomach which wasn't hunger—I never ate much during that time in Syracuse—and I tried to convince myself that I would emerge—from this gray, cold, sorry city in its necklace of bright suburbs—with a postgraduate degree in fine arts and a future consisting of work I liked among people who thought me excellent. The graduate courses met mostly in the late afternoon or early evening. I worked my jobs to afford the tuition I wasted by coming to work instead of to class. But, then, can you name an art student who is not in need?

Early in February, after the January thaw had hardened into mud-colored ruts of ice, when it was not only cold but always damp, so your elbows clicked and your fingers worked without precision, during what you might think of as the dinner hour, a maroon-haired girl opened the door and climbed the rough wooden steps built clumsily from unmilled spruce planks to tell me, "Knock knock."

Now, what I detested most in life could be summed up as people who stand in your doorway and say, "Knock knock." So I stared, in no friendly way, and said nothing she could mistake for a welcome.

Her hair was ear-length and its very bright maroon, at the top of her head, seemed to go golden and then into a trace of blondish bright green. She stood in the doorway under her shiny head that was everything Titian knew never to be about, and she looked like a fugitive. Her jeans appeared damp, even soggy, and her tan lace-up boots were dark with moisture.

I said, "You intend to donate your hair to someone in need?"

She wore a shade of lipstick that represented an effort to match her hair. It failed. She was very pale, and the color of her hair made her skin look muddy.

"Do you think I could warm in here a few minutes?" she asked me. We had electric baseboard heaters, and I kept the thermostat high. She clasped her hands in front of her and shivered. Sleet and granules of hail, in epaulets, lay along the shoulders of her jacket. When I was a kid, they were called Eisenhower jackets, and I recalled them as made of unlined wool. Bad girls in my high school wore their boyfriends'. Now, I supposed, hers was a fashion statement. She didn't look terribly Commander in Chief to me, so I nodded. She nodded back, and she took two steps in and squatted near an electric can opener that made the can-opening noises but didn't take the top off anything: the can hung in place and shook, not unlike the maroon-haired girl.

The way she crouched there annoyed me, and I said, "Come here, for Christ's sake."

"Where?"

"In this chair."

"Are you getting out of it?"

"You do not have to sit on my lap to get warm. Correct."

She nodded again, I nodded again, I shifted from the chair, she passed carefully in front of me, and then she sat down with her arms across her chest while I took a Phillips-head screwdriver from the metal shelf near the door and began to work on the can opener that, so far, was useful only as a paperweight.

She was very small, with short, stubby fingers and almost-chubby hands. She looked, at first, like a child. With that hair, she could have passed as a child's doll. But her face was lined as well as dirty, I saw, and her eyes were hazel-colored and quite grown up.

She coughed and wiped at her nose. Then she clasped her hands on the desk and seemed to study the animals I'd left there.

"You make these?"

I said, "It's like doodling. It kills the time."

"Boring, huh?"

I said, "It's a job."

"I get jobs," she said.

"Good."

"Then I lose them. I have this way of messing things up." Her voice was rich, and coarsened by cigarettes, I thought.

"We must be from the same family." I looked up, prepared to smile, but she kept looking at the animals.

"I don't think so," she said.

"No, it was just a kind of joke."

"My boyfriend says I never get the joke, so the joke's on me." She looked at the figures and said, finally, "These are weird animals.

But you being a guy and all, I'd have expected you to have them locked in mortal combat."

"Mortal combat," I said. "No, I hate that stuff." I asked her, "Who hits you?"

"What am I," she said, "some kind of a waif? And you're the whatever—the rescuer guy? The protector? I'm begging you for a little *warmth* in here is all."

"You're getting it," I said. "You got it. Forget I asked."

"Yeah. 'Who hits you?' And then forget it." She lit one of my cigarettes and coughed as the unfiltered smoke hit her lungs.

"Help yourself," I said. "And nobody hits you."

"What—it shows?"

"Just the little yellow thing along your jaw. Next color is brown. Then greeny blue. Then your basic black and blue. The makeup never works. Anyway, you're too light-skinned to wear enough of it to do a very good job. I could try for you. Have you got your stuff?"

"What, are you, like, gay? You do makeup with your friends?"

"Right," I said, "I'm gay."

"No, you're not. I could tell."

"Okay," I said, "I'm not."

"I know you're not."

"That's right."

"So how do you know about putting makeup on girls?"

"My mother was kind of a girl when I knew her."

"What?"

"She was young, that's all. What's your name?"

"What would you guess?" she said, moving the clay figures about as if she were a child at play. Her expression wasn't playful, though, and I wondered if when she dreamed or, say, chased a bus on Erie Boulevard, she forgot enough of her life to look less wary.

"With hair like that," I said, "it's a definite Monique. Possibly a Lauren."

"Lauren Hutton," she said. "With that gap tooth? My boyfriend's horny for Lauren Hutton."

"Is he the guy who hammers you?"

"But it's Jill. Dumb, huh? Who're you?"

"Edward."

"Ed?"

"No. Edward. I never got too much into Ed, or Eddie, or any of that."

"Yeah, you're a formal guy. I can tell that. Edward. Okay."

"How old are you, Jill?"

"I thought they'd have nuns in here," she said. "Parish priests and nuns. You know: 'Rescue Mission'?"

"I think maybe you want a church," I said. "Some kind of sanctuary? You want me to help you get to a church? Or the women's shelter?"

She stood. She very carefully flicked her finger into a cow with four horns and sent it softly over. "Been to the shelter. Been back from it. Thanks for the heat, Edward."

"Good luck," I said. The can opener whirred. I tested it on a donated tin of fruit cocktail. "Take care of yourself, Jill."

She said, "Same to you." She righted the clay mutant cow, put her hands in her jeans pockets, and left the trailer, passing me as she did with a little light-footed nonchalance neither of us believed.

I had wasted the fruit cocktail because I'd sliced my left thumb on the open can, bleeding a red that clashed with the rusty color of the maraschino cherry. I considered drawing with my blood instead of ink, but I was simply too old for a stunt like that. I cleaned my mess and began a sketch, while holding my left thumb up in the air, like a parody of someone who indicates to you that life is just dandy. I drew with my right, and I got through the rest of the late shift without talking to anyone except a teary, tall woman who brought her dead father's sport coats and slacks in a couple of plastic bags. You give me the dead guy's clothing, I give you a receipt and I either say *Thank you* or *Sorry*, depending on your attitude. Then I go back to the picture. Then I turn down the heat, switch off the lights, lock up the trailer, and drive my corroded Chevrolet station wagon, its paneling held on with duct tape, across the lot to the twenty-four-hour market. That night, I strolled among the solvent and well nourished and bought myself a six-pack of Anchor Steam beer, which cost me a couple of hours' wages, and then I drove home, about six miles west, then two blocks up, and quite a few socioeconomic notches down, to my apartment.

I drank beer and worked some more on a sketch I'd started before locking up the Mission trailer. It was not a cartoon for a grand canvas by Tintoretto, nor was it the trail of a masterful hand like Ellsworth Kelly's, but it was not too bad a sketch by someone who worked the late shift at the Rescue Mission trailer and who could clearly benefit from the instruction he managed to avoid. *My boyfriend says I never get the joke.* And *I have this way of messing things up.* I heard them like lines in a love song on a jukebox in a bar. Like lines in a love song, when you think you're dying from the love, you understand them, you believe, because you're an expert. You know they mean more to you than to anyone else, and you are so tipped off, and so clued in, that you could weep to celebrate your wound and your awareness. But all you are, of course, is high on a very high dose of yourself. This was how I sneered at myself that night, drinking beer, and switching from pencil to conté crayon. But I did know what she meant, and I knew what her boyfriend meant.

The next day was Friday: me in the Mission trailer from two in the afternoon until eight. I woke up early and drove to the university, where I threw clay in the hope of being seen by my sculpture teacher. I didn't know why I made occasional awkward efforts to stay a part of the degree program when I attended few lectures and came to no critiques. I thought I was holding myself in readiness, I believe. I believe I was telling myself about open options, about pouncing on opportunity in case it came to the door—"Knock knock"—when what I was really doing, I guess, was panicking in slow motion.

Jill came back to the trailer at something like five, her khaki Eisenhower jacket open, her white T-shirt stained, her eyes enormous and miserable, her pale skin chapped-looking, mottled. I was accepting, from a man who kept a little white dog on a long lead, a portable television set he had taken away from his son whose grades had slumped.

"Knock knock," she said from the doorway.

"Damn it," I said. "Why don't you just knock on the goddamned door? Instead of *saying* it?" The man pursed his lips and raised his eyebrows, and I asked him, "What? You want to donate the dog?"

Jill said to him, "Edward always cracks jokes." Her face was a mask of amiability: she wanted so much to appear to be my friend, to be able to know and explain me to small men in charge of small dogs who could never know me as well as she. I thought

I could smell her across the trailer and over the ripeness of slow-leaking canine gas. She bore a vegetable smell, dark as old carrots and onions, a funk of fear and, I figured, of pain. It was the smell of the end of the long flight.

The man smiled at neither of us, indicated with his head that his dog should follow; he left and the dog went, the lead looped between them on the floor like a signature on a contract.

"Smart dog," I told her. "How's life?"

"I'm in a little bit of shit," she said, looking away from me. "That TV work?"

"The guy said it does, yeah. You want it?"

"I don't think I have a plug, anymore, to plug it into."

"He threw you out."

"No," she said proudly, looking young while she tried on old expressions, "I got the hell out on my own."

I said, "It's staying the hell out, right? That's the hard part?"

She said, "It's staying *in* that's hard. No. I don't know. Who says any of it's easy?" Her eyes were red, and the tears stained her face as if they were mascara tracks. They weren't, but they dropped, very visibly, straight down to the corners of her narrow mouth.

"Heavy tears," I said. I got to her slowly and was raising my right forefinger with care to touch a tear. She flinched anyway, and I put my hand at my side.

"Sorry," she said.

"You didn't do anything. You don't have to let people touch your tears. Where did he hurt you this time?"

She pulled up the sleeve of her jacket, and I saw the two red patches on her upper forearm. "Indian burn," I said. "He put both his hands there and he twisted one of them up and one of them down. Right?"

"Native American burn," she said, laughing while she cried. It sounded like a cough.

"Is he Indian?"

"Native American," she said. "Part Onondaga, some French-Canadian, some I don't know. He's beautiful, though. He's got this, like, copper-colored skin, almost. It's beautiful."

"That's what you said when you told your parents about him before you left."

"My mother," she said. "I stopped talking to my father."

"Did your father hit you?"

"Sure," she said. "What else?"

"Exactly," I said. "What else. Exactly. Well, they do rape you, sometimes, fathers."

"You know about this shit."

"Would you like a hot shower and a meal?"

She held her breath, then let it out. "Nobody ever tried to fuck me with a lead-in like that." She almost keened the words, and each syllable was pitched on the same sharp note.

"'Lead-in'? You're a singer?"

"I used to think about music college. I used to think about singing and music college up in Potsdam. You're not trying to fuck me because who'd want this?" She held her hands out, indicating the best evidence—herself—of her unworthiness.

"Name your favorite food," I said, backing away and indicating the desk, where she might sit and warm herself.

She went there, and she sat. I had shaped, in clay, a large mouth, belonging to no creature I knew about, from which protruded, instead of a tongue, another bestial mouth. She held it, then put it down, and wiped her hands on her sleeves. "You're crazy," she said. Then: "Oatmeal."

"That's it? Oatmeal?"

"Yeah." She nodded. "Yeah, that would be my favorite. With brown sugar."

"I'll make oatmeal for you."

"You can cook?"

"I can cook that much," I said.

"Is that what you do? Like, I'm a waitress and a punching bag, you're a rescuer and a cook?"

"No," I said, "but I used to run deliveries for a fancy food place in New York. So I had a small connection to food."

"New York's cool. Why aren't you there?"

"Had to come up here."

"For what? Come on. Come on. What?" Her face was furrowed with impatience, and she looked, then, almost my own age, middle twenties, instead of like a full-time high school cutter of classes.

"You want anybody else's story, right? Anything except yours."

"You're in trouble, right?" She said, "You're in hiding up here. You're in the deep end of the deep shit, like me."

"I got on-the-job training," I said. "I may be stranded here, but I'm a total authority on being you."

She sat very still. I thought she was going to erupt and leave. But her face went placid, almost as if she had fallen asleep, or as if she were a child who listened to a story. Once upon a time, there was you. . . .

I said, "My mother got herself knocked around a lot. Kicked. Punched. Cut. Slashed. Broken. Fucker broke her arm two times. Broke her jaw. Broke her nose. She stopped looking like her."

"Did she make it?"

"So you do know the chances are good that you'll die of it," I said.

"The lady at the shelter told me. First thing. 'Know that they tend to kill you,' she said, like she was telling me the weather. I knew it was a set-up deal. But still. You know: *dying*. I heard around. You hear things at work. I work in bars, restaurants. Ruby Tuesday's, Bennigan's, Colorado Mining Company. Theme parks with food. You know, where you can just get by without a master's degree. You hear it, though. Like it really happens. But the way she said it, at the shelter—like it was a pitch for something."

"That's what it was," I said. "She was trying to sell you some staying alive."

"But did your mother make it?"

I shook my head. "She only got involved with men who hurt her. So I had to come up here for her."

"Because she died?"

"I had to identify her body."

"Jesus."

"At the county medical examiner's building."

"They just go, like, *here*? And you go, that's right, it's my mother, thanks a lot for inviting me over this afternoon? What'd she look like? Jesus, Edward. How did you *feel*?"

"I suppose the way I would feel if I had to walk into this living room setup they have. A room off the lobby of the building, you walk in, and there's a rug and a coffee table, I think, and a sofa. I do remember that. And some chairs, and a set of dark drapes. Who installs the drapes? Who picks out the furniture? I kept wondering if they knew why. I remember the chairs are this terrible blue, this optimistic, cheerful, cerulean blue. It's like a TV show, except Dad's not reading the paper and Mom's not folding laundry and being cute about life. They ask you if you're ready, and then the guy pulls the drapes. They're blue, too, except very dark, and very shiny. It looks metallic, the cloth, the drapery looks like it weighs a couple of hundred pounds. And I guess I felt the way I'd feel if it was you. An off-yellow sheet around your body and your face uncovered."

"And it would be me," she said.

"There you'd be," I said. "Dying's a cliché," I said, "because she honestly looked like she was sleeping. Everybody says that, I hear. Well. It's true, though. Well. Except her jaw was thick where it used to be fine, and her nose was knobby where it used to be thin. And her forehead was all yellow and brown where he broke it. I could see the caved-in part. The medical examiner said he tried to fix it a little before I looked, but he couldn't. How could he fix it? Her boyfriend broke it with a steam iron. You don't fix it when they come to bat with the big-league swing. But maybe you and your boyfriend don't have a steam iron in the house."

"House," she said. "It's one of those apartments on Kinney."

"We're neighbors," I said. "I'm on Polk Street."

"I take the laundry when we have enough money, you know, out to the cleaner's. *They* iron it."

"Well, then, that's a weapon he wouldn't have access to."

"Right."

"Jill," I said, "I wish you could hear us."

"I *do*, Edward, I hear us. You think I'm stupid?"

"No."

"Nice?"

"Yes."

"Cute?"

"Sure. Cute."

"You think I'm a furball."

"I'm offering hot oatmeal, a shower, clean clothes, twenty-four safe hours, no conversations you don't want to have, and no extracurricular activities. All of it almost around the corner from you. In the navel of bleakness."

"It's pretty in the spring."

"In the spring, if spring ever comes, it could be pretty. And I'll throw in a guarantee: no more descriptions of my mother."

"Who got beat to death."

"Who—yes. That's right."

"Who got domestic abused to death."

"Yes."

"If I took a shower and washed my hair, I'd be cute."

"Jill, I don't care if you're cute."

"You should. Edward, are you *sure* you aren't gay? Makeup on your mother. Clay stuff. Drawings. That's pretty gay stuff."

"Okay," I said, "fine, I'm gay."

"You really did her makeup?"

"We were both young. It was how we talked about it without talking about it."

"Your old man?"

I nodded.

"He beat on you."

I nodded.

"But she didn't put makeup on *you*?"

I shook my head.

"So that's how you got not to be gay."

"That's how I got not to be gay. We need to shop some oats later on," I said.

She fell asleep sitting at the desk while I rewired a lamp that was made from a ceramic batter jug. At eight o'clock, I woke her and turned the heat down and the lights off and locked the trailer. We drove over to the market, and she was asleep before I'd finished locking her in the car. I thought it was at best a halfway probability that she would be there when I returned with oats, brown sugar, butter, raisins, and Anchor Steam beer. Inside the market, I saw three men with interesting skin, one of them a little scarred at the forehead and with a chin whose flesh looked almost golden. He had big hands on long arms, and his hair was glossy black, gathered in a ponytail, and he looked dangerous. Of course, you look hard enough for dangerous people, you're going to find them in abundance. The golden man's scars were yellow-white, and it was difficult to look away from them because you don't always see that clearly what people like us might be passing. But there they were: the gifts from parents or other elders which we handed on to girlfriends or wives or kids. I wondered, of course, if I would do the same, as a father, as a lover, as a man who didn't live alone. That was a reason I lived alone, I think—to keep the gifts to myself.

I was staring, and the golden-skinned man looked at me. I was disgusted by how I flinched and turned to study a bottle of fermented soy, holding my breath—truly: not breathing in or out, as if I cowered in the brush of a dark forest—until he was past.

The air, which had been damp as well as cold when I went into the market, was almost liquid now, and the temperature was falling. Fog was beginning to freeze on windshields and light stanchions and trees. The night was turning white. The city, black and brown with slush and with filthy, coarse snow in roadside mounds, started to look clean. Jill was sleeping when I returned to the car, and she slept as I drove us on Erie Boulevard, past the kind of joint she waitressed in, and cut-rate furniture stores, and burger franchises, and then up, past the sex club which that night was featuring a naked dancer named Cricket.

"Home," I told Jill.

She woke up with huge eyes, fluttering lids, she made a sound like a sick sigh. I knew she didn't remember where she was. I knew it all, didn't I?

"Edward's place," I told here. "Oatmeal."

"With brown sugar," she said. "Right. Okay. The Rescue Mission Man."

You walked down a narrow flight of stairs from the entrance on the side of the three-story building—my apartment in the basement, one larger apartment on each floor—and you entered my little living room, which led into the kitchenette straight ahead or, to the left, my bedroom and bath. None of it was filthy, but little of it was worth looking at except the walls and refrigerator, on which I had taped reproductions of pictures, postcards from museums, some of my own sketches, and a letter from my mother's final boyfriend's lawyer.

I said, "Familiar, huh?"

"Nice pictures," she said. "I'll bet you one of these days we'll live better."

"Really?"

"Sure," she said. "Why not? Hey! This is me!" She was looking at my sketch of her, taped onto the wall near my calendar.

"It's supposed to be, anyway," I said.

"No, it is. It's good. Except I look weird. Am I supposed to look, I don't know, sick?"

I was putting a saucepan of water on to boil. "No, you're not."

"Well, I look it."

"You're supposed to be sleeping," I said.

"You saw me sleeping?"

"Tonight, but not when I made the picture."

"You imagined me," she said.

"I did."

"That's pretty intimate, imagining someone asleep."

"I didn't mean it to be."

She said, "Oh, no?" I shook my head. "Well, as long as I'm not a weirdo made of clay, or dead or anything," she said.

"Clean shirts, undershirts, boxers if you want: in the bureau in there. Long shower now, and I'll make oatmeal." I said it with the modesty you use before stepping into the operating theater for a little neurosurgery, but it was mostly reading directions on the can, stirring the oats into the boiling water, and being alone for a few minutes to think about the heavy, tearing noise the drapes made when they scraped open and harsh white light fell on her gray and yellow skin, her broken head.

Jill called out, "I was thinking you'd be a jockey shorts guy. Whoops. I don't mean I was, you know, going around thinking about your underwear."

I actually said to the man who pulled the drapes, "She looks like she's asleep."

He didn't say anything. Then he opened his mouth. I heard his lips pull stickily apart and I heard him say, "I wish she was, buddy."

That was when I cried. When he tried, that way, to be kind to me.

I sat at the table and smoked cigarettes until Jill came, wearing the same clothing she'd worn into the bathroom. She'd made a decision, and I was relieved that she wasn't small and cuddly in my big bathrobe, or available in my boxer shorts. She smelled of deodorant soap and, I'd have sworn, my shaving cream. I disapproved of the pleasure it gave me to think of her in my bathroom, rubbing my stuff on her face. At that time, I didn't want to receive anything from anyone nor, I suppose, to give much, either.

I put the oatmeal in front of her. She watched me pour milk and sprinkle the sugar on, then stir it again until the raisins were coated.

"This is what you eat when you're a kid," she said, blowing on a spoonful.

"And you're a kid," I said. I went to the other side of the table with a bottle of beer and my cigarettes.

"I haven't been a kid for years," she said. She ate and stopped, closed her eyes, swallowed. When she opened them, they were wet.

"Hot," I said.

"Hot."

"Your mother made it for you?"

"No," she said, "my mother never made it for me. I don't think I ever ate it before in my life. No, I had this girlfriend in school— well, she wasn't my friend. We went on a date together with these guys who were friends, one of them had a car, and we both kind of gave it up at the same time, her in the front seat and me in the back, so we had to act like friends so we wouldn't think each other was a slut. That would be my analysis, looking back at it. But we both acted pretty much like sluts, no way around that. And this girl, her mother always made her oatmeal for breakfast, she said. I was so jealous. Imagine your mother cooking breakfast for you. Jesus." Her face was smooth, that instant, and then it clenched again. She said, "You're really a trip, Edward, you know? And I—"

She went so pale that I stood, a cigarette in my mouth, the bottle of Anchor Steam still in my hand. "What?"

She raised a finger to her lips. She swallowed. She shook her head. "The door?" she whispered.

"No."

"Yes." She covered her mouth with her hand, and it was as if each belonged to separate people. Her eyes blinked and blinked, and I thought she was going to faint. I figured that the golden-skinned man with the scars had followed us from the market. I realized that was who was at the door. He was going to smile when I opened the door, and show his healthy teeth, and say, "Knock knock." But of course it was my father who had come to the door like that, before he shook his head and gritted his teeth and shook his head faster and faster and made the long, wordless sound, like a circular saw biting wood, and began with his fists.

It wasn't my father at the door, I remembered. It was the man from the market. And I didn't have to let him in.

I didn't have to let him in.

"Maybe he isn't mad," Jill whispered.

"Maybe," I whispered back.

"He's gentle, you know, sometimes."

"I know."

"You do?"

I sickened myself. I hated myself. I said, "Yes, I do. It's the same damned thing again, Jill. So I know it. But I don't think I *heard* anything. Maybe you really *didn't* hear him? You think?"

She closed her eyes and stirred the oatmeal. Then, her eyes still closed, she set the spoon against the side of the bowl. She lowered her face almost into the oatmeal and finally she looked at me. I drew in most of the cigarette and dropped the butt into the beer bottle. I sat down. I lit another one.

I said, "It could be habit. It—because you aren't used to being alone that much. Because he needs you with him all the time, doesn't he?"

"He needs me all the time, that's right."

"And maybe you only thought you heard the door. And, anyway, even if it *was* the door, maybe it wasn't him."

"So open it," she said, staring at the oatmeal. "Just open it and let him in. I mean: why not?" I moved from the table and she said, "No! Edward!"

"Open it like 'I dare you to open the door'? Open the door, Jill?"

"No," she said. "Please. Edward, please."

"Because I *will* open the fucking door," I said. I went around the table and across to the door and I set my hand on the latch.

"Edward, why are you *angry*? Don't be mad at me. Please don't open the door, Edward. Please don't be mad."

It stopped me. I took my hand away from the latch. I said, "I'm not mad at you."

"You looked very angry, Edward."

"No," I said, thinking of all of us who passed our gifts along. "I'm not angry, Jill. It's fine, it's all right, and nobody's here. But I won't open the door. You're safe. You can stay here, if you need to, and we can both be safe."

I listened to us, breathing hard.

But I had taken away the safety, and she said, with her own anger, "And you can put my makeup on for me. And cook me oatmeal."

"I wasn't mad at you," I said. "I was mad at myself."

"And make me little clay cow things and mouth things. But you were mad at *me*, Edward. It's not like you're not a good guy. You never put a move on me, and I'm walking around here taking off clothes and putting them on, naked in the shower and defenseless and everything. And the oatmeal and all."

"Which you didn't eat."

"I think I wanted somebody to make it for me more than I wanted to eat it. If that doesn't upset you."

"No way you can upset me. Would you like a cigarette? A beer? Glass of milk?"

"No, thank you," she said.

"I have bread, I could make you toast."

She shook her head. "I think I better go back, because what if it *was* him?"

"You can stay here," I said. "Or you could come back. You could always come back, if you needed to." She stood in front of me, several steps away, and looked up out of her light eyes surrounded by furrow, all of it under that hideous, metallic maroon. I didn't feel any emotion, I thought. "So you could let me know," I said.

"Let you know what? I don't *know* anything you don't."

"Please let me know you're okay."

I didn't think she could trust me again, but I waited to hear—at the apartment, and at the Rescue Mission trailer, and at school. Every now and again, I drove, though not too slowly, down Kinney Street. For a while, I bought the *Post-Standard* and looked for news of small, beaten women. There were several, of course, but none that sounded like Jill. I was watchful, always, for a golden-skinned man with scars, but I never saw him. And, though I thought I had come to a kind of an ending, I surprised myself by living through the season in that city, and then through the year, and then the others. I always hoped to see her, but I also always thought—and I think Jill always knew—that it would finish for her at the window where, when the drapes drag apart, one of you will look inside, and one of you will look like she's asleep.

GOOD TO GO

"Your father says you bought a gun. He says you bought a surplus army gun."

"We used the M16A2. This one, they call it AR15. It won't fire auto."

"What's that, Patrick?"

"Automatic, Momma." From the mattress where he sat, wearing camouflage trousers and a khaki T-shirt, his back bisected by the corner of the room, he said, "You know. *Blam-blam-blam-blam-blam-blam-blam.* That's semiauto. You need to squeeze off one round at a time, but the rate of fire's good enough. Anyway, I didn't buy enough ammo to fire full auto for long. I don't need that much."

"For what, dearie? Why do you need a gun?"

"You talked to Pop?"

"He telephoned." She took her raincoat off and set it on the back of a short wooden chair. "Les answered the phone and of course they jawed."

"Jawed?"

"That's what Les calls it. He says it's like a couple of bull moose with their antlers locked and their forelegs set. All they can do is make noises."

"Now, what would Les know about two mooses?"

"Oh, dearie, he's a traveler. He's been to places. He's more like you."

"Travel. Here to Hawaii, and then Kuwait, then fucking paradise. Goats and camels and sheep and sand. And then I never barely came home."

"Dearie, yes. Yes, you did. Here you *are*."

"Here I am," he said. "That's right." Then he said, "That's right." His eyes were closed. She took one step nearer the mattress on the floor where he sat in his scuffed, sand-colored boots and his camouflage pants, his hands knotted around his knees, pulling them up against his chest.

He opened his eyes. What's the 'more like' supposed to mean?" he asked her. "More like me than he's like Pop? Except Pop's your *husband*. Legally, he still is, right?"

"Yes."

"But you want that part of it over," he said.

"Yes."

"Your life's moving along," he said.

"It is, yes."

"Mine isn't, anymore."

"You've just come back from a terrible time," she said. "You were in *danger*. You got *hurt*. You didn't have a shower for weeks and weeks. Those moistened baby wipes—I must have sent you a hundred."

"I didn't get them. I told you that."

"I'm sorry, Patrick."

"The mail was fucked. Everything was fucked."

"Would you like to come over to my—to where I'm living?"

"With Les and the mooses?"

"You could sleep on a sofa bed on clean sheets. We'd leave you be. Maybe you'd feel safe there."

"Oh, I'm safe, Momma. I'm safe. It's other people in danger." His face looked bony. He rubbed his cheek with the tips of four fingers of his left hand as if he wore a mitten. "I'm good to go."

She sat on the chair where she'd put her coat. She watched him look at her legs the way men look at a woman's legs. His etched, thin face was different, and so was his close-cropped hair. She realized that some of it was gray. He wasn't twenty-five yet, and his hair had gray in it and he wore a stranger's face, she thought. And he sized her up when he looked at her. She knew he wasn't her baby anymore, but now she wondered whether he was still her son. Her husband, Bernard, had said, "He's in trouble. I can't get hold of him anymore. He's out there. Have you *seen* him?"

She'd said, "You know how angry he got with me when he came back."

"He's loyal to me," Bernard had said.

"If that's the way you want to put it."

"I don't want to fight with you anymore. You're out of my life, and I'm out of yours. We're getting on with it. You wanted your freedom, you got your freedom, and now I'm—I'm shut of the whole damned thing."

"Aren't we all free," she'd said. At that moment, she had felt inventive and full of effective words she had every right to call after her husband as he vanished from her life. "But here you are on the telephone," she'd said. "You didn't vanish, after all."

"What vanish? What are you *talking* about? Patrick's in an

awful lot of trouble, and we need to be useful, or something. I
don't know what to *do*."

"No," she'd said, still feeling wiser than Bernard. "Tell me how
to find his place."

"It's a slum," he'd said. "I didn't know they let people live in
those places. Down where the Earlville feed mill used to be,
where the train station was in the old days. Somebody bought up
all the old buildings down there. I wonder did they even bother
to *look* at the wiring."

"I'll get down there. It'll take me an hour or two. I'll go in the
morning. Is he sick? Did he come home, I mean, with some kind
of illness? A lot of them had fevers when they came back. A lot of
them had dysentery."

"'Saddam's Revenge,' he said the troops called it."

"And what did he say about the gun?"

"He said he felt the need of a weapon," Bernard had said. "I
asked him why he did, and he mocked me. He said, 'Danger
lurks.'"

"'Danger lurks'?"

"It's what he said. I can only tell you what I heard and that's
what I heard." Then Bernard had said, "So, your new life's agreeable to you."

"It is, thank you. How are things for you?"

"Well, considering. My wife leaving me, and the lawyer's bills,
and of course I've got the sleep apnea thing. I keep waking
myself up."

"I remember it well."

"Dr. Bittman says it can sometimes be fatal."

"Let's hope it isn't."

"You could sound a little concerned."

"Well, I am a little concerned. I'm sorry you don't like how it sounds. And this is about Patrick right now, isn't it?"

"Yes," he'd said. She said *sullenly* to herself, and the description pleased her. She had felt, when they hung up, as if she had won a small contest. And then the fear for her son had poured in, like the sudden sound of the nurses laying out instruments when the orderly pushes your gurney through the OR doors.

Patrick lit another cigarette. He looked so much older than when he'd left. And she couldn't find recognition in his eyes. She couldn't find herself. Before she thought she'd speak, she was saying, "It's *me*, dearie."

He looked her over, the way a man looks over a strange woman, and he blew out smoke as he said, "Hi, Momma."

Although his shoulders were wedged against the walls, she wanted to find a way to get her arms around him. But how could you protect a man this large and hard, in his terrible, dim room that smelled of rotted vegetation, when he looked like a stranger made of only angles and skull?

He smiled, and she saw how white his teeth were. She thought of trips to the dentist when he was eight or nine, of the coupon book for payments that the orthodontist had issued them when Patrick was thirteen. "We're paying the son of a bitch to buy a goddamned *boat*," Bernard had said. Each month, as he tore out the coupon and wrote out the check, he had said, "Here's for the goddamned boat."

"I thought of you," Patrick said. "I did. I thought about you and Les in your new house and you in your new job. I thought about Pop all alone. He'd be so bad at that, I thought. And I was right. He eats bologna on white bread with mayonnaise. That's his dinner, some nights. With a can of light beer to wash it down in front of the TV."

"He knows how to eat intelligently. He knows how to cook. I'm not his mother."

"No. You're mine."

"Yes, I am."

"And that's why you're here."

"Yes, it is."

"Because I own a Colt Arms AR15. If I didn't own it, you wouldn't be here, right?"

"I'd have waited until you invited me."

"You're always welcome, Momma." He looked to her like someone else, and she wanted to cry out a warning to him, tell him that he was disappearing, that he needed to return. "Just like I should know I'm always welcome in your house in your new life with Les, who is such an experienced traveler and he knows about mooses."

There was one window in the room, a beautiful twelve-over-twelve with crazed glass and mullions probably gone to pulp. She imagined that it would sell for more than a month's rent if the wood, through some miracle, hadn't completely rotted. The light that came in was like the water you look up through when you open your eyes at the bottom of the pond. She could see him by it, and, turning, she could see a knapsack and a duffel bag hung from nails spiked into the walls. Behind them and across the wide room was an old, dark veneer closet with no doors, and, in a corner of the closet, as she looked over her shoulder, she saw the weapon's ugly mechanisms, dull but a little lit by what was left of the window light that spilled into her son's room.

"Do they give you a bathroom here?"

"Downstairs, in the back corner. You want me to show you?"

She shook her head. "I'm all right."

"Momma, you are always all right. You land on your feet."

"Dearie, no, I didn't fall. I just kept living my life is all."

"Pop said you fell in love. That's falling."

"It wasn't falling, though, so much—what I'm saying about the next thing? That's what it was. That's what it felt like. 'Oh! We're *here* now. We aren't *there* anymore.' It wasn't about your father, all of a sudden. It was Les. I even tried to not let it be, but it was. And it couldn't be Bernard. It couldn't be your father. No matter how I wanted things to work."

"Shit just happens and have a nice day. The kid used to say that, PFC Hopkins, the one that I lost. He used to say that when he fired his weapon or when they opened up on us. 'Have a nice day, motherfucker.' He was the boy that I lost in Falluja, doing house-to-house."

"No, *you* didn't lose him, dearie. *They* shot him. The officers told you what to do and you did it and he got wounded."

"No, he was plain damned killed. He bled out while he kept on moving his feet. Never stopped until, you know, he *stopped*. I was fire team leader and he was my SAW gunner and they just hollowed him out. I tried to stop the bleeding with my hand, but there wasn't anyplace to put it. You're supposed to apply pressure. Right. Apply pressure. But on *what*?"

She knew that tears ran down her face. She wished that Patrick could cry, too, though she had her suspicions that crying might not do all the good she used to think. It did help you realize that you were miserable, she knew. Maybe that was useful information. But she wanted to stop crying because she didn't know what tears might goad him to do. This was new between them, part of the so much unfamiliarity. That, she thought, was also something worth weeping about.

"Patrick, what's the danger?"

He motioned with one hand, sweeping it before him. He smiled, but his dark eyes told her nothing.

"Really. You told your father there was danger lurking."

"And he told you?"

"Well, we're *worried*, dearie. Guns make people worry. And you came home troubled. So naturally we'd talk about that. As your parents. As—because we love you."

"But you didn't send Les," he said, "your new next thing, with his travel experience, and knowing a lot about life."

"This is about us," she said, thinking that the words had come out in a whine.

Patrick said, "Wrong us. This is about reservist PFC Arthur M. Hopkins of Rome, New York. And rifleman Sweeney Sweeney of Madison, and PFC Danny Levine out of Gloversville, the ones who were not KIA. And me. I was the corporal let us get separated from the squad. I was the one directed our fire onto a little square sheep-shit hut, and I was the one got us shot to wet fucking rags. That's the us."

She said, "And that's the danger? Why you needed to buy the gun?"

"Why not? It's a reason. It'll do. That better not be Les," he said, his emptied face lifting as slow, heavy footfalls sounded on the raw lumber stairs.

But she knew the weight and pace of the sound of the steps, and she knew that Bernard would appear at the door, a little out of breath, a little wide-eyed because he stared so hard when he was worried—a tall, broad, decent man she had tried to live with after losing every reason except gratitude, regret, and this lean, sad man who was their boy once.

"Hi," Bernard said. "I had to come. I couldn't not come. Is that okay?"

She stood and went to the doorway and kissed his cheek. She knew that he'd close his eyes. "You smell nice," she said.

"A different soap is all."

"Well, good," she said, patting his chest, then stepping back. "Patrick was talking about Falluja."

"Terrible," Bernard said.

"That's because of the sweeps they had to send us on," Patrick said. "House-to-house is terrible in any place. The hajis are good at ambush. You get your unit isolated, and you are pretty fast all fucked up. They smell how all alone you get to feel. Not PFC Hopkins. He just said, 'Have a nice day, motherfucker,' and he sent over one long burst of 5.56 and then he died, all scooped out, that kid." Patrick lit a cigarette and said, "I wish I had another chair for all the parents that are here."

"We're good," Bernard said.

She said, "It's fine, dearie."

"Okay," Patrick said, "good and fine, then. But you don't have to hover here, you know. I think I know what I must sound like. I think I sound like I'm blaming you for not being there, in Falluja. I'm not. Really. I wouldn't *want* you there, all scared and doing your duty and shit. I don't want anything bad to happen to you. This is—I must be scary enough." She heard his throat close down and she watched him blink and blink, his dark eyes suddenly as wide as his father's.

Bernard said, "Is this the post-traumatic—"

"Private First Class Hopkins didn't mention any open-sphincter stress syndrome while he was getting dead," Patrick said, "so I would just as soon skip it, Pop. Nothing personal. I didn't mean to insult you, right? You're my man. Only . . ." He crushed the butt into the coffee cup with the other butts and he lit a new one. "I apologize, Pop."

"No," Bernard said, "I'm good."

"And Momma's fine. And I am good to go. What?"

Bernard had walked across to the veneer clothing cupboard. He squatted, and she heard his ligaments take the strain. "This is it," he said. "I don't see the clip. This does take a clip, am I right?"

"We call them magazines," Patrick said. "Mags. I've got a couple."

"It's safety precautions, keeping them separate from the weapon," Bernard told her.

"I don't see anything safe about it," she said. "It's ugly. It's frightening."

"It's efficient," Patrick said. He drew in smoke, then said, "You're thinking I'm going to open that window and set a pillow on the sill, then insert a mag and lean the weapon on the pillow and do some wild-ass-vet-on-a-rampage deal with people out there suddenly all falling down. But no way. Do you know where we *are*? Greater downtown Earlville, New York, folks. There's nobody *out* there."

"But Patrick," she said, "you wouldn't do it anywhere. You wouldn't do it anyway. It isn't *you*."

"No, Momma."

"Patrick, boy," Bernard said, "you bought it. You went some-place on purpose and you bought it for plenty of money that you had to set down onto some gun dealer's table."

"You're right, Pop. I have to admit that."

She remembered them standing side by side and looking up at Patrick as he leaned over a rifle that he aimed at them. They were in the side yard of their first place, a tall Victorian farmhouse on a half an acre of land in a little hamlet that wasn't very far from Earlville. It was summer, and Patrick had been working for weeks on his fort. As an eleventh birthday gift, they had opened an account in his name at the lumberyard, and Patrick had purchased small lots of planking and studs, an expensive framing hammer, galvanized nails. He had built himself a fort in the crotch of a young sugar maple outside the dining room, and he was up in his safe place after dinner in June, she thought, or early July—the sun was still high, and no one ever talked about autumn coming on—and she and Bernard looked up at their son. He looked down over the sights of his wooden scale-model Garand M1 rifle.

"You didn't see the ambush," he'd said.

"No, we didn't," Bernard had answered.

"You don't need to worry, though, on account of I won't shoot."

"You know, I knew you wouldn't," she remembered telling him. She remembered, now, in the old feed mill, looking at her grown and damaged, dangerous son, how disappointing to the boy her confidence had been.

"You knew?" he'd said.

"I mean I was hoping," she'd told him.

"We hoped you wouldn't shoot," Bernard had said.

"Please don't shoot," she'd called to him in the shadows of his fort.

"No," he'd said, "I won't."

Across the room from their boy who was now grown up, Bernard stood slowly. He leaned against the wall and put his hands in the pockets of his khakis. He always wore khakis and a blue button-down shirt under the white medical coat he put on when he was in his pharmacy, filling prescriptions. He said, "I'm worried about you. You can understand that."

"And I'm sorry," Patrick said. "I am. But now I think you need to go. You did what you could." He'd gone onto one knee, his forearm leaning on the opposite thigh.

"What does that mean?"

"You said what you thought you should say, Momma. And it was nice to see you and Pop be friendly with each other."

"And does something happen now?" she asked him. "Is that what you're saying? Because I won't leave here if it is. I won't."

Bernard said, "Me either."

Patrick flushed very dark. His lips were set in a bitter line. In the underwater light of his awful room, with his gray-flecked hair and his unfamiliar eyes, he seemed to her to be a new creature she must care for. She knew that she didn't know how. But she walked slowly to the cupboard, expecting each time she stepped that he would order her to stop, and she was breathless when she stood near Bernard and the gun she was afraid to look at.

Patrick said, "Please." His voice was flat, as expressionless as his face.

Bernard shrugged. She watched him take a deep breath. She squared her shoulders and waited.

"I *am* warning you," Patrick said in the flat voice.

"Dearie," she called to her son, seeking a level, low voice with which to address him.

"No more conversation now," Patrick said. "I warned you."

After twenty-five years, she thought, all they knew was this: standing in their separateness to hold their ground against their son. And what kind of achievement did that amount to?

"I warned you," Patrick said. He said, "Here I come."

He leaned forward, but he was far less graceful than she'd expected. He tripped off the mattress and then he caught himself. And she remembered this. She remembered standing in a room on an overcast day. It had to have been in their first house at the start of a long winter. Patrick was little and grinning. His chin was covered with drool. He'd raised his arms to the level of his shoulders. Then he reached higher. He lurched and then he righted himself and he made his way across the room in a wobbly march. She remembered how they'd clapped their hands to celebrate their boy's first step. She remembered thinking that there, stumbling across the room, came the rest of her life.

FROST LINE

I didn't drive upstate in a rented car because from the time I heard of his father's death I saw myself in the back seat of a taxi. A stranger was coming to town, I thought, and she ought to be driven in whatever might pass, up there, for style. It was dark when I took a car service Lincoln from my apartment on Carroll Street to Grand Central and then, five hours later, under the lead-colored morning sky, I found a cab outside the Utica station. It smelled of cigarettes and hot metal, and I looked out through a window smeared by the damp muzzle of somebody's dog at the abandoned-looking streets of Utica beneath several feet of dirty snow and twisted slush that had melted and frozen, melted and frozen again. We left the dark station that was constructed of shadows, echoes, chilly dampness, huge white marble stones, and long, dark, empty wooden benches, and we drove into the city with its bright onion-bulb Orthodox churches. I felt as though I'd arrived in eastern Europe and was setting out toward the border of little, sunless nations nearly at war.

My driver, whose cheeks were stippled with high, fleshy blackheads, told me to call him Sylvie. The certificate that was held by duct tape on the face of his glove compartment called him Sylvester Damschalk. The charge for the trip away from the station and onto the Kosciusko arterial highway and then to Route 12 and finally the funeral would cost more than twice the rental of a car. But I was where I had planned to be, sitting in the back of a long, dark car, not visible behind the wheel. I wanted to be delivered there. I wanted, then, to be driven away. I had wanted to see myself that way as it happened, and then when I thought of it a week afterward, and then months, and then years: an unrecognized woman is driven to the funeral rites of the man who prevented her marriage to his son. She arrives and departs. It is long enough since she has been here so that what her lover called her voluptuousness, and what she thinks of as her baby fat, has burned away. She arrives behind a mask of boniness about the eyes and mouth. Hidden by the quarter-panel windows of a big old Mercury cab, its blackness scoured by road salt, she enters her history unseen.

"So you know the area," Sylvie said. "From the way you talked about the snow and how you know the way there."

"Maybe I just looked at a map," I said.

He studied me in his mirror, adjusted his thick, horn-rimmed glasses, raised and lowered his brow, and said, "You mind if I smoke?"

"I'm sorry. Yes. Among the things I no longer do, one of my favorites is smoking."

"Yeah?"

"I'd like not to be tempted into asking you for a cigarette."

"How about if I promise not to give you one, ma'am?"

"How about if you do?" I said.

"That's a yes or a no, ma'am?"

I didn't answer, and he didn't smoke.

At the two-story motel, Sylvie took cash. He had a lighted cigarette in his mouth and it bobbed as he spoke, agreeing to return in the morning. "Back to the station," he said. He nodded for me before I answered. His skin was yellow-white and it creased into thick folds around his eyes. The blackheads were far apart and broad, each on a little island of skin. He held the cash between us and counted the bills from his right hand, also jaundiced-looking, onto the reservation desk. Then he scooped up the pile, as if he thought I might take it back.

"What's the name of the station?" I asked him.

"Well, Jesus, I don't know," he said. "It's the railroad station is what *we* call it. Don't you worry. It's the only one." He stared at me with his magnified eyes as he folded the money and stuffed it into a pocket of his khaki jacket. "I'll get you there and then you'll go home."

"Maybe this is home," I said. "Maybe it was."

He leaned his head to the left and studied me. He exhaled smoke through his nose and said, "However you like it, ma'am. Maybe yes. Maybe so."

I turned from him to stare at the surface of the desk, and he left as I had hoped he would.

I put my bag in the upstairs room, which offered a view of a municipal garage, and refused to work on myself in front of the mirror. I walked the few blocks to the church. I felt victorious as I walked because no one passing in a car or on the street seemed to notice me. And I had wanted to arrive invisibly, like a ghost coming home to observe his family's supper. The town was heaped with snow that was pitted by car exhausts and objects kicked up by the little plows that cleared the sidewalks and the giant orange plows that were shaping islands in the roadways for backhoes and dump trucks to remove. The house roofs had two or three feet collected on them, and I remembered how by the end of January the weight of the upstate New York winter had worn people down. Part of that weight was the understanding that there would be cold and snow through March and into April, that every morning would be the start of another struggle to defrost slushy water lines and haul ice-crusted firewood and coax a car along unreliable surfaces.

The church was named for a saint who was skinned alive. Mac, for MacNeilly, and I had argued about saints, flayed and otherwise, and the central tenets of most major faiths, as we had argued about national foreign policy, the state education budget, The Artist Formerly Known as Prince, the defensive line of the Buffalo Bills. I remember his saying, as he poured wine at dinner with Norman and me, "It's plain bad sense not to say the Rosary and pray to the Blessed Virgin if you can. It's like not accepting the Host. Because what if it works? What if it's true? You miss a terrific chance at something. I mean, you're saving your own life!" He watched me with his almost-clear, pale blue eyes. They suggested no feeling. It was always his mouth, rarely still, that gave you a clue about his feelings. "What's trivial about that?" he asked.

"I never called it trivial, Mac," I said, looking at his son, my lover Norman who later that night, to the surprise of no one, would insist that we marry.

"No," he said, "but you thought it. I know your face, darling. I know those two lines you get above your nose and the way you chew your lip. I've always thought it's to remind yourself not to tell me what an opinionated, dark old savage I am."

I shook my head. "You're not that old," I said.

He laughed with a shout and drank his wine. I knew he'd want to pour more, and I held my glass close to myself, beyond his reach, as he leaned toward the bottle. It was sour and unresonant, something from Bulgaria he'd found for six dollars a bottle. He'd spend good money on excellent whiskies, but never on wine. His handsome, square Irish face was red. His thick, iron-colored hair fell onto his forehead and he shook it back into place, a small, continuous signal of his vanity.

"Not so old," he said. "Meaning I'm all of the rest, then. Dark, opinionated. Well, you're a tough one."

I said, "I'm not as tough as you, Mac."

He drank and closed his eyes, like a child finishing his milk, and when he opened them, he set his glass down and leaned forward. "No," he said. "You're not. Or do you think so, Norm?"

Norman blinked. He looked handsome in his dark gray suit, but a little wearied by us, I thought, a little bruised. His ginger-colored hair and his pallor could make him appear unwell in a dimly lighted room. By candlelight, as tonight, he looked afflicted. His father and I taxed him. I wondered whether we didn't owe him better. Wouldn't a man want more from the woman he slept with, even if the sex was all right? And it was. At least it was for me. Norman labored so earnestly for what he thought of as my happiness. And so, I'm afraid, did I. And I wished that Norman might have more from me than I gave.

"Jean can take care of herself," Norman said, maybe with a little regret.

"But it was in relation to my own cold heart," Mac told him. "I've been saying I don't think she carries too much more than a splinter of the necessary ice in hers. Though it's more than you've been blessed with, poor guy."

"Who said it was necessary?" Norman asked his father.

"Ah, then we'd have to argue the premise of the need to survive."

"Isn't it a sadly short distance," I asked, "from the love of Christ, as transmitted by the Virgin, in response to the worrying by the supplicant at his prayer beads, down to the brute survival of an organism that needs no more than to breathe and copulate? Isn't that what your 'survive' implies?"

"And surely to have a thought or two," Mac said, "and just possibly do something more than fuck."

I said, "Possibly."

"We're off the topic," Norman said. "Let's drink more alcohol."

"Ah, Normie," Mac said, "rest your fears. She and I won't leap over the table at each other's throats. Will we, Jean?"

I said, "I wondered, Norman, what you thought the topic *was?*"

"And I never learned from either of you why a splinter of ice in the heart was necessary," Norman said.

"Ask your father," I said. "To survive, he thinks. You know: to protect yourself."

"And you?" Norman asked.

I drank the wine. "Honey," I said, "I'm afraid that he's right."

His father's face shone, and Norman looked inconsolable.

He was a little heavier now, a bit softer at the jowl, but he'd kept most of his hair and it was mostly still red. He wore metal-rimmed glasses, and they gave him a severity that I didn't mind at all. He looked at the pews nearby as he passed me and took his seat at the front. A short woman with a beaky, passionate nose and a good figure that she dressed very well came behind him with two girls. I had always thought he'd be a generous father.

Then the organ grew louder. Then the pallbearers marched in, six elderly men in business suits who seemed defeated by their not having lofted MacNeilly's corpse and hauled him down the aisle themselves, instead of preceding a dark, shining coffin on a wheeled cart, propelled by men from the funeral home. Eventually, I knew, the reedy but round-faced priest would lay a shroud on the bier. I was grateful for the cover of the casket over Mac. I didn't want to see his face.

The congregation called responses to the priest. We stood and we sat, and there was the singing of psalms. The priest read the service, and all were assured that believers would be reunited, and death would be overthrown, while those of us who didn't believe, I gathered, would die and rot and keep rotting.

Fair enough, I thought. We've been warned.

Then poor Norman had to read his eulogy. I watched him walk with care to the lectern. In spite of the weather, his black shoes were glossy. As a businessman he had obviously given talks, I thought, for he tapped at the microphone quite professionally before he unfolded his remarks. He said that his father had lived here in central upstate New York, two hundred miles from his birthplace at Tenth Avenue and Nineteenth Street in Manhattan, all of his adult life. He talked about his mother and her early death. He talked about his father's long widowerhood, and his real estate business, and his devotion to his faith. I smiled at him, though he only looked down at his eulogy or up, above his listeners' heads, because he had made his father's religiousness sound like a business practice and his marriage a well-constructed deal. I wondered if he'd meant to.

I thought again of his father's insistence on the splinter of ice in the heart. He had called the general office at the high school

where I taught before I went to Cooperstown to study curator-
ship and then New York City to practice it. His message said only
that I ought to call at once. I did, concerned for Norman's safety,
and he told me only that Norman was fine but that he was not.
He asked me to meet him on the edge of a construction site,
south of town, where a strip mall was being built. He had sold
the land at an enormous profit, of course. So afterward I thought
of the place as the scene of the crime. I parked behind his long,
maroon Lincoln town car. I walked over to sit in the passenger
seat while he, looking only forward as if the car were moving, as
if he were in control, took up a large thermos with nested red
plastic cups on top and poured us each a cup of hot coffee that
smelled as if it were sweetened with cognac.

"A four-in-the-afternoon pick-me-up, Mac?"

"Dutch courage for me," he said, "and a kind of a toast to you.
Join me, please."

"This could look unhappily like an assignation, you know. If
anybody looked."

"It would be an honor," he said. Then he said, "You don't
think so."

"Speaking only for myself," I said.

"I can appreciate that. How's your coffee?"

"After seven hours of policing hormone rage and searching
for undone homework," I said, "I would drink transmission
fluid."

"You're an agreeable toper," he said. "You can keep up with
me. I always leave poor Norman panting. Do you leave him panting, Jean?"

"You're asking about me and your son and our sexual
practices?"

"You have some, of course."

"Do I have to answer this to get to drink my drink?"

Still looking ahead, at upended wheelbarrows and long, thick rusted wires for reinforcing concrete, he shook his head but didn't smile. We weren't going to be joking, then, after all. I was aware of the smell of his cologne, which I found too sweet, and of the lavender sachet he must have kept among his starched-stiff dress shirts. The smell of coffee and cognac struck me, then, as cleansing. I sat with my nose above my red plastic cup. I wondered if he was going to make the move on me that I had half expected for a long time. He liked women, and he didn't mind if they saw, finally, how little he feared them. There were women who understood that in him. They responded nevertheless, or maybe because of his disdain, and then he responded to them. Mac would enjoy sharing some time in bed with his son's woman.

"I need you to reconsider your romantic liaison with my son."

"You should also tell this to your son."

"He'd listen hard. Then he'd hate me. I'd be sacrificing not only what he might think of as his happiness, though I believe he'll get over you sooner or later. Maybe later, Jean. You're a considerable . . . person. But I'd also be sacrificing his feelings for me. I won't do that if I don't have to."

"So you believe I'll be more—"

"Reasonable."

I said, "Is it because my parents are not only dead, are unable to dower me, as I've little doubt you would put it, but that they died poor? Or because *I'm* poor—an underpaid teacher in a noplace New York town?"

"I think the world of our town," he said. "And Norman will have money."

"Then because my mother was Jewish?"

"Oh, not your father, then?"

"He was a frightened atheist, though he had the balls to stay one," I said. "But it's the Jew thing, isn't it? You and your Rotary friends just don't *do* what you have to all call intermarriage. Right?"

He drank his coffee and sighed. His warm breath flared a momentary fog on the part of the windshield in front of the steering wheel. "You're a bright girl, Jean."

"And you're a bully, Mac, with the social intuition of a bear."

"It's no wonder to me that he's drawn to you."

"In marrying him, I'd be marrying you. With your ten-cent bigotries wrapped in your ten-dollar tea dance etiquette. But didn't Norman tell you that I didn't say yes when he asked me?"

"He did. And I assured him that you finally would."

"Because I wouldn't be able to resist the lure of my father-in-law?"

"Because it would raise you up, Jean, a little closer to what you ought to have been if you'd had any luck in your parentage. The Lord knows how you, of all, deserve better." His voice was strangled. He did sound as if it caused him pain to hurt me. I was learning then what I know now for certain. Suffering and apology aren't more than custom to a man like Mac, who always operated in sequence: first he insulted you, then he felt pain, and then he gracefully apologized. I thought of tossing the coffee on his lap. I thought of taking in a mouthful and spitting it at his face. But I was always pleased that I simply set my cup on top of the dashboard and returned to my car and drove off.

In the church named after the saint who was flayed, Norman told us that his father was probably in heaven with his mother now, berating her for not having gotten in a stock of Jameson's twelve-year-old. The listeners laughed and the woman beside me sniffed and whispered, "That's right. He liked his whiskey."

I thought: Not heaven, Norman. Not that from you.

He came from the microphone and surprised me when he did not pause to turn and kneel to the Cross before he took his seat. Instead, he turned to his right and looked at the coffin, which was now beneath its cream-colored silken cloth. He slowly bent forward, stiffly, from the waist. His motion became a bow that he held before he walked to sit beside his wife.

The priest led us into a good deal of smiling and embracing and shaking of hands in celebration of fellowship and salvation. As someone not on the road to heaven, I was reluctant to join in, but the very small woman to my right, wearing a fox coat and a pillbox hat with a lifted veil, insisted that we hug. There was more bulk to her long coat than to her body, I thought, and her smell was familiar. The lines of her grainy face were filled by rouge, and her little teeth seemed unnaturally white. While I asked her for a ride to the cemetery, I realized that the smell of her toilet water reminded me of the lavender sachet of Mac's shirts. I wondered how well she had known him.

The priest walked forward, up the aisle, followed by the coffin and its unburdened bearers. My neighbor put her hand to her lips as the coffin passed our row.

"There he goes," I said.

"How did you know him?" she asked.

"From when I was young," I said.

"Well, you're still young. But there won't be anything at the cemetery, dear. The frost line's too deep. The ground's frozen hard for six or seven feet, at least. They couldn't get into the ground.

And they wouldn't be able to maneuver a backhoe in those tight spaces. He'll have to wait until spring."

"To be buried?"

"Oh, yes. You had to have left here when you were very little, not to know that. It's part of what winter here is made of—the departed in their coffins at the cemetery vault, waiting. They wait all winter. There's a ceremony and they're interred in the spring, you know, when they can dig down into the ground."

"Is that strange?"

"Well, yes, I suppose it is," she said, "but that's life upstate. Wouldn't you say?"

My mother had died in the local hospital during the summer of my nineteenth year. My father killed himself in Columbia, South Carolina, in the autumn of my senior year at Stony Brook. I'd traveled south to collect his ashes and had returned to throw them into the winds off Old Field Point, on Long Island.

"I suppose it is, yes. Upstate."

"Where are you from?"

"Downstate," I said.

"I'm May Grange."

"Jean," I said.

The priest chanted his blessing of MacNeilly, and a handbell rang. The priest called again, and then again, and, each time he did, the bell sounded in the darkness behind the church. When the priest walked forward, up the aisle, to be followed by the body, he trailed incense, and it all became powerful to me, mysterious, and I felt that for an instant I could sense the primitive astonishment behind the declarations read to us without very much feeling by the thin-voiced priest. We walked out together and May took my arm as we navigated the slush at the foot of the stairs. I asked her for a lift to the luncheon announced by the priest, and while she drove a small car very slowly, with great uncertainty, I talked about my job. May had never been to New York, she said, though she had heard of the Metropolitan Museum.

"If you can get up to 1000 Fifth Avenue, I'll give you a tour," I said.

She was frightened by winter, pale, overpowdered, and buttressed by her faith. Their sodality group would soon travel to the veterans' home in Oxford, New York, she told me. "By bus," she said. "It's best, you know, not to drive long distances in this weather. Don't you think?"

"I try to take taxis," I said.

She was warming up on MacNeilly and his devotion to the community, and how disappointed he was when his son went to work at the bank in Binghamton and bought a house there. She told me the name of his wife—Donna—and their daughters—Lana and Hannah—and I'm afraid that I giggled. After I'd helped May hang her coat near the bar of the banquet hall, I walked among the long tables, each with six places set on a side, and then I walked through the room with the steam trays. It was what you'd have to think of as country food: bright and glistening with gravies, sauces, and syrups. A small bar served wines and spirits and because it was MacNeilly in the coffin stored in the vault, and because of the nights I had kept pace with him at his table, I asked for Irish whiskey with no ice.

"It's the only place you *don't* need ice to ease the sting of human transactions," Mac said to us at one of the usual dinners for Norman and me and his father, cooked by Norman and me in the kitchen built for Mac's wife.

Norman had said, that night, while he peeled the potatoes he was going to roast with rosemary and I trimmed the rack of lamb we would bake in a mustard and bread-crumb coating, "This is the only haunted *kitchen* I've ever heard of." His shirtsleeves were rolled to the elbows and his glasses had slid down his nose. He couldn't push them back up because his hands were wet. I pushed them up and kissed his nose. He said, "More, please."

I kissed his mouth and he said, "Folk remedy for haunted kitchen: carnal relations among the potato peels."

We got partway there, and then went back to cooking the meal. I often thought, as we cooked together, that the silence between us was a good deal of the pleasure of our relationship. Norman and I were good at silences, and that always entered into my calculations when I worked out reasons for our remaining a couple. It was after that meal, when he was pouring aged Irish for us, that Mac returned to his refrain about the need for an icy heart. It became the kind of conversation he appreciated most, with Mac declaring the rules for engagement with life while Norman sat back, buffaloed into silence, and I leaned forward, pinched into disputation, all of us more than a little drunk. Mac measured out the Jameson, reminding us that ice was essential to the human heart but extraneous to the consumption of spirits.

"Maybe it's just an argument for cruelty," I said.

"No," he said, "it's a recognition of cruelty."

"You're both so highfalutin," Norman said. "It's simply begging for mercy." He held his finger in the air to emphasize the point.

"From who?" Mac asked.

I said, "Whom."

"You see?" he said to his son. "*That's* ice. It's just what I mean."

"No," I said, "but who from? What kind of mercy? What's at risk?"

"Oh," Norman said, his lips working hard to shape the words, "that's the great secret that everybody knows. It's yourself."

"You great sot," his father said. "You'd better have more, because you're so far gone tonight, there's *no* going back."

"But really," I remembered myself asking them, "what kind of mercy could you mean?"

"I'm Donna MacNeilly," she said to me. I finished my whiskey and set the glass onto the bar. "His daughter-in-law?"

"Hello, Mrs. MacNeilly," I said. "I'm Jean."

She was very attractive, I thought, sensual-looking, and with makeup perfectly done. The blunt cut of her dark brown hair exposed her muscular neck and accented good shoulders. Her smoke-gray suit was expensive. She had hazel eyes and a direct look, so I could watch her figure me out.

She smiled unpleasantly when she finally said, "Oh, I know who you are."

"I'm the quasi-ex."

"No, there's plenty of ex to go around. You're the genuine, full-fledged ex, all right. Hello."

We shook hands. She had to tilt her head back to look at my face and I was certain she resented that. When I asked after her children, she half turned to point a perfect sleeve toward the back of the room where the two girls of maybe six and eight, sorrowful and clearly tired of sorrow, sat flanking Norman while they ate franks and beans. "It's a tough day for them," I said.

She nodded. Then she shrugged. "He was such a wearisome, pushy, mean old bore." She started to laugh, then stopped herself. "I'm sorry," she said, "but he really was."

"He'd hate to hear a woman saying that."

"Right," she said, "that's the same MacNeilly, Senior, I'm referring to. The Courtly Rapist, I used to call him. Not that he raped anybody that I know of. But I always thought he could have. He had that hard, heavy—I don't know."

"It sounds familiar."

"You got married, I heard."

"Separated."

"Ouch," she said.

"It's the way I relate to men," I said. "I leave them."

"What a perfect reminder for me, of course, that you'll want to say hello to Norman. Unless he knows you're here?"

"Why would he?"

"No," she said. "Of course not. I was wondering, though, why you'd come back."

"Well, I used to live here, Donna."

"Did you ever come back before? I mean, after you moved down to the city. Isn't that where you went?"

I looked over her as some of the hundred or so people in the hall arrived at his table and Norman greeted them with great seriousness. "The city is where I went. And I haven't come back until today. Do I really need to come up with a package of reasons for you? I knew the man awhile. I lived here awhile. I'm leaving tomorrow morning."

She stared at me, then stuck her hand out, and we shook again. She had a strong grip. "Welcome home. The family thanks you for coming." She looked at me as if she wanted to remember my face. Then we dropped the handshake and she walked away. Norman looked up to see her, and then his glance went past her and he recognized me. His face went still, then tight, then only still again. He stood, and Donna went to him to hold his elbows, to lean in against him, to kiss him on the mouth. So now we've all been reminded, I thought. He shot his cuffs and pulled his suit coat down as he approached. I saw Donna turn to her children, as if she wanted me to see how unconcerned she was.

Norman came closer than I thought he would, and he kissed me on the cheek. He sniffed loudly and said, "Coco Chanel. Some things don't change. Did you drive up? Is your husband here?"

"Amtrak to Utica. Alone."

"Utica," he said. "How did you get here from *there*? Where are you staying? I thought you got married. You did. I heard about it."

"I took a cab to the Howard Johnson. I did get married. I'm getting un-. I'm sorry your father is dead. You are, too, yes?"

His face reddened. He said, "*Are* you?"

"I didn't exactly love him."

"He was nuts about you," he said.

I said, "You know that, do you?"

"He always told me it was a permanent wound when you left. He went back over how long it would have taken you to apply to graduate school, plan where you'd live, make the arrangements for leaving. And he'd say, 'All that time she knew she'd be off, and us not suspecting.'"

"The stealthy girlfriend steals away," I said. "I never imagined he approved of me so much."

"You must have. He all but begged you to marry me, he said."

"All but," I said. "How are you, Norman? Are you all right? With all of this?"

"The death?"

"And Donna and the rhyming daughters."

"Ouch," he said, with Donna's inflection. "Would that be a bohemian verdict on the estate of a longtime but admittedly middle-class friend?"

"You're so much nicer than I am. You always were. I apologize for my—jumpiness? It took a little courage to come up here. And plenty to walk in *here*. Look, she's a strong, terrific person, Donna. And your girls are beautiful. They adore you. This really worked out so well." His light blue eyes were the only part of Norman that could overpower me. And they seemed at times to look directly past my pretense of the moment, and here, at the reception for the mourners of his father, when he ought to have been flabby and drained, he seemed to understand that I lied, and he seemed to find it unacceptable. "I didn't come here to give you a rough time," I said.

"Seeing you, though, isn't easy."

"I'm sorry."

"Is it regret, Jean, would you say? Is there any regret to what you're feeling?"

"About you and me?"

And of course they were his father's eyes, looking out of the son, and understanding me.

"I should be moving along to the other guests," he said.

"Right."

"*Is* there any regret?"

I said, "I was in the church. Did you see me?"

He shook his head.

"I have to tell you this. It isn't what I came seeking. I don't know why I came, and I don't really know if I was seeking anything at all. But when I heard, and it was just by accident, from a friend of a friend in New York who used to live here who still gets the rag they call a newspaper—when I heard it was your father, I reached for the phone and I reserved a ticket for the train. I don't know if I came up here to see him off, or to watch you send him. But your beautiful bow, after the eulogy. The lovely, formal grace of it—more graceful than anything your father ever did in his entire life, Norman."

"No," he said. "Wait." His hand was up with the palm toward me, and I reached for it as I had used to do, putting my fingers between his, which felt cold. Of course, I let go right away. His face grew grim. He said, "But my father—"

"I know who he was. Believe me."

"That so-called bow, though."

"Do me the vastest of courtesies," I said, "and don't tell me what you meant by it? What I saw was, I don't know, it was old-fashioned, it was elegant. Now, maybe it was just another act of obedience, though I intend to think of it as a great deal more. I felt something, then, that I hadn't felt for a long time. I ended up mourning *that*. And I'm grateful for the opportunity."

"'*Another* act of obedience,' you said?"

"Did I say that?"

"Didn't you, though."

"I'm sorry, Norman."

"We both are."

"Yes, we are."

He said, "I have to move along to the others."

I said, "Goodbye, honey."

The smaller daughter watched me from behind an angry expression. May was talking to the older sister with what seemed to be great pleasure, and I envied her for offering comfort from out of such a worried, small life. I walked among waiters and

waitresses and guests, most of them drinking and quite a few
working on plates of little meatballs or lasagna, and no one knew
who I was or, anyway, cared to brace the ghost. A waiter phoned
for a cab that took me back to the motel.

I watched parts of two movies. One was full of exploding
trucks and burning cars and gunfire. I fell asleep and, when I
woke, changed over to a film about a man who was a croupier in
London and lost everything. I watched several programs featuring smug hosts and dysfunctional guests who were starring in the
fifteen-minute unfilmed movie of their life. I cried when a
mother and daughter were reunited long after the mother had
sold the child for crack cocaine but had gone on to find a prison
term, rehabilitation, faith, and then her child. The daughter
seemed to forgive her mother, but I didn't. I washed my face and
put on jeans and sneakers and a cotton pullover and went downstairs to the Trolley Car, which was what they called their restaurant. The waiter simpered when I ordered a bottle of wine with a
salad chaser. It was an alleged merlot from New York State, and it
tasted no better, I thought, than the eastern and middle European
wines that Mac used to buy. For dessert, I asked for an Irish
whiskey, any brand, straight up. Instead of offering a sentimental
toast—and, really, to what?—I sipped it and imagined Norman at
home with Donna and their daughters. He probably had a den, I
thought. She probably starred in civic little theater, reveling in
the sexy costumes she could wear.

Upstairs, I lay on the bed to read. I was working my way
through *The Good Soldier* because a woman who worked with
me had said it was the great modernist novel. I remembered
thinking about modernism as part of fascism when I was in
college. I wondered if I was waiting for Norman. If I had the

thought, then maybe I was. I tried to figure out the meaning of such considerations, but I fell asleep.

I woke a little after midnight because there were sounds at my door. I saw him, distorted by the spy hole in the door and looking queasy in the hallway light. I opened the door and stepped back, but he stayed where he was, so I went closer to the threshold. We did our hesitation in whispers.

"Are you all right?" I asked him.

"As all right as this can be. Yes, thank you, I am. Are you?"

"I'm okay," I said. "I'm okay." Then I said, "I ought to be saying, 'But Norman, what about your wife?'"

In the bad light, and in what I'd have to call our excitement, those clear, pale eyes were on my forehead, on my own eyes, on my mouth. He looked distressed, but he was smiling when he said, "'And what about your kids?' you ought to say."

"Yes, of course. But here it is, Norman," I whispered. "Here's what your father and I knew about each other: the virtue of the icy heart. If you have it, you can do what isn't fair, you can do what isn't anything in the neighborhood of right. And you can survive the pain of causing so much pain."

Norman made a wincing sound, though he kept his face expressionless.

The cabdriver Sylvie, with his magnified eyes, his corroded skin, his odor of stale cigarettes, took my bag and we walked out of the motel lobby in the bleak, gray day to his taxi. He opened the back door for me.

"So how did it go?" he asked.

But I saw Norman's clear blue stare as he drew himself up in the corridor.

"For a High Mass featuring a dead man," I said, sitting in the back of the dark cab as I had intended from the start that I would, "it went all right."

But I was seeing how Norman, as I stepped back, came forward into my room, and shut the door behind him, then faced me, then bowed.

ONE LAST TIME
FOR OLD TIMES' SAKE

Her husband suffered the cancer, but her lover was also going to die of it, her lover thought. In their motel room, during the last late afternoon MaisieRose would permit them to share, she slowly wandered the small hired space that was left to them while he talked and talked—he heard himself with shame—and could not stop. And neither could she stop fleeing, he thought, as he watched her wander from closet to bureau to door, moving without pause past the broad bed.

"When I was just out of college," he said, "I was living in New York, on Charles Street in Greenwich Village. There was this man, a friend, I guess you'd call him, from school, an older guy. He was one of those people who people like me wanted to be like. A sturdier person, already a man. I even liked it that his hair was thinning, a little, because it meant he was closer to the secrets."

"Which ones?"

"The ones that boys just out of college want to know: about desperate sex, about intense pain that you prove you can handle, and of course about death. Death was the favorite word. We kept using it. Of course, this was when nobody my age really *believed* in death, but we kept hearing about it. We took courses in it, didn't we? All that existentialism? *That* was it, maybe. The set of his lips. He looked like Camus, a little. He smoked his cigarettes like that, too. Like he knew. And the thing was, he wasn't a phony. He'd done two years in the army, in Europe someplace. And he clenched his jaws so the muscles always rippled. Girls loved that, and some of us imitated him, but he did it because that was what he always did, you know? And the cigarettes: he smoked unfiltered Camels and he *liked* them, you could tell from how he sucked the smoke in, deep. And he could cross his legs and lean over his lap and smoke, his forearms crossed on his knee, and he'd look like some kind of soldier of fortune, or some writer off a tuna boat in the Gulf."

"Gabe, he sounds exactly like you," MaisieRose said, "except for the cigarettes and the soldier part and the boat and of course the part about knowing everything." She walked a few paces from the end of the motel bed to the door that opened onto the second-floor balcony below which their cars were parked. Gabe worked the stopper out of the bottle of Calvados she had brought and poured some apple brandy into each of the plastic bathroom cups he had unwrapped. "Stand still," he said. He carried a cup to her. "Stay there."

"You think I'm running away?"

"You do keep moving," he said.

MaisieRose leaned against him, holding the cup at her side. She nodded her head against his chin, then kissed him, then kissed him harder, and then she stepped sideways toward the small, round table between the bed and the window that looked onto the balcony. She sat, and he went to the bed, sitting on the side, his legs uncrossed, sipping at the brandy while he watched her.

"If I stuck my hand out like this," Gabe said, "and if you reached over, we'd be holding hands. If our hands were open instead of clenched."

She shook her head and held up her broad, long-fingered hands, as if in surrender. "No fists," she said. She said, "Lovely Gabriel."

He said, "I'd just as soon you shot me as wooed me."

She nodded. "I am wooing you," she said. "I admit it. Only it's short-term woo. Can you think of it that way?" As if they timed it, she shook her head as he shook his. "I know," she said. "I can't, either." Then she asked, "What about the Camus boy from college?"

"No," Gabe said, "he was a man. That's part of the point. I was a boy, but he was a man. He was maybe twenty-four, and I was a few years younger. But I was a child, compared to him. I had this place in the Village, on Charles, very close to Greenwich Avenue. There was an engine house around the corner, and I lived with all these wails and shrieks from the fire department's sirens and klaxons, and I got so I never noticed them. I worked at New Directions, which was on Sixth Avenue in those days, and I saw major-league artistic folk, and I got so I never noticed *them*. The publisher was a famous genius and literary figure, a guy who really mattered, and there were all kinds of important writers who I carried coffee in for, and, by the time I'd come home at the end of the day, I'd forgotten that I'd seen them. Jesus, Maisie, I've forgotten being the me I was in those days. But this guy I'm talking about, Marshall Waring—Marshall F. Waring II, in fact, a prep-school kid, a flunker out of Yale and finally an honor student at Lafayette after his army tour: I think of him a lot. Always."

"You never mentioned him."

"Marsh. No, I guess I never did. It's hard to know what to say."

"I guess he's all about secrets," she said. "Where is he?"

Gabe said, "I don't know. That's part of the . . . the mystery in him. After he had this immense affair, he showed up, and then he disappeared."

"Immense affair," she said. "As in . . ." She gestured at the room, at him on the bed. "As—"

"Yes," he said, "as big as all of this, I think."

"Gabe, I don't want to disappear from you."

"No," he said, "I don't want you to. Or me from you. But we will."

MaisieRose set her cup down and placed her left palm on top of the back of her right hand, which was pressing on the table. She lowered her chin to the back of her left hand.

"But maybe not," Gabe said.

"Don't you be chipper, you chipper son of a bitch," she said.

"Oh, Maisie, I don't really feel too chipper."

She said, "I know, honey. Shh. I know."

He watched her and rubbed at his face, as if suddenly wanting a shave, and then he said, "It's at least two in the morning, maybe later, and I am in one of these four rooms of mine that opens off a single corridor—that was the kind of apartment they used to call a railroad flat—and I was either smoking my Kools or reading or looking out at the other apartments in hopes of seeing a gorgeous woman who would come to love me or, in the spirit of *Rear Window*, the murder of a gorgeous woman who had missed her chance at loving me. The door pounds twice, then there's nothing, and then, when I open it, there's Marsh. His face looks like a Delmonico steak. He's holding one arm against his ribs. And of course he's got a Camel in these torn-up lips. And he's smiling, a shy, minimal smile I always associated with him and those secrets I wanted to know.

"He says, 'Hey.'

"'Hey,' I say, low-keying it because I would have given my liver to be as elegant as Marshall Waring.

"And by the time he's had a shower and a couple of beers, I learn—"

"The affair," MaisieRose said. "The husband caught him?"

"Of course. What else? He worked for the husband, who had played football for Penn State, he was this vast left guard who wasn't cut by the Los Angeles Rams until the last week of training camp. He ran a landscaping business in eastern Pennsylvania. He had a wife named Dina. She and Marsh got in big-time trouble together—you know those affairs? The older husband, the younger wife, the love affair with a guy who never, ever, intended for them to get involved?"

"Imagine," she said. "And you're smoking Kools, to boot. And they got caught."

"And the football star caught them, of course. He pounded Marsh like a stake, the way Marsh described it: 'Like a stake,' he told me, smiling around his cigarette, 'straight down into the ground.'

"And why had Marsh come to my apartment, on Charles Street, in New York City? Because of my virtues? My readiness for promotion to the vanguard of existential men in dark T-shirts vaguely resembling Jackson Pollock? Not quite. I was the only person, it turned out, who he knew had a phone where Dina could call him. He's the existential galoot on the phone-free prairie, and there I am with my telephone, which is more valuable to the man I thought I wanted to be than I was.

"He lived in my place for part of that summer, and then he went back to Pennsylvania. Before he went back, while he was healing, they kept in touch with phone calls, and I imagined this tall, willowy woman, pale and anxious, calling him from phone booths in the rain. Sometimes, when I answered the phone, and it was Dina, saying, 'Hi, Gabe. It's me,' I imagined being loved by a woman I was doomed to love—you might appreciate this— because the love was impossible. Marsh went back there to meet her at—you might appreciate this—a motel. It was supposed to be—you might appreciate this—for the last time. He was like a soldier to me, volunteering to return to the front. He'd been beaten purple, his side had been swollen, his shins a kind of cor- rugated green-black where the football guy had kicked him once he had him down. He had these raccoon shiners and, I swear it, there were what looked like crusty *dents* on his fore- head. And he was going back because of 'Hi, it's me.' Goddamn it, MaisieRose."

She raised her head from her hands. "Well, you became your hero," she said. "Would it be useful to know you're my hero, too?"

"I want to be your lover."

"You are."

"I want to keep on at it."

She bit her lower lip and smiled and shook her head.

"I'm sorry," he said. "And for the story, too. It was a shaggy Mar- shall story. It doesn't really end. It peters out. He disappears. I never heard from him. I always figured I never deserved to. You know, because I wasn't cut from the same cloth. I wasn't heroic—"

"No," she said, "you maybe weren't *romantic*. Back when you were what you keep calling a boy. But you *got* romantic, Gabe.

You got considerably more fucked up by fortune. Marshall would be proud of you now. Let's drink a lot more. Let's drink to you being romantic at last, and let's get—what did you call it?"

"Chipper?"

"Let's be that."

"Except you're the one who said it. Let's don't be chipper, you said."

"That was when I was going through my anti-chipper phase. In the period of my life when I considered it possible to decide to not be with you anymore." She said, "Shit. Do you think Marsh and Dina got together? I mean: stayed together."

"I always wanted to think they did. And I never believed it."

"No. But maybe, huh?"

He said, "I hope so."

She said, "How would Marshall and Dina have said goodbye? Some kind of Ingrid Bergman–Gregory Peck goodbye, I imagine. Right? But those glamorous bastards always have it easy: the cameras, the music, the makeup. They don't have me snuffling in the background."

He said, "The older you get, the harder it is to say goodbye."

She said, "Really?"

"I don't know," he said. "But possibly. It's what somebody told me one time. I just remembered it. This was a person who was a painter, in New York. She married a man who needed her to not be a painter anymore, and she went along with it. They moved upstate to where he had a job, and she stopped painting and learned how to do their laundry."

"It's never that simple," MaisieRose said, sipping Calvados.

"No," he said. "You're right. And it surely wasn't with them. I guess she loved him, though. Maybe he loved her back. He sure as hell needed her. And she sure as hell stopped painting after a while. But she had this father, and he was dying, and she took the train out to the Middle West to visit him several times. And just before it got very bad—Jesus, Maisie, why am I telling you this thing about people who die?"

She shook her head with her eyes closed. When she opened them, she smiled. "Because you can't help it. Because you're the morbidity man. And it's all we can think about, unless we think about the other aspect of it, which is worse. You might as well tell it."

He raised his own plastic cup of Calvados but didn't drink. He set it on the bedside table, next to the telephone, and he rubbed his hands together as if they were cold. "She was leaving to go home again, she was kissing her father goodbye. You know. All of that. And her father said—he whispered it, she said. He told her, 'The older you get, the harder it is to say goodbye.' I hated hearing it, but mostly because it made her so sad. We were pretty young, and it didn't occur to us that everyplace you looked, you'd find death. We lived, you know, like it was there, but in pockets—a little here, a little there, just enough to make distant circumstances seem, I don't know, glamorous. Nobody believed it was . . . whatever it really was."

"Part of the package," she said.

"Yes," he said. "No. I mean: you're right. That's what we thought we knew. It was *around*, but none of us would catch it, we thought."

"And here it is."

"It's fucking everywhere, isn't it?"

"He was right," she said, "your friend's father. Wasn't he? Were you lovers?"

"You think I have this pattern of going after other men's wives?"

"You wish. You'd love to be a rogue," she said. "Wouldn't you? But were you lovers?"

"Yes, I would like to be a rogue, instead of a middle-aged marshmallow. And no. We weren't lovers. Well, we were—well, yes."

"What about the affair is confusing to you? Did you or did you not get naked together under bedclothes?"

Gabe said, "Not under bedclothes. Not naked. It was a little more furtive than that. It was hastier than that."

"Once?"

"Once. Drunk. High on, actually, some extraordinary hash, and drunk on gin, and full of despair. I had decided to be in love with a jazz artiste who didn't quite love me back—"

"Sarabeth," she said, "the smoky black chick from Atlanta who went to London."

"The same."

"And the painter consoled you."

"It was one of those mutual consolation things in an outbuilding at a party in Putnam County. You know, where nobody ever mentions it again?"

MaisieRose nodded toward his apple brandy and he raised his cup and she raised hers. "To mutual consolation," she said.

"I can't."

"You have to," she said. "It was the agreement. We would sit down together one more time and we would get a little lit and say goodbye *properly*. That was how you said it. With the old-time Gabriel Stone proprieties all buttoned into place. Because you knew I could never say no to you for almost anything, and especially when you did that imitation of Colonel Blimp but with an erection." She sat, looking at the plastic cup, and then she looked at him. She raised the drink and swallowed it.

He drank, too, making the face of a child compelled to swallow medicine. She watched him, then looked away. She shook her head. "Your friend, the standing-up lover in the outbuilding, wasn't she right."

"Wasn't she," he said.

"I have one. I have one for you."

"One what?"

"One of these things we're saying because we're frightened about having to leave in different directions."

"Those," he said. She reached for the bottle of Calvados which he'd stood on the bedside table and she poured a little into his cup. "I used to love it," he said, "when we were eating dinner and there was wine—even that Belgian beer, once, in a quart bottle. You would hold it in both hands like that and pour it for me, and I found it very intimate and comradely and *offered*, and all at the same time. Just like this."

She went back to the table and poured a little for herself. "I know," she said. "That's why I did it." She sat and drank and said, "My mother had a friend, once, who was dying. It was the first time I got dragged off to a dying person. I was about sixteen, and she thought I owed this dear soul some final attention. She was right. But it was very frightening. But she was right, and I went with her to the hospital. This was Decima Bellstead, who was my mother's dean at college. The old dear was maybe eighty—seventy-eight, seventy-nine, eighty, in there. And her husband, this wonderful tall, skinny old man with a plume of very fine white hair, he was there, standing at the foot of the bed, and we were standing at the side. This was in St. Elizabeth's, in Bingham-ton. And she began to drift away. You could see it. She got flatter and flatter on the bedsheets. And her husband hit the bed and shouted, 'Dessie! Dessie! What do you need? What can I get you? What do you *want*?' Because that's what his whole life had become: getting her what she required. There's a long pause. And then it's like this ghost, this dead person returning. Her eyelids go up, a little color comes back into her face, and she stares the length of the bed at him. 'Sex,' she says, and she closes her eyes."

"Dead?"

"No. But that isn't the point of the story."

"No. No. I understand." A horn began to bleat in the parking lot of the motel. Its rhythm was that of an infant crying, a regular expulsion of noise that said nothing but need. Someone had rocked a car equipped with an anti-theft mechanism, and the sound would continue for hours unless the owner came to silence it. "That's the twenty-first century," he said. "Cars that sound like fucking babies."

"What baby? And don't swear so much, Gabe. It tells me how upset you are. I don't want to know how upset you are. I don't want you to think about whether I'm upset—"

"*Whether?*"

"There isn't any need to say that, I mean. I mean, we know. So we can talk about subjects *besides* the obvious."

"Oh," he said into the cup, because he was finishing the brandy, "you mean everything about departures. Parting. The varieties of leave-taking. Well, all right." He watched her shake her head and then put her lips together hard. "All right," he said in a softer tone. Then he breathed in and sighed out the air and said, "Right."

"That's my boy," she said.

"That's me."

"That's you."

He said, "I knew a couple—these local people I know. They're very corrupt. They tell stories on each other even now, years after the divorce. They could have kept respecting each other afterward, because they'd gotten so close. The marriage went under, but they had real regard for one another, I think, and then they got bitter. I would love not to get bitter."

"Please," she said, "please don't. This is not a divorce. And I don't want to lose everything."

"I hope we don't," he said.

She looked at him until he bowed his head.

"No," he said, "we won't. But these people did. One of the stories he told about her was how, when her mother was dying— it was very clear: she had days, very few days—and they were in some hotel in Ocean City, New Jersey, they'd just returned to the room from the hospital and they were standing in the room, looking around, the way people do after a car crash, you know. Dazed, stupefied. All of a sudden, he liked to say, 'She all but tore my clothes off.' And they made love very passionately, and she wept and wept. Except, of course, he has to tell it this way: 'She made me fuck her till she cried.' But that's how it happens to people with all this dying going on."

"Except for us," MaisieRose said. "We've done everything *except* make love."

"On purpose, do you think? I mean: do you think we came here intending not to make love?"

"Not me," she said. "I intended to beat you into the mattress and leave you weak. One last time for old times' sake, and remembered forever."

"Maisie," he said, "it's the forever that's killing me." He closed his eyes and tipped his cup, but it was empty.

"Here," she said. She stood before him and tilted the bottle over the cup he held out.

"How much time's left?" He put the hand that didn't hold his brandy on her stomach and she stood still. Then she leaned against his hand, then returned to her chair.

"I didn't wear a watch," she said, "because I don't want to know. Before you got here, I unplugged the clock radio and stuck it on a shelf in the closet."

"We're the clock."

"I am really hopeful that we won't get metaphysical," she said.

"We're saying goodbye, MaisieRose. So you can nurse your husband to his death. We're leaving each other, not for any reasons I can understand or bear to accept. And we don't want to get meta*physical?*"

"So I can look him in the eye when he dies, Gabe. And that is a decent reason."

"Yes, it is. It is. And I'm being selfish."

"Good. In a way, I mean. Because you love me."

"And isn't *that* rewarding for us," he said. "But what if we figured out a way to mourn his death and *then* be happy? But a lot later on. A decent long time afterward. Why couldn't we try that? Why couldn't we hold out hope for that?"

"This was not supposed to be the conversation of the evening."

He said, "It's really evening out already?" She went to the window and drew the blinds over. Then she turned on the wall switch, and the sconces and the table lamp went on. They could have been in any state or nation, at any time of day or night. "Thank you," he said. He said, "I think I'm finding this mildly impossible."

"You won't leave—"

"Of course not. No. So maybe—I remember our agreement, I remember—but maybe it's a sign that we shouldn't leave each other. Damn it. Fuck it and goddamn. You're consistent. I have to say it. You're the same woman. You were never disrespectful of him, you never complained, you never made fun—"

"He's a decent man," she said. "He's a good person. People *like* him. I loved him, I believe. I married him, I stayed with him. We tried to have children together. We lived an entire lifetime together, almost. It was you, Gabe. If you hadn't happened, then I'd have been an ethical, passable wife. It was you."

"I'm not sorry for messing things up. Jesus, Maisie, I'd leave a dozen wives and children."

"No, you wouldn't. It's one of the—you're loyal. You're the loyalest man I know. You'd walk outside, if I needed you to, and you'd lie down in front of a moving car because of me. That's why, it's one of the reasons why, this is so difficult for you. Because you absolutely understand what I'm doing. That's why this is killing *me*, Gabe."

The car horn continued while she covered her face with her hands and sat straight at the table, as if to offer him her pain as some kind of proof. He stood, then leaned against her where she sat and cradled her head to him. After a while, he said, "I can feel your breath through my clothes."

She moved her head, and she breathed out harder.

"MaisieRose," he said, "Jesus."

She turned her face and kissed at him. Her cup went over, and so, then, did her chair. He pulled her dark blue blouse up from her corduroys and kept pulling it, buttoned, so that it came off her in reverse—tails over collar, sleeves inside out, an earring momentarily caught in a buttonhole, and, once it was worked loose, he tossed the shirt behind him. He undid her chestnut-colored slacks and knelt to work them over her brown lace-ups, and then, kissing her and pulling with his teeth at the hair of her groin, he took her underwear down. She undid her brassiere and he worked at his jeans and cotton sweater as she stood before him in shoes and navy-colored socks. Then she knelt as he had knelt, returning her breath upon him.

They moved together to the bed. They turned each other, moved under and atop each other, pushed the other's limbs and pulled at one another's heads. They moved furiously while they remained in place. And what were they, he asked himself, except another story? Once upon a time, he thought, there was MaisieRose and there was Gabe. They were one more man and one more woman caught in somebody's story—one they might even tell about themselves, perhaps, but many years later and in separate lives: the story of the couple who, confronted with the prospect of a distance from each other that seemed a kind of dying, and then with actual dying itself, suddenly needed to touch and seize and bite and swallow each other.

The car alarm sounded its single note again and again. He made a noise as if in response.

She said, "Shh."

"No," he said, "when this—"

She said, "Honey, I know." She said, "Shh." She said, "I know."

THE SMALL SALVATION

He saw her at the start and finish of playschool mornings as the children gusted about her like blown leaves. She seemed to him to smile like an actress playing a part. He thought of her as the pretty girl in high school and college who had starred in every play but who hadn't gone on to anything but earnest, sweaty civic little theater since she'd been condemned to grow up.

Her large dark brown eyes looked merry. He couldn't tell if she was pleased or feeling ironic. She sat on the small, low child's wooden chair in the center of the preschool playroom and indicated a little chair opposite. Her bent knees, parallel and pale, struck him as graceful. His long legs were locked, and he tried leaning back while he extended them.

She hiccupped a laugh and said, in a bright and ringing voice, "Poor man. Should we stand?"

I've forgotten my preschool skills," he said. "But I'll be fine. This is fine." He took a deep breath. He found himself staring at the silk scarf of cream and gold and black that was tied at her throat. He thought of it, or maybe he thought of her thinking of it, as a brave little scarf.

She nodded. She clasped her hands on the hem of her dark, figured jumper. She raised her brows, and he realized that he was supposed to begin.

He said, "My grandson—"

"Jeremy's lovely."

"Jeremy is," he said. "But he's shy."

"Don't worry. Look at you: *you're* shy."

He felt himself flush as he said, "I am?"

"And you're a fully functioning grandfather. Shy's all right." She smiled as if he were Jeremy's age. She might not have intended to, he thought. But what did it mean if she had?

"Yes."

"Was that the problem you called about? I mean, that's utterly swell, if it is. I'm happy to address it with you."

He shifted his legs and felt that his knees had come to the height of his face. In the basement of the village's Baptist church, on an errand that was sad and even ridiculous, but inescapably important, he addressed this younger woman on behalf of his daughter's child and he was certain that he was a fool.

He said, "Someone took Jeremy's cape."

Her face creased in sorrow. She shook her head. "Oh, it *saves* him," she whispered.

Jeremy's mother, his only child, had cut the cape from a piece of white corduroy. She had stitched a red *J* on it and sewed the grosgrain ties with which she fastened it around him. He wore it every day. He had stood, solemn and invulnerable—less vulnerable, anyway—as Nora tied it on.

"And somebody took it," he said.

The teacher responded as if to the child. "Do we *know* that someone actually stole it? Could we have mis*placed* it?"

"Mrs. Preston, he came home without it. He was as pale as a

piece of paper. He couldn't talk. He went to his room, he threw up his lunch—"

"Ill? Perhaps he's ill."

"Illness doesn't jettison a cape. Getting the cape swiped made him feel sick."

They sat too far apart for her to reach him, but she leaned in his direction with her arm out. "Of course. I understand," she said. "You're a good grandfather. Is Jeremy's father back?"

"This is such a small place, this village," he said. "No. No, he isn't. I think that he won't be."

"It's good you're here visiting, then."

"It's why," he said.

"You're Pop-Pop, yes? He talks about his Pop-Pop. Your daughter, Nora, she's lucky to have you. I understand the place she's in."

He wondered if he was supposed, now, to ask her for details.

She looked at the linoleum between them, then she looked at him from underneath her brow. His eyes skittered from hers but he forced himself to look again at her resigned, sad face. He thought, frighteningly, of slapping her to punish this theatricality. He thought next of holding her face between his palms. He looked away again.

She said, "Both my parents were dead when *my* husband left. My sister visited a brief little while, but of course she had a life to return to. What do *you* return to—ah, is there something to call you besides Pop-Pop? Do you prefer Mr. Royce?"

"Bing."

"As in Crosby?"

"I'm afraid so."

"It's an upbeat name. You inspirit us all, Bing."

He said, "You've been wonderful to Jeremy, Mrs. Preston."

"Muriel?"

"Thank you."

"Thank *you*," she said, smiling what he thought of as a gracious smile. He wished she would simply *talk* to him instead of demonstrating what she intended her words to mean. But he also liked looking at her, and she clearly wished him to.

"The cape's gone. Nora and I looked at home. You didn't find it here, or you'd have said so."

"Poor man. And poor, poor Jeremy."

"Muriel, would you mind terribly if I stood up? My knees are strangling."

She made the hiccup of laughter again and put a hand over her mouth. She stood, saying, "Here." She extended her cool, small hand and he took it and she tugged. When he was up, she slowly let go of his hand and said, "There's so much of you. You just kept coming. Unfolding, I meant—you know."

Her eyes met his. She was pleased to have said it that way, he was sure.

"Thank you," he said. He looked away, at the walls decorated with pasted constructions on rough paper, at crayon drawings of towering stick-figure parents and little sheltered stick-figure kids. He was afraid of seeing Jeremy's. He wanted Muriel Preston to find another reason for taking hold of his hand.

"You said that you understand Nora's, ah . . ."

"Plight?"

"Yes. Plight. Did you mean you're a single parent?"

"Whose husband left. I raised the boys myself. Tim's in the navy and Barry goes to Hobart. He—my husband—said that he felt like all the air in the house was gone. After *that*, he told me about his girlfriend in Syracuse. She was salesperson of the year that year for the Stickley furniture showroom. Yeah. So I know how Nora feels, more or less. How is she about it?"

He closed his eyes and spoke slowly, but still his voice was unsteady when he talked about his child. "Not confident."

"Getting left will create that effect," she said in a dry monotone. "And not just on Mommy. Behold: Jeremy's cape."

He looked at the chairs against the near wall and at the clothes closet, open to display its low, bare hooks. "Oh," he said. "You meant—"

"*Voilà*, I meant. They both need a cape."

"And his is gone."

"And so is hers," she said. "Does Mrs. Bing Royce visit our perhaps claustrophobic municipality? Jeremy never mentions her."

He thought again of striking and of cradling the sweet, insincere face. He shook his head: acting *could* still be sincere, he thought. And he thought that he was hoping so. He said, "No. Not for some years. She died."

"I'm sorry."

"Yes. Thank you. Well, it sounds like we're all pretty damned sorry, Muriel."

"It sounds like we all need a measure of comfort," she said. She looked directly into his face. She seemed sad, not bold, but her voice was even and determined when she asked, "Should I tell you the way to my house?"

He knew the village well and didn't want to. He thought of Nora as trapped here. He thought, often, of insisting that she come to live with him in New York, and he knew that he was afraid she might give in. He believed—it might, he thought, be all he believed—that he could not share his bereavement yet. His sadness seemed all that was left of Anna, his wife. So here he was, fugitive comfort to his child, driving through the village large enough to contain several churches, one of them fundamentalist Protestant, one Roman Catholic, one the traditional Baptist that housed the nursery school, a small Presbyterian church of elegant white clapboard, and no synagogue, of course, or mosque. The Methodists had established themselves in the next village to the north, five miles up on the commuting road to Syracuse. People here drove to Syracuse or Utica, or they repaired computers locally, or staffed the insurance company or hospital, cut cord-wood, ran a snowplow, and a few on the outskirts still farmed.

He thought a lot about churches these days. He wished he could believe in leaving his sorriest thoughts in the dim, com-forting coolness of one. But he couldn't. All he left, in the base-ment of a church, was his worried grandson, and all that Jeremy had left behind was his cape. His daughter's husband was an architect in Syracuse. He lived, now, with an interior designer who had worked on one of his homes. They went to church every week, Nora had told him with scorn.

"But maybe it's not supposed to be like taking out the pails for the weekly trash pickup," he snarled as he drove. "You're supposed to be a pilgrim in church. You're supposed to *love* something. Or somebody. *Acknowledge* the damned cosmic whatever-it-is." He didn't know whether he was disgusted with himself, or Nora, or her nearly former husband, or this theatrical woman whose limbs he thought of, whose jumper and sweater he described to himself as he drove the village, taking far longer than he needed to reach her house. He thought about her brave little scarf and was con-fused by the cruelty of his thoughts about her since, obviously, he was also drawn—through these well-tended streets—to Muriel Preston. He went past one after another Greek Revival, Cape Cod, and Queen Anne house, most very well kept and all of them brightened, now, by the orange maples and copper oaks and yellow poplars that flared as the year swung around October and dropped toward another upstate winter in which Nora would worry about Jeremy's health and Jeremy would worry about everything. And Bing, he knew, would think not only of them, as the snows sealed the village in again, but also of Muriel Preston, no matter what happened.

It was about to happen now, he thought, parking in front of the narrow gray shake-shingled house with its small porch littered with wind-blown, bright leaves. It was going to happen now.

Her living room was small and shadowed. She still wore the jumper, but had removed her white cotton turtleneck sweater, and her chest above the bib of her dress was red with warmth. The scarf was knotted loosely about her neck. It was a grown-up woman's neck, with some less-than-taut flesh beneath the smoothness of the scarf. He thought he could smell her bare shoulders and arm when she brought him his wine.

"I like red wine," she said. "Is that all right? It's a big, rich Pommard that I can't afford. Except I love it. I've saved it for a special occasion. So here we are inside of it. In the occasion, that is, not the wine. You understood that."

"I understood that." He would have sipped laundry bleach or buttermilk. He'd felt a little drunk while parking the car. Make that unsteady, he amended.

She was barefoot now. Her toes were stubby on small feet. She sat on the sofa, two white linen cushions to his left. There were muddy-looking canvases in gilt frames, and photographs of boys and the young men they'd become. Lemon peel, he thought, and the almond soap they give you in the bathroom of the Georges V in Paris, that was what the skin of her shoulders smelled like.

She sipped her wine and smiled. "It'll open out plenty more," she said. "Give it a while."

He looked at his watch but didn't note the time.

"Bing," she said, "give it a while."

He nodded. He smiled. He drank the wine. As if he were about to sign a document that was the engine of great consequence, he wondered what was going to become of Nora and Jeremy. What was in store for him?

She poured more wine for them, reaching to the coffee table and scenting the air of her living room. Her eyes moved sideways at him as he breathed her. He couldn't tell whether he was intended to see her observing him or whether she had merely looked. She smiled as if to herself when she sat back. She was careful, in the adjustment of her hem, to cover her knees.

"Does Jeremy talk to you?" she asked.

"About—you mean about his feelings?"

"He says you're wise. That's his word for you: 'wise.'"

"We talk a lot. When he asks about his father, it destroys me. It's like watching a sick puppy, or a wounded bird. Words don't work when they're devastated like that."

"No," she said, "you're wrong. You do give him comfort."

"The goddamned cape gave him comfort. I beg your pardon."

"Oh," she said, "I've heard that locution before." She sipped wine. "I survived it."

They sat, they drank, and then she stood to pour a little wine they didn't need yet.

He said, "You think of yourself as strong, then."

"Bold, I think you mean. Licentious, even. Do you feel . . . rushed?"

"No," he said. "I didn't mean that."

"It's all right if you did, because it's possible I am a little forward with you. Anyway, I do feel competent, I'd say."

"Yes," he said. "That's what I'd say, too."

"At what, would you say?"

"Living your life, I guess." He moved his arm, and it touched her jumper, for she still stood, holding the wine bottle. "Making your way."

"Try me," she said. "See for yourself." She set the bottle on the table's dusty wood beside their glasses, and later he remembered his concern that the bottle might have made a permanent ring. He put his arm about her thighs and pulled her against him, pressing his face into her jumper. Her hands, on his shoulders, drew him in, but then she said, "Upstairs, all right? Come up."

In her room, on the maple bed that groaned as they shifted and slid and bucked, she actually said—he would repeat the words in his thoughts of the afternoon—"Oh, my darling." He thought it as arch, as premeditated, as stickily poetic as anything he'd heard. He wanted romance, he thought with pity for himself. He wanted this to be as fresh and just invented as her words turned it scripted and somehow untrue.

He thrust very hard to stop her from saying it again. And he felt, at the time and later, that his motive betrayed her even as she made their passion seem a little ludicrous. Neither her words, nor his response, nor her tears, nor his wondering whether she truly wept, prevented them from marching on together, with strength and with what struck him as a comradely regard for what felt best for each of them. He realized that he wanted her to say those saccharine words again. He wanted her to mean them. He asked, with his body, whether she did. He demanded that she did. He held her down on top of him as he slammed up. He closed his eyes and heard her grunt and maybe, then, whisper a protest once, though she moved and moved and moved with him. He demanded, with his body, to know what she had meant. But it was Bing who gave in first, surrendering to his angry pleasure, knowing only a little of what he had intended and knowing nothing more about her own intentions, to lie beneath her like a victim, emptied of himself.

He didn't know if he had slept and dreamed in the chilly, dark room when she moved on him and then climbed out of the bed. "I would like to wear your shirt," she said.

"Please do. But it's a little big for you."

She stood beside the bed to pull it on. Its tails hung to her knees. "I know," she said. "That's why I wanted to wear it. Stay there, please."

She returned with their glasses and the bottle of Pommard. "I think you'll find it's opened more than generously," she said, smiling what he thought she might think of as a wicked grin. She sat on the bed, touching him, still wearing his shirt, as they drank.

"I flushed it down the toilet," he finally said.

"Yes. And you're noting, when you say that, how I kept a condom in the drawer of my bedside table."

"No," he said. "Yes."

"Is this the first time since—"

"No," he said. "There was another time. An earlier time. Well, of course it was earlier. I was awful at it."

"How did you think you did here? Just now?"

"Could we talk about the World Series?" he asked her. "Or how you like the Knicks for the upcoming year?"

"You are the rare man I would talk with about the World Series if he asked me to," she said. "So that should tell you how we did here together. If you'd like to know. How would you say we're doing?"

"Muriel," he said, "I got lost in you. I didn't mean to say anything like that—about the apparatus."

"Apparatus! That's wonderful. I wish I could be indiscreet about it and tell someone." Her voice sounded sad when she said, "I don't trust anyone that much. Maybe one day I'll tell it to you. Do you think?" She drank and settled back against him. She said, "I believe these things are meant to happen as they insist on happening, and it isn't given to us to necessarily understand why. Do you agree?"

Her hand moved over his belly and groin, and he moved to be available to her. What she said seemed absurd to him, like the flabby talk that disappointed him in churches. But he said, "Yes."

"Yes," she said, leaning to kiss his mouth. She sat back and said, "I wasn't just left with my boys. I was left when I didn't have a job, when there wasn't money in the bank for us, when it was a brutal winter and I ended up selling shoes in Utica. The store went out of business. The strip mall it was in went bust. One of my kids, Timmy, was caught for shoplifting, but I begged and begged for him, and they let him go. That's why he had a clean record when it was time to try for Annapolis. Do I think of myself as strong? Yes. Do you?"

"Yes. You raised your sons," he said, "and they're all right."

"Oh, yes. They are."

"And you're young."

"Young enough, I suppose." And then she said, "For what?"

"A life? I don't know."

"Well, I always had one, Bing. *That's* the being-strong part."

"Of course."

"No. Please don't *of course* me. It's a little complicated for that."

"Yes," he said. "Muriel, for what? I'm confused."

"Yes, you are, I'm sorry to say." She set her glass on the floor and stood, removing his shirt. He wondered if she indicated by shrugging it off that his obtuseness was ending the day for them. But she stood before him an instant and then climbed into the bed, pulling the comforter over them and climbing onto him again. Then she raised herself up, with her hands on either side of his face. "I want to look at you," she said. He closed his eyes in embarrassment. "No," she said. "Bing." He forced his eyes open, and she gave him a rueful smile which, he thought, was precisely how she had intended, hours ago, to complete their afternoon.

Then he saw her eyes flicker and close halfway. She made a surrendering sound, and she kissed him deeply—as, he speculated, she might possibly *not* have planned.

Downstairs, in jeans and a baggy T-shirt, she held the cream-colored scarf as if she meant to knot it on her neck. She raised her face to be kissed goodbye.

"I'll see you tomorrow," he said. "You know—with Jeremy."

She said, "Darling." She held the scarf against her cheek as if he had just presented it to her.

As he parked in the driveway behind Nora's old Volvo station wagon, his legs felt tired, as if he had walked great distances. His body hadn't ached like this since before Anna died. He was only past the middle of fifty and she was in her forties, but he thought of her as young. He thought of her, too, as confusing. Yes, he thought, but remember the sounds she couldn't help making. Those were not, he thought, the noises she planned for him to hear. He snorted. He shook his head. He tried to feel only experienced about the flesh, and not excited, but he couldn't pretend. He still smelled her, and he felt her in his shoulders and thighs. He thought he still smelled the mixture of them. He paused at the back door, wondering whether Nora would smell them, too. He crackled his chewing gum to cover the excellent wine with artificial cinnamon scent, then spat the gum away and went inside.

It seemed a normal early evening. Jeremy assembled unbrilliant constructions of locking plastic bricks while not watching the television set that brayed bad news in the little breakfast room. Nora, he could see, was listening to the news and sorrowing for the fall of mutual funds, for dying rivers, for soldiers wounded, for migrant families pursued through a southwestern desert by federal officers armed as heavily as soldiers sent off to war. Her thick eyebrows sloped down, her lids were low, and her narrow lips frowned. She looked like Anna, he thought. And what help was that to anyone?

"So where were you?" she asked, not listening, he thought, for an answer. He waved to Jeremy and the boy waved back, his fingers together so that his hand looked like the paw of a cub. Jeremy's smile was real but disappearing, and he looked as usual: worried, small, and slumped against the end of a harrowing day.

Facing Nora in the kitchen and murmuring into the sizzle of the small chicken she'd just lifted up from the oven, he said, "I spoke to Jeremy's teacher. The nursery school woman."

"Muriel Preston."

"Yes. She didn't see the cape. I think she thinks maybe one of the children stole it."

She said, "They don't need it."

"No."

"Jeremy does."

"Yes, he does."

"I mean he *really* needs it."

He nodded, then went to the counter on the far wall for the hardwood cutting board and the carving knife and fork that he and Anna had given to them when Nora's husband, Jeremy's father, was home. He dripped juice from the bird on his shirt and along the floor.

"Sorry," he said.

Nora said, "That's all right." She tore off pieces of paper towel so that she could clean up the juice, but she held the paper, watching him, and she finally set the crumpled squares near the sink. Bing told himself to remember to wipe the floor after dinner.

"I'll let the chicken sit awhile," he said.

She said, "I should have bought some cloth someplace."

"For what? A new cape?"

"Maybe I could have persuaded him. I asked, but he flew into a rage. He said it wouldn't be— Hey, Jeremy, honey. Hi."

He held something like a white, yellow, and red pistol made of the locking plastic bricks. He solemnly offered it to his grandfather.

"Look at that," Nora shouted.

"Good job," Bing said, holding it as you'd hold a handgun.

Jeremy said, "It's a angle iron."

"Of course it is," he said. "What do you do with it, honey?"

Jeremy took it from him and held it against the side of the refrigerator. With the eraser end of a pencil, he made measuring motions. "You get it straight," he said.

Bing said, "Yes, you do."

"I love how you didn't mark the fridge up," Nora said too loudly. "Thank you."

"It was pretend. Arnie does it real."

"God, doesn't he," Nora said. Arnie Holland was the country man in his thirties who was as celebrated among the women of the village for the effects of his shirtlessness while he worked as he was for his achievements at rough carpentry.

Bing, slicing a drumstick and going to work on the thigh, said, "Arnie was here, then?"

"At Lindsay Delano's."

Bing had dropped Jeremy there after school so that Nora could stay on at work in the hospital admitting office, where a flu had cut into the staffing. He had driven from Lindsay's back to school, then from school to Muriel's house, and from there to the Quik-Mart for his guilty cinnamon gum, and from there to his daughter's. He was becoming a local, he thought. It was time to go home. It was time to get back to work. He hadn't checked for messages, he hadn't called the office, he hadn't even opened his briefcase in nearly a week. He was moving with his usual long-legged, slow-motion lope—that had been Anna's description of his progress through the world—but he was really on the run.

Nora said, "What, Daddy?"

He looked up to see Jeremy staring at Nora as Nora stared at Bing. He had separated drumstick from thigh and thigh from the carcass. He had cut off the wing. He had carved the breast meat into semicircular slices, and he stood above this orderly disposition as if he had come upon an accident, a wreck.

"No," he said, "I was thinking."

Jeremy said, "You looked sad."

"Sir," he sang at the boy, "I was *glad*. I was glad to know you and in a transport of delight to be carving up this great big slice of bologna for your platter. *That's* the matter."

He waited for a smile. He had hoped for laughter, but a little smile across the dull white cheeks, pushing at the dark pink bags beneath the eyes, would have satisfied him. Jeremy only watched him with his usual care, and Pop-Pop served up breast meat. Then he talked to Nora about a textbook they had to revise, for school board adoptions in Texas and Arkansas, because the sections on evolution referred to the *immutable cycles of mutation*. "Far be it from me to deny a biology professor his zippy little pun, his toothsome academic oxymoron," Bing said. "But that Texas guy with the bullwhip on his office table in Congress—truly, a big black bullwhip—summoned us to Washington. I didn't go. I refused to. But I did have to send two of the kid editors. Adoption means huge sums. Do you care about this, honey?"

Nora's eyes, as dark and liquid as Anna's, looked miserable. "Like you said before," she said, "I was thinking."

"About what—besides textbook adoptions?"

"How you're telling what somebody else ought to be hearing. But that can't be, can it? And how I'm listening to you while I ought to be hearing a different somebody else."

"Somebody else," he said.

Nora said, "Somebodies. The case of the missing somebodies."

"But that can't happen," he said.

"Apparently not."

He said, "Apparently not. *But*," he said, "do I *not* get to gobble Jeremy's dessert?"

His grandson looked up expectantly, but not with resistance in his eyes, or a willingness to joke that moved on his chapped, bitten lips. He was waiting, Bing understood, to find out whether the world intended to take away his wedge of pineapple upside-down cake.

"Oh, baby boy," Bing said.

Nora sat with Jeremy while Bing cleaned up dishes. He worked in a trance of hushing hot water and the simple process of scrubbing at pots and the roasting pan while the dishwasher made a grating noise behind which he sheltered the way some-one is private behind a high hedge. He thought he understood everything about his loss of Anna—the complaints, the physical exam, the tests, the results, and then the roaring speed of it. He knew what he thought and felt about every grim inch of the cornering, the pinning-down, every day, into a smaller and smaller space, of the tall, tough Englishwoman he had known for so many decades. Whatever he understood about his life was through what she'd seen in him and how she had told him of what she had seen.

But something had happened, and no one but he and Anna had witnessed it, and he thought he would never understand. It filled his chest, it pressed him breathless, to realize that he could ask only his forever-vanished wife what she had meant in the artificial dusk of their bedroom as she, on their bed, opened her eyes to find him in a chair beside her, weeping.

He sighed, now, in Nora's kitchen, as he recalled the discovery. Anna's mouth had tightened, and her dark eyes had scratched like fingers at his face. He remembered straightening in the chair as if expecting a blow. And he'd received it.

Her weak whisper spat from the yellow crepiness of her face. "Jesus, Bing," she'd said in the darkness, "can you give me a *break* here. Give me a *hand*, old boy, and push me off."

So why not think of synagogues and mosques? he thought,

turning his hands beneath the water. Why not wonder about churches? Besides the nighttime hauntings at home, were those not where the truths of the dead were said to reside? No one but Anna could tell him what she had wanted of him, and what it was that he couldn't provide. She hadn't asked him to kill her, he thought. Or had she? If he had understood that, would he have agreed? Had he tried, out of fear, not to understand? Was that the way he had let her, in her agony, down? Or was it something different, maybe even something, somehow, more?

He had never told Nora. He wouldn't, he knew. Jeremy knew the most, he thought, about feeling failed. His hands opened in surrender under the hot, rushing water. If he and Jeremy made it another twenty years, he thought, he might try asking his grandson the meaning of the loneliest moment of his life.

On the way to the car with Jeremy, each of them wearing a sweater in the chill of the morning, he saw the pink, shining offal, like a tiny brain, that he had spat out before entering the house the night before. He kicked it aside, saying, "Yuck," to Jeremy, who hadn't noticed because, Bing suspected, he could see only the bleak patterns of the morning ahead at school. Whatever they were, they were unspeakable, and Jeremy didn't try to describe them.

As Bing buckled him in, Jeremy echoed, "Yuck."

"Yuck what, old sock?"

"New sock," Jeremy replied, dutifully socking his Pop-Pop's arm.

"Yowch!" Bing howled, but Jeremy didn't smile. He would return tomorrow, he thought, and he would see—while he drove, or while he added fares to his Metro card at a subway station, or while he looked at proofs—the ivory cheeks, chewed lips, and anxious eyes of his child's child. There he sat, pinioned by buckles and straps. Bing thought of last night's roasted chicken, now a half-stripped carcass. He thought as he started the engine that its flavor filled his mouth, as if a sour bubble of grease had come up his throat to burst behind his teeth.

"You are my hero," he sang to the tune of "You Are My Sunshine," "my lovely hero—" He said, "Did you know you were my hero?"

"No."

"Do you know what a hero is?"

"No," Jeremy said. Then he said, "Yes."

"What, honey?"

"They have blue pants and boots and a red shirt," the boy recited.

Bing prayed: Oh, don't.

But Jeremy continued. "And they have a cape," he said.

All that Bing could say, then, was, "I love you, honey. Pop-Pop loves you to bits."

Jeremy whispered, "Yuck," and then they were silent for the rest of the ride through the tidy village, and then while Bing found someplace to park, and then while he lifted his grandson out and onto the pavement, and then while they joined their hands and walked to school.

Muriel greeted her students outside the basement entrance of the Baptist church. She wore an unbuttoned navy blue raincoat over her shoulders. He saw white tights and a short, dark skirt, and he thought—as he had so often during the evening and the long night—of the smoothness of her thighs. She smiled at them, and Bing felt himself smile back goofily, as happily as adolescent boys can smile at adolescent girls who have been kind to them.

She wore a raspberry-colored silk scarf, he noticed, that was held in place with a cameo pin. He thought of it as little and brave, but he felt only pleasure—his, but also hers—in the observation.

She said, "Good morning, Jeremy. Good morning, Pop-Pop."

Jeremy looked at Bing before saying, "Morning."

"Yes, ma'am," Bing replied.

"Yes," she said. She said, "I have something, Jeremy. I think you might need a new cape. This one is very powerful." She drew a bundle from under her coat and shook it loose. A cape unfolded, a different shade of blue from her coat or skirt, but clearly part of an outfit she had planned while she planned this moment. She held it out, and Jeremy, after looking it over—Bing saw its *J* in white and lavender paisley—silently turned his back toward his teacher so that she could fasten its paisley ties about his neck.

When she turned him back around and kissed his nose, he looked at Bing.

"Looks good, old sock," Bing said.

"New sock," Jeremy told him and punched him with power on his offered upper arm. Bing winced and yelped, and Jeremy grinned very broadly.

"Thank you, Mrs. Preston," Bing insisted.

"Thank you," Jeremy said, moving away from them and toward a cluster of children who had been watching.

Bing said, "That was a great—I don't know. Courtesy. Favor. Small salvation, for goodness' sakes. Nora asked him if she should make another one, and he said no. He cried. He was angry, I think. Because the magic of the original was gone. But there you were with this—"

"A different magic is all," she said.

He knew that he had to return to his car and drive to Nora's and then leave. But he also had to stand among the copper and the orange leaves with his grandson's teacher. "It was generous," he said, "and a beautiful gesture in friendship. And it was gorgeous in and of itself."

He felt himself reddening as she flushed up from the knot of her scarf along her cheeks and then her forehead. Her eyes were full. A father and his child were half a block away, followed by a mother who wheeled a stroller, and he sensed that they were aimed toward Muriel. Bing felt a desperation about being forced away from this final intimacy with her.

"Gorgeous," he repeated.

"It's when someone decides that the difference in the magic is acceptable," she said. "And by the way: an action isn't always a gesture." She looked at the approaching father and she said, "A person needs to know the difference."

And he didn't. Maybe she knew that hesitation in him. Maybe it was why she was, apparently, alone—because others also didn't know the difference in her. He saw his grandson's long blue cape as the boy, under its protection, dared the dangers of his peers.

She turned from him. She turned back. "You might take some time and decide," she suggested.

He said, "Yes."

She smiled a sunny, theatrical smile. She said, "Teachers. They're always giving homework assignments."

"Nora's coming to get him after school," Bing said. "I have to get back."

"Back," she said.

"To New York. I have a job."

Yes," she said. "We never talked about our jobs very much. We were in a hurry."

"Yes."

"Too much of a hurry, do you think?"

"Not too much of a hurry," he said. "No. I wish—I wish we could start in a hurry all over again."

"We could continue in a hurry," she said.

"Maybe I could phone you during the week," he said, with a thick-tongued dullness he hated.

"Dear man," she said, "I think you could do anything to me." The spasm of anger he felt for the theater in her voice was frightening. He stepped back. He looked away and he waved at Jeremy, who moved his cocked arm back and forth—all he dared, in front of his friends, to display of farewell. "But you're already gone," she said. Her face grew serious and it seemed smaller. He thought he saw what she might look like, grown older.

Even he, Bing thought, could hear the sorrow in his voice. "Not that far," he said, because he wanted her to smile. "Not as far as you'd think."

Waving goodbye to her across perhaps ten inches as Jeremy had waved to him over a dozen yards, he turned away from the school. He prayed. He addressed no heavenly father stitched from children's dreams. And he didn't believe that his prayer could be heard. Still, he prayed, because now, he thought, just possibly, he understood some of what his wife might have meant in the rigors of her dying.

Anna, he said to her as he walked through the leaves to his car, could you do me a favor, dear girl, and give me a bit of a push?

THE BOTTOM OF THE GLASS

The cousins made a rough crossing, they'd have said, if they had thought to complain. They mentioned but didn't lament the time in the air, the late arrival at de Gaulle, the bus ride to catch the train at the Gare Montparnasse, or the long wait for the Très Grand Vitesse to Bordeaux. They did joke about the man in the car rental agency at the Bordeaux terminal who spoke no English and who resented that they spoke some French. He cost them a half an hour of futile searching for the car he pretended to direct them toward, nearly shouting his exasperation: *"Les voitures, il restent la, à droit—la, monsieur! La!"*

Eleanor could imagine them, with their several heavy bags, their sacks from the duty-free, their great, damp slabs and mounds of muscle and fat shifting and trembling as they panted in and about the station and, finally, through the darkness of the garage beneath it where the rentals, *les voitures*, were parked. She imagined Eugene's French, with its awful accent and its wonderful vocabulary, as he breathlessly sought to entertain the traveling salesman who, speaking French with native fluency and English with a transatlantic businessman's ease, had offered to lead them to their car.

Now Eugene sat at the table in the kitchen of the rental house, which he called, quite properly, a *gîte*. They had never met, and her husband had never spoken of these enormous creatures who, it seemed, were kin. Eugene had embraced her on arriving in their sporty convertible, climbing out from behind the wheel with slow, laborious motions to hold her neck in a yoke of moist, thick fingers, kissing her head with the greatest delicacy until Bertha had pulled her away to smother Eleanor's bowed face in those enormous breasts that shifted as if they were independent creatures trapped beneath the baggy tan traveling dress she matched with tan strap pumps and a tan leather handbag that looked as though it were weighted with stones.

"No la, no la-di-da, and surely no parked vultures, dear girl," the cousin of Eleanor's dead husband chanted. "The fellow knew we'd never find them. The Sino-French gentleman, a manufacturer's agent for *plastics*, if you can believe it, unless he meant explosive *plastique*, now that you mention it, finally showed us where to go. He'd been there before, of course, and he was waiting in the corner of the rental office with that polite tranquility of theirs—"

"Not that my dear husband wishes to be mistaken for a racialist," Bertha warned.

Eugene smiled damply at the table in the kitchen they had planned, she and Sid, to use during the rest of June and all of July. While Madame Panifiette, their landlady, took the advice of her husband and several friends in the area to consider whether— here she had made a number of faces involving downturned lips, raised brows, and a half a shake of the head—given the legalities involved, she could release Eleanor from the remainder, as she said it, of "your obligation to me."

Eleanor had said to the tiny Madame Panifiette, with her alabaster complexion, in front of Eugene and Bertha, "You never liked me, did you?"

"Well, now," Bertha had said, in sweet, slippery syllables, "we don't want to necessarily accuse anyone of anything, do we?"

Between them, Bertha and Eugene weighed seven hundred and fifty pounds, Eleanor would have bet. On a better day, she'd have guessed it at six-fifty. But this was only a few days after Sid had looked up from the little corner table on which he leaned toward his white, lined pad with his fine-point fountain pen. She had been sitting at the pine dining table in the tile-paneled kitchen, writing postcards home at maybe eight in the morning. She looked up as Sid did. They caught each other's eyes. She thought he was going to say something rueful about his work. She was ready to smile and cluck and go back to the cards that told what a fine time they were enjoying. But it stopped, inside his eyes, and they went out. He fell sideways from his chair. She went to him, she called to him, she blew her breath past his teeth and felt it going nowhere except back up at her mouth. That night, after following the ambulance to the regional hospital and after talking to a man from the gendarmerie who seemed too young to drive, much less take charge of her husband's death, she used Sid's address book and her own to call home and speak to eight or nine people. She did not call her daughter, Margo, and every day that she failed to, it seemed like a more impossible task. It was an overdue account, accruing a terrible interest. Of the people she did call, Sid's cousins, whom she'd never met, insisted that they come to her. They flew from Baltimore to Roissy–Charles de Gaulle, they took the train to Bordeaux, and they navigated their rental car over the small roads of the wine country of southwestern France, and here they were, managing, among other elements, her grief. Over some days, the details of their journey emerged, and she came to think of them as her big, fat heroes.

They were probably sixty, she thought. Bertha was as tall as Eugene, with beefy shoulders and thick, rounded arms. She dyed her hair black as if to match it to the hair of her shaved moustache. She wore either dresses or skirts with matching tops, nothing tucked in, which was a vanity that Eleanor found moving. She could see the breadth of Bertha's vast thighs as she walked briskly, in dressy high heels, through the echoing, cool, white or white-and-rose tiles of the floors and walls of the *gîte*. She "straightened things up," she said. "Not that it isn't as neat as a pin. But one tries," she said, "to help. The best, the most useful help, they say, is order. So one picks up."

Eugene, who ran a rare-books business in Baltimore, on one of the streets near the revived waterfront area, looked every day at the few French books Madame Panifiette had supplied, as well as the couple of stacks that had taken up too much of the space in Sam's and Eleanor's rolling duffel cases. When he wasn't reading in books he clearly didn't like, or looking at titles he didn't want to open, Eugene spoke on the telephone, using his credit card, to arrange in his blatting but quite correct French for the passage home of three vertical Americans and one who would, as soon as his body was released by the authorities, travel prone.

"Assuming," Eleanor told him as he hung up and sighed, "that Fifi LaPue over there lets me out of the lease. She had a little hankering for Sid, by the way, would have been my bet. What the drug people call a jones? Though I don't know her position vis-à-vis the African-American dead."

"Perhaps, then, she'll be glad to see you go, now that you're on your own. I *am* so sorry," he said. "Forgive me. Sidney—"

Eleanor nodded. She didn't know what else to do with her face, so she put her hands over it. Sidney and I, she nearly said to his cousin, would not have made it from the June we are in to the start of autumn. They'd been a middle-aged couple in a second marriage for each that was going as sour as the wine their land-lady's husband produced in what was little more than a very large old stone garage. Now Eleanor was a middle-aged widow whose husband had died of what the very sweet young doctor, who smelled of a citrus soap Eleanor had thought clean and sexy at once, called *une attaque*—a stroke.

Then the doctor had added, not hesitantly at all, for she was a sophisticated woman of France, after all, "*Les neiges . . .*" She did pause on Eleanor's behalf to say "Do you know this word of ours for, er, the Negroes, madame?"

Eleanor took a deep breath in order to shout at her, to screech, she realized, about her experience as a teacher of French at the sixth-snootiest prep school for girls in the city of New York. She was going to scream in impeccable French. But the woman's kind, tired light green eyes, her obvious concern for the dead man's wife, silenced her. She touched the doctor's forearm with the fingers of her right hand, and she nodded.

She let her breath out, and she said, "*D'accord.*"

"*Eh, bien,*" the doctor said. "*Donc. Les nègres, il sont tres vulnérable des attaques. Je regrette, madame.*"

It had seemed to her before he died, and it seemed to her afterward, that they had remained in love. The sorriest part, she was beginning to believe, was that love did not necessarily make it possible to live, together or alone. And a desire to live, some-

thing beyond the animal drive to not be killed off, she had reluctantly come to think, was the most necessary and most elusive of
feelings. Thinking of the size of Sid's mistake and hers in marrying, she wondered if Eugene suspected something of the great
error in which Sidney and she had courted and married and
traveled abroad. Here he was, because he thought it right to
come to the aid of his nephew's white wife, this gentle, vast, and
elegant pear-shaped cousin from Baltimore, sweating through his
white duck trousers and his dark blue long-sleeved shirt, waving
his white, broad-brimmed straw hat as a fan between them while
they sat at the kitchen table and checked their little list of what to
do after a husband's death in a rural rental house among the rows
of the Panifiettes' sauvignon blanc vines at the end of a very
warm June. She knew that Bertha's whiteness could be all or
some of an explanation, but she doubted it. His hairless café-au-
lait head shone from the heat, and she thought she could feel it,
like his decency, radiate from him across the yard or so of polished pine.

"I'm sorry the weather's so uncomfortable," Eleanor said.
"And I'm so glad you're here, you and Bertha, that I feel *treacherous* about my relief—on account of your discomfort. But thank
goodness."

"You're a cousin. A cousin-in-law. I do not know *what* you are,
in legal definitions, Eleanor. You are our family. If you want to be.
If you do, then you are. If you don't, consider us a very, very large
pain in the ass until we see you safely home."

She took his beefy, moist hand, the one that rested on the table
near his coffee cup, and she set it against the side of her head.

"Dear girl," he said.

Bertha walked in, moving as gracefully in spite of her size as

Eugene did, whether it was to lift a cup of coffee or cross a room. Eleanor could imagine them as they somehow, helping each other quite cordially, made their slow, breathless way up the stairs of the Très Grand Vitesse and stowed the bags at the end of the first-class carriage. She could imagine them murmuring to one another— "Are you all right, dear? If you'd give me your hand . . ."—and could envision them as they faced each other across the little table of their compartment, stomachs folded doughily over the table's edge, great arms flattening on its top, arranging bottles of Evian and sandwiches, wedges of cheese, perhaps, and chunks of fruit that Eugene cut for them with a folding wooden-handled picnic knife while the train gathered speed. She saw his vast hands manage with delicacy the division of a Cavaillon melon or a crescent of Brie, saw hers distribute napkins and plastic cups.

"I have just been having another word with Madame Panifiette," Bertha said. "She was most accommodating of my accent." Her smile might have excused Madame or indicted her own French, but it was kind, somehow. "She expects to 'achieve a resolution' quite rapidly."

"I'll bet you money," Eleanor said, "that it costs us extra money."

"I will expect her to do better on our behalf," Eugene said, with a little steel in his voice. "But some money might pleasantly change the equation. I *could* see that."

Bertha asked, "Did Eugene tell you that we were cooking tonight?"

Eleanor shook her head.

"Well, we're cooking," Bertha said, "so you might prepare yourself."

"Is that a stressful situation?"

"No, dear," Eugene said. "It's noisy, a little, and sometimes quite messy, but I wouldn't call it stressful. You are in one of the superb culinary districts of the world, and not at all far from St. Émilion, such a great wine center, as I'm sure you know. We're off to shop, and then, when we return with food and drink, you are invited to a meal prepared by relatives. Are we your in-laws?"

Eleanor shrugged. She tried to smile brightly.

"Outlaws, then," Bertha said, and she laughed like a girl, though her eyes seemed sad as they slid toward Eleanor and then away.

"Outlaws it will be," Eugene said.

Begging her pardon for seeming intrusive, they moved about the room, opening cupboards and inspecting the refrigerator, each naming items for a list while Eugene wrote down, on one of Sid's green-lined white legal pads, what they would need to buy at the open-air stalls in the square of St. Macaire and at the supermarket in Langon.

Eleanor, who was tall and broad-shouldered and, according to Sid, "the slightly repressed all-American lifeguard at the country club pool," was thinking of Margo, also tall, slender, and broad-shouldered, who suddenly, it seemed, was in graduate school for the study of some kind of cell physiology that her father, a medical doctor, seemed to understand while Eleanor could only decipher the meaning of "cell" and "physiology," without formulating an intelligent sentence that used both words. She was remembering how, early that winter, Margo had come home from Madison, Wisconsin, to Eleanor's place on West Ninth Street to stay the night and register her opinion about Sid and her mother before spending the weekend at their old apartment, now her father's, uptown.

She said, "Mother, for Christ's sake. Have an *affair*. It's an itch, so scratch it. Get over the thrill of it. Then learn how to live alone like the rest of us, for Christ's sake."

"And have you considered that it could possibly be more than sex?"

"When a forty-five-year-old divorced white woman gets a jones for a slightly younger, fairly hot black man who writes books, one of which she happened to read *before* he picked her up at the Metropolitan Museum show of those Vienna Whoevers who did the highly sexualized paintings? Ma: *duh-uh*."

"I don't know where to begin," Eleanor had said. She remembered stumping back and forth on the broad, painted planks of her little Village living room. "I don't know whether to shout terrible things about your not knowing the Vienna Secession, or calling their paintings 'sexualized,' like you're the Dean of Correctness at a second-rate college, or portraying me as this over-stimulated matron who just wants to get *laid* by the nearest black man, who, like all the rest of them, you know, *you know*, is a phallic engine who cannot stay away from dumb and oversexed white women. Margo: *duh-uh*. How could you? And why are *you* so lonely, handing out that living-alone stuff? And since whenever do you say I have a *jones*? I don't know where to begin."

"Don't say anything I can't forgive, Mother."

Margo had called her Mother since the divorce, which they had conducted like a small war while their civilian casualty was in the eleventh grade. Eleanor said, "Margo? Are you really that alone? Are you saying that *I* am? Are you accusing me of being in despair? How desperate do you think I *am*?"

"How much do you weigh, Mother?"

"How much—"

"How much do you weigh?"

"One thirty-three."

"I thought it was, like, a hundred and forty-five?"

"No comment."

"Right. So I'd call you roughly a hundred and forty-five pounds of desperate. That's how desperate I think you are."

Margo sat in silence, then, and watched her wander in the living room, from the wall of bookshelves to the long sofa to one of the windows onto Ninth Street. Finally, Eleanor let a long sigh slide between her lips and she said, "I've been holding my breath. I've gotten so strung out by you, I forgot to breathe."

"Then you know the principle of blowing dope. Hold it and hold it and then let it go. I could roll us a joint."

"Of marijuana?"

"What did you think it involved, Mother?"

"I don't want to know."

"All right."

"Do you smoke it a lot?"

Margo looked at her with the pity of the young. Eleanor had seen it on her students' faces. That it was undisguised made it cruel, as if they had never considered the possibility of an elder understanding the gulf between them. You decayed before their eyes, it said, and you didn't know how close to dead you were.

"I think you're learning to value yourself is all," Eleanor had said when they told each other goodnight. "It's not easy. I know."

"And do you?"

"Do I what?"

"Mother, do *you* value yourself?"

"Of course. And I know that Sid values me. Oh," Eleanor had said, "not a great answer, is it?"

"You're still learning, too."

"Life is long," Eleanor remembered telling her.

"It better be," Margo had said, about to go inside the guest room, "because you are one slow learner."

Which apparently was true, Eleanor thought as, in the French rental, Sid's great cousins prepared to drive into St. Macaire to purchase butter and cream and duck breasts and two kinds of mushrooms. "We can bake in those little ramekins instead of metal molds," he said. "Absolutely no harm done. And that's a reminder," he instructed Bertha, "about milk for the timbales. We cannot forget the milk."

"You're making the list, dear."

"Yes, I am," he said. He told Eleanor, "The preparation of food, you will not be surprised to learn, excites me. I get forgetful."

"He can also be dictatorial and quite like a master chef— decidedly cruel," Bertha said, smiling. "It gets quite dangerous when we cook."

"The danger," Eugene chanted, as if from memory, "lies in running short of reliable duck confit, not in any slightly bruised feelings among the sous-chefs."

"Who said that?" Bertha asked.

"I did, of course."

"You can see," she told Eleanor, "he grows brutal."

There was a rustling of linen clothing, a seizing of lists, and a counting of currency, and then they were off in their black convertible, down the stony drive to turn left onto the little connector road, then right onto the paved secondary, and then to wander the turns past vineyards and the sheds that sheltered stainless steel storage tanks and the descent into St. Macaire with its ramparts and its small, plain cathedral, and its narrow streets. She thought for a moment of the cousins as they loomed over the small, taut French while they inspected the wares of the seller of Basque sausages and cheeses, or the local man so proud of his harsh Armagnac, and the butcher who always seemed to sneer over his duck legs, his unplucked chickens, his thick loins of pork. She could hear their murmurs to each other and their charmed, polite replies.

In the master bedroom, which like the dining area opened into the vineyard, she moved folded clothing about and tried to pack. There were two large bags and two small ones for carrying books and bottles of water onto the plane; they hadn't brought more than thin summer clothing and a cotton sweater apiece for a cool night, but there seemed to her to be too little room in their luggage. It felt important that she leave nothing of his behind, although she suspected that, eventually, she would give it all away in New York. For now, though, she wanted to bring him home with everything he'd carried abroad.

Did that include her? She wondered if they would have returned together, assuming the small matter of his not having died of an explosion of blood in the brain.

"Probably," she said to the chugging of insects outside, the slow droning of fat bees in the waist-high pots of rosemary next to the house.

"Of course," she said.

Looking at the herbs and thinking of the cousins at their list-making, she thought of the preparation of food. She remembered the first formal date with Sid, who had taken her for dinner to Jarnac, the restaurant in the West Village. He had insisted that they order the cassoulet, which was better, he said, than the cassoulet, with white beans and duck and pork sausage, that he had eaten in the Fifth Arrondissement of Paris the previous year. A stocky, jolly, but tough-looking woman came out of the kitchen while they ate, and she circulated through the small room. She and Sid embraced, she patted Eleanor on the shoulder, and she moved on.

"The chef," Sid said.

"I can't help it," she told him. "I'm impressed."

"That was the idea."

"It was?"

"Oh, yes. You're who I'm determined to impress."

His thin face, which she thought had as many muscles in it as an athlete's arm, was a little darker, with a little more putty color, she thought now, than Eugene's. Sid kept his coarse hair short, and she had enjoyed inspecting the beautiful shape of his head. She could imagine a mother holding her hand around the back of that head. She could imagine her own hand there. He saw her speculating, and he suddenly grinned, a big and boyish, happy smile.

"What?" he said.

"Never mind. Although I suspect you can figure it out."

"I hope so," he said.

"I'm considering matters," she said. "So tell me something."

"About what?"

"About anything besides me. Tell me something about your work."

"You said you know my work. Now I'm disappointed."

"What you are is like a boy about it."

"I'm like a boy about everything else, too," he said.

"Never mind. Tell me about what you do. I read the one about the women who robbed banks. Very cool, as my daughter might say. A bunch of right-on women, she'd say, except for the part about shooting people. Your detective cries. People seem to like that."

"Margo. Your daughter."

"Yes, Margo. So what are you working on now?"

"Why, you."

He had never mentioned any relative except his mother. He had certainly never referred to his cousins, the vast Caucasian Bertha and Eugene, the giant brown purveyor of rare books who would return chirping to the house to prepare something involving magret de canard in order to nourish the widow. And here was the widow, trying to fit too many clothes into too few cubic inches of luggage that, a couple of weeks ago, had accommodated everything.

Eleanor slept among the stacks of neatly folded undershorts and T-shirts and olive-green cargo pants and the socks she had bought him at Brooks Brothers. She had been frightened while she slept. She had awakened herself by calling out, had looked about the room and closed her eyes and gone to sleep again. Now her mouth was gummy and foul, her face felt greasy, her left hand hurt from clenching it. She showered but put on the same clothing she'd worn—khaki shorts, a wrinkled white camp shirt. She brushed her teeth and worked her hair into a ragged bun. She went barefoot into the kitchen, where she drank iced spring water while watching the sun hang huge and orange over the hills at the far edge of the grape vines cultivated by Monsieur and Madame Panifiette. The sun appeared not to move, though the insects chirred louder, she thought, and the bees worked harder now, and the hills began to go dark, almost as if they were a silhouette, even though the brilliant orange sun appeared to be directly over them. You would think it would light them up, she thought.

"Stand by, Eleanor," Eugene called. She heard the throbbing of the engine of their Saab, and then she heard the slamming of doors, the rustling of plastic sacks, and the panting of very fat people moving across the hot slate walk at the back of the house.

She and Sid had not slept together during the week before he died. They had agreed, though they'd said nothing aloud, to continue to sleep in the same bed, to kiss each other good morning and goodnight, to walk naked from the shower to their bedroom, to use the toilet without hesitation or shame, and to in every other way manifest their intimacy. The making love had stopped as though a mechanism had broken without any other symptoms. They had malfunctioned without a fight, only slightly acknowledging the increment of tension between them. Sid was making some progress with the book, his fourth, about a black detective of the upper middle class who solved crimes out of his affection for the victims, but never quite learned how to love the woman who, by the end of each book, loved him.

On the night of her learning about the breaking down, they lay in the dark in bed, he in pajama bottoms and she in sleeping shorts and a sleeveless, scoop-necked top, not touching, at the start of their sleeping this way every night.

"I keep wondering," she said. "I mean, about how, where you are—at the start of it—you could go off to France for a couple of months and work on a book that depends on being in New York, where your people are—"

"My *people*?"

"Now, you know what I mean. Your *characters*. You couldn't have meant—you didn't think that *I* meant anything about race."

"No, El, of course not."

"It doesn't sound like us," she said, "talking that way. I mean, making that kind of mistake about each other."

"No."

"We don't do that."

He shifted. He sighed. "We surely didn't used to," he said. He teetered on his side, and then rolled onto his back again. "We didn't. We mustn't." He turned toward her and kissed her upper arm, letting his teeth gently close on her flesh.

"You're trying to turn me on," she said.

"I am."

"So that—so that what, Sid?"

"So that you know."

"It's a part of the argument, then?"

"We aren't having one."

"What are we having?"

"I don't know."

"A power struggle," she said.

"El, come on."

"Well, I'm not hard to get," she said.

"That's not what I meant."

"I don't know quite what you meant," she said. "But I do think we're a little old to be wasting our time on so much talk about what we aren't doing when what we *could* be doing is making each other happy."

He lay beside her, he didn't move, and the orange sun hung in the early nighttime sky.

"Except we aren't," she said. "Am I guessing it right? Happy, I mean. I mean, we're *not* happy." Here they were, she thought, two adults who functioned in terms of language carefully chosen, and it was as if neither spoke the other's native tongue. But the attitude of his body, his distance though he lay so close, his silence, now cut through the words they didn't or couldn't select. It's as simple as that, she thought. We are not. "What we've been doing, maybe," she said, "has been hoping. Maybe what we did was mostly hope."

"Mostly hope," he said. "Nothing ignoble in that."

"We tried."

He said, "We did our best."

"Oh, Sid," she said.

After a while, he said, "That's right. Oh."

And finally, she had returned his kiss, on the hard curve of the top of his shoulder, letting her lips come away slowly from his bronze-tan skin that always smelled to her like spices—and she thought of their names, although she never cooked with them and really didn't know one from the other: mace and cloves and nutmeg—because it seemed likely, she thought, before she turned over to face away from Sid and from the enormous, ragged sun, that they had just kissed goodbye.

Bertha and Eugene cooked, and they did their best to entertain her. They made drinks of Campari and soda over ice, and Eugene warbled bad renditions of tragic French arias while Bertha complained about the mysteries of the stove mechanisms.

"I am using dried cèpes," she told Eleanor, "along with chopped shallots and milk and no more than one-half a cup of heavy cream to make a kind of gateau of mushrooms. They're really called timbales. You know the term? After we combine over heat, we'll bake. You'll find it echoed in the heavy cream, the port, and the shallots of the woodland sauce that my husband, the fascist chef, is coercing together for what will, after all, be simply sautéed duck breasts. Are you hungry, dear?"

Eugene was gliding from the sink to the table to the stove, wiping at his sweaty forehead with a dish towel hung about his neck. The evening breezes came in over the grapes while the air of the kitchen took on the aroma of the reducing canned chicken stock he apologized for using. "We bought it at the hypermarché outside Langon," he said. "It's a travesty, of course, but there hasn't been time to make real stock. And we had better hope, by the way, that the co-fascist to my left"—and here Bertha actually performed a half a bow, her huge breasts falling against her dress—"knows that I require some of those cèpes for my sauce. And, darling," he said to her, "can you scoop me five tablespoons of butter?"

She said, "Eleanor, would you mind awfully grating some nutmeg?"

Eleanor said, "Why?"

Eugene stopped washing parsley at the sink. Bertha, panting as she sautéed mushroom strips and chopped cèpes, with a knife in one hand and a tub of butter in the other, paused, then turned to Eleanor, looked at her face, and said, "An unpleasant association?"

She almost spoke, but only shook her head.

"It's hardly necessary, dear," Bertha said.

Eugene danced, immense over his relatively narrow, small feet, toward the table where she sat. "I must make you another Campari-soda," he said.

"No," she said. "No, thank you."

"Some of the dinner wine? If you know me, then you know I brought enough. I have Chateau St.-Georges-Côte-Pavie, which is a St. Émilion from nearly up the road. It's supposed to be very fleshy and full of blackberries. It's breathing on the counter, let me pour you a glass."

"I can grate the nutmeg," she told him. "That's all right."

"And I can pour you a glass of wine," he said. "And *that's* all right."

She held her palm out and Bertha deposited the little tin grater with its small compartment that held the nuts. Eleanor leaned to sniff at the compartment. That was the smell of nutmeg. She said, "I wonder if you could excuse me?"

"Dear girl," Eugene said, "it's all too, somehow, celebratory, isn't it? We were afraid it might feel that way. Although one *could* celebrate Sidney. Perhaps one ought to, even. My brother's boy. And aren't genes *so* treacherous? Arthur, my brother, also died too young. And he was healthy. Anyway, he was slim. Broad at the chest, but slender all the same. He was a dancer for a couple of years, a professional chorus-boy hoofer in Philadelphia and New York. You'd have thought that one of us was adopted, my mother used to say, because we were made so differently. Of course, I happened to them twelve, nearly thirteen years after my poor mother thought she was done with bearing babies. Arthur believed I was this pick-me-up-off-the-street creature, but I wasn't. I was born to them, and we were brothers, the poor soul. We both of us adored Sidney. He was more like a brother to me than Arthur, now that you mention it, who was, if you'll forgive the psychology, a little bit more of a *father*, if you can believe it, as we got older. So maybe the meal's for him. But it's also for you, Eleanor, because Sidney loved you and you loved him. God bless you both."

Bertha said, "She's all done in, Eugene. She's exhausted. She should sleep. Eleanor," she said, "you must have a nap. At once. We can worry later about food. Do you hear?"

Bertha insisted on shepherding her from the kitchen table and past Eugene, who leaned to kiss the air beside her face, around the corner, and down the short corridor that separated her bedroom and Sid's from the room in which the cousins slept. She smelled the nutmeg, she believed. And she smelled Bertha's heated skin, and a floral talc, and the astringency of a deodorant. Bertha held a vast, round, heavy arm about Eleanor's shoulder and she murmured to her, making noises but not whole words, little cooing sounds of encouragement, as she saw her through the bedroom door. Inside the bedroom, as she lay on the bed beside the open French doors, Eleanor heard them moving across the tiled floor of the kitchen, heard the sputtering of sautéed food, the clatter of implements against crockery and pots, the thump of the oven door, the gurgle of liquids measured out. It all calmed her, and she let herself listen to the sounds of their cooking as, when she was a child, she heard, from her room, the noises made by her parents as they cleaned up in the kitchen at the end of a dinner party, her father's voice tired and grainy and deep, her mother's voice rich with satisfaction as she gossiped about her guests.

Eleanor woke to the sweet smell of grapes outside the bedroom, and the creamy, thick odor of the chalky soil in which they grew. Over those smells lay the dark richness of roasted vegetables and seared, sauced duck. She was lying on Sid's side of the bed, among his scattered clothes, closer to the open doors onto the fields, in the darkness of a cloudy sky lit coldly now by the pale, small moon. It would rain in the morning, she thought, and the day would be humid. Eugene and Bertha would be uncomfortable in high humidity, and they would soak through their traveling clothes. They would suffer, and so might she, she thought, but none of them would look up, like Sid, and then, like a lamp extinguished, go out.

She put on clogs and went into the kitchen, passing the closed door to the silent extra bedroom. A bottle half filled with the St.-Georges-Côte-Pavie glowed in the low light the cousins had left on. She tugged at the cork and poured some into a kitchen tumbler. In the refrigerator she found sliced duck wrapped in plastic, and she sat at the table and ate. The wine was fruity and rich, and the taste of the duck made her hungry for more. But when she thought of the smell of nutmeg, although she couldn't make out its taste in the duck, she removed the partly chewed meat from her mouth and threw it into the garbage pail under the sink. She took a swig of St. Émilion and spat it down into the drain.

Walking past the great pot of rosemary, and among lavender bushes, she slowly carried her wine down a row of grapevines. Something flew close to her head, but when she looked up she saw only the rows of cloud, like the serried layers of flesh on a fish, lit from above by the dim moon. She squatted, suddenly, and coughed, waiting to be sick. Nothing happened, though. It was as if they had eaten the corpse, she told herself, and she gagged again. But nothing more happened except a strangled cough, and she turned from what she thought of as her theatrics, sipped at the tumbler, and then walked the short distance back to the French doors of the bedroom, where she sat cross-legged on their bed and emptied her glass and thought of the sorry sweetness of their confession to each other that, at barely their beginning, they were failed.

A night bird at the far edge of the grapevines called, another answered, and then she heard Bertha's rich voice. It had made a kind of whinny in the bedroom across the corridor. She moved from the bed without thinking, and she crouched at her closed door. Breathing raggedly, shallowly, she pressed the empty glass to the door and her ear to the bottom of the glass. She heard the whining of what she knew were bedsprings in the extra room. She heard the shuffle and brush of bedclothes, and she heard their skin. They were probably running with sweat, she thought. They were naked and their bodies were wet and they were making love. She had never thought of them this way. She had considered them delicate of feeling, gentle of motive, bound inside themselves by their fat and the difficulty with which such large creatures moved, no matter how graceful they might appear. But now she heard them whisper with pleasure, she heard the smack of lolloping, floppy skin, the suction of their flesh as they moved together and apart and then together again.

Eugene said, low, "Oh, for God's sake, my *dear*est girl."

Bertha made a sound of pleasure at her wickedness.

"God," he said.

She thought of the hundreds of pounds of flesh that shifted and slid, of the way a mounded stomach was stuck by fluid and friction to the loose, damp canyon of a crotch. She was excited by what she heard, but she was also suddenly aware that what she ached with now was not the grief of this morning or of the days and nights before. It was envy, she thought. She didn't breathe out, and didn't breathe out. She knelt at her door, one hand closed on the knob and the other holding her eavesdropper's glass as she listened to the long silence in the room across the hall. Then one of the sweat-slicked, gargantuan lovers held by death at bay whispered words she couldn't distinguish. Then one of them shifted great weight, the guest bed groaned, and Eleanor began to breathe.

NOW THAT IT'S SPRING

They flew from New York to Dublin, from the long late winter of ice storms into an early spring. But spring, if that meant the weight on the neck of the sun, had come and gone, the air hostess told them on the fifth hour out. "You're in for the wet," she'd said, smiling, "and I'm sorry for you."

An hour after arrival, before they trundled the bags outside, they dug into them on the dirty floor between customs and the taxi queue and they helped each other put on the bright anoraks, one yellow and one red, that marked them as citizens of L.L. Bean. Then they found the cab that would struggle through geyser splashes from potholes, around fluorescent traffic cones at construction sites, and past the shuttered shops of half past seven in the Irish morning—the city felt gray, raw, and unwelcoming— while their dark and frowning driver talked in jolly tones about the forecast of more chilling rains.

He said, "It's a lovely old section of the city."

Claire said, "Sorry?"

"I'm referring to your destination, missus. If you care about the Vikings, you're in for a treat. You'll be walking, anyways, on cobblestones for certain."

She said, "I can't, Richard. For Christ's sake."

He made conversation for her and he watched her slide a little on the seat of the cab, hiding underneath the blanket of his chatter. "I remember," Richard said. "It's very historic. Right? The whole . . . district."

"There are some lovely little houses round and about the office blocks and them."

"Charming, then, would you say?" Richard said.

"My word for it exactly," the driver said, looking as though he might knife them on arrival but sounding like a waitress in a tearoom. Richard realized that he hadn't been inside a tearoom for twenty years. "And we have to allow for the plight of the farmers," the driver instructed them, "for it's said they need the rain something terrible."

To make up for Claire's silence, and what he knew without looking to be her frozen expression, Richard overtipped the driver. The house was one of eight, connected by brickwork and each with a wide, wooden door. The shadows of higher buildings darkened the brick and made the rain feel colder. There was very little traffic passing in front of the house, though it growled in some surrounding streets. He found the keys they'd been sent by his author, one small and one that was thick and long and heavy, which fitted the keyhole before which he had to stoop while jiggling and shoving the key until it turned and the red wooden door swung in. Past the small vestibule was a dining table, and in an alcove parallel to the vestibule were a sofa and an easy chair before the only window. In the not quite dark of the house, they could see a little kitchen in the rear of the house and, to their left, entering onto the kitchen, a staircase.

Richard said, "It's very—"

"Depressing," she said.

"Generous of him, I was going to say."

"Yes," she said. "I mean of course. I know how generous it is. I know I'm being a bitch."

"Being a little bitchy," he said. "We're just in the foothills of the dangerous mountain range of High Bitch known to wary travelers as Claire Pottinger."

"Weary of me or wary—or *worried*, maybe?"

"He said they'd leave some stuff for us in the kitchen. Let's make coffee and find a little bread for toast."

"No," she said, "let's sleep and then go out into the god-damned rain."

"For what?"

"So we can *talk* about it. Like the stewardess, like the man at immigration, like the cabdriver. God, it's cold in here. It's cold, it's dark, everything smells damp, and, yes, it is very generous of him to invite us to stay here, I agree, and the charming cobbled streets."

He took off his rain jacket and hung it on a peg in the vestibule. Then he took off hers, unzipping and pulling at it as if she were a small child, and he hung it up next to his. He took her hands in his and rubbed them, then held them before his mouth and hushed his breath at them. "You're all icy," he said, doing all of the little bit he could do.

"Hypothermia," she said. "Or rigor mortis."

He led her upstairs: a bedroom at the head of the steps and one to the left of the top banister. In the room with a double bed next to a window that overlooked the street, he pulled the heavy white sheets back, unfolded two thick blue woolen blankets that were draped across the foot of the bed, partly pushed and partly held her until she was draped in bedclothes and, still wearing her dark framed glasses, asleep. He took off his shoes and lay down beside her. The rain was hard against the window and it drummed on the roof. He removed Claire's glasses and set them on his bedside table. Then he lay with his nose against the thickness of her hair and listened to the drainpipes gurgle, and to the effortful climb and then fall of his jet-lagged wife's deep breaths. He thought briefly of the symposium where he would earn their airfare. Then he thought, with a lurch in his gut that he felt each time, of the lawsuit against his wife and of the long, cold year they had lived since the legal complaint had arrived to sicken their household.

Bill Robinson, a sixty-five-year old essayist of narrow reputation, had written a memoir of his father called *The Gentle Gunman*. It was making Robinson, and Richard's publishing house, and several others in Europe and the UK, a lot of money. And he was a very decent man who had insisted on lending them the little house he'd inherited from one of his brothers. And they had flown to it to escape the choking ice that had ended their winter, and the legal bill of particulars that had frozen Claire's professional life. "Now we'll get well," he said silently, in what he suspected was a lie, "now that it's spring."

Claire was asleep when he wakened to darker streets and heavy rain. He huddled against her and smelled her skin and breath, touched the edge of her breast near her rib and, like a lightbulb just before the current dies when a storm has taken the lines down, a pulse of lust lit him. She rolled into his hand and then escaped from it to lie at the edge of the window side of the bed. He heaved himself in the other direction and went downstairs with his shoes in his hand. There was dark Dutch coffee ground fine and an elegant note of welcome from their host. He gave the phone number of his house on the northwestern coast, and Richard was relieved, trying the phone, to find that it wasn't connected. He couldn't imagine calling the man in the midst of his work to discuss, say, how you turned the broiler on. He found good French wine in the refrigerator and Irish whiskey in the cupboard. There was fresh bread, two cheeses, and a packet of ham. He explored the broiler on his own and managed to toast bread. He made sandwiches, and he poured whiskey into hot black coffee. Then he carried it all upstairs, because he couldn't find a tray, on an oversized art book, photographs of the Vezelay basilica.

Claire wasn't in the bed. He looked in the other bedroom, which was also empty. He looked out its window on a narrow alley, stacked with scrap wood and building materials, that ran behind the house and its neighbors. From their bedroom she said, "Lovely coffee, all spiced up with wonderful hootch. Good Richard. *Good* Richard. Come eat and drink!"

She sat on a stool at the foot of the bed, sipping coffee and chewing. With one hand she clutched a blanket around her shoulders and the other guided the cup. There was color in her face again, and she looked into his eyes instead of away and in at her anger.

He sat on the bed and watched her eat and drink. "I got worried," he said. "I couldn't find you."

"You always find me."

"I thought we'd both gotten lost, you know, from each other."

"I went downstairs to the bathroom. I walked right behind you, when you were twiddling the knobs on the stove. The bathroom's through the kitchen, and you make a left."

"I found it earlier," he said. "It was you I couldn't find."

"You always find me. This is incredible ham."

"You have to read the note downstairs. The man's probably in the process of winning a half a dozen prizes, and he finds the time to lay in food and recommend the Powers whiskey. There's an unopened Meursault in the fridge, and half of something very grand-looking that I never tasted. And that beautiful Irish butter."

"And you'll tell these academics and newspaper guys and the publishing dollies in their little skirts how terrific he is. And now you can talk about his taste in French wines. But you won't mention that you were the one who found his manuscript, and you were the one who put it over and made him a little bit rich before London or Dublin or Berlin."

"I don't think that's why he did it. I know it isn't. He really doesn't care about that."

"Everybody cares about that," she said.

"Probably. You're probably right. But he doesn't *want* to. I think he thinks he shouldn't. So he keeps himself in check, inside the harness. He's quite damned proper in the best sense. He's a man in charge of himself. You know him—you know what I mean."

"I don't know him the way you do."

"Well, for that kind of knowing," Richard said, "there's just his ex-wife and his wife."

"And of course the woman in the States. The musical woman. I forget her name. His well-known, sordid affair that, frankly, sounded pretty terrific to me. What's her name? I can't remember names anymore unless they're my lawyer or the lawyers of the people who sue me or the people who do the suing. I won't say the suing person's goddamned name. I refuse to."

"You should have another half sandwich. I'll go downstairs and make more coffee and bring it back up."

"Too late. I already ruined the picnic, didn't I? I'll come downstairs and watch you boil water."

They pressed switches downstairs, and brownish yellow lights leaked onto the dark carpets and packed bookcases and threw shadows on the framed prints that hung around the living room. Claire found the thermostat, so there was heat now, and she set clothing into drawers upstairs and hung some in the one closet of the house, in the bedroom next to theirs. Richard made them more coffee with a little seasoning of the Powers, and now they sat near the single downstairs window with its skin of rainwater while Claire, still wearing the blanket like a coarse, heavy shawl, read aloud from sections of the book about Dublin. Her face was animated now, and her glasses slid down her nose to make her look like a studious girl. Richard prodded the buttons of their cellular phone and found that he was unable to call their symposium host, or Bill Robinson, or their daughter in Washington, D.C.

"'. . . and is one of many enticements to the traveler to walk the Liffey's length,'" Claire read.

"And is the reason I will cancel this telephone company's *ass* when we get back," Richard said.

"So we can't get in touch with anyone?"

"It's only the afternoon," he said. "We'll go find a post office. We'll buy a phone card. We'll make calls with it, and then we can get takeout food and carry it home."

"Over the quaintly cobbled streets," she said.

"You never forget."

"And I never forgive," she said. "Guess who I mean."

He nodded. "Me neither," he said.

"No, you're reasonable, Richard. I admire you. I envy you. Because I'm either sick with fear or sick with rage. One way or the other, the goddamned country-mouse hack who is *convinced* he's capable of writing *anything* that anybody could believe I would remotely consider worth stealing has gotten so deep inside my life, I think you ought to be chasing him for fucking your wife in her mind on your own bed." She looked at the guide-book. "That's vulgar," she said. "That's a pretty bad stretch of a bad figure of speech. It's lousy language. The creep is a *midwife* for lousy language."

"Worthy of the plaintiff," Richard said, "but not of you."

She nodded. She looked at the book. "I never realized they had so much to do with the Vikings over here. You know, their history."

"Fancy that."

Her face was crimson, which was preferable to the pallor he had seen so much of during Claire's immersion in the plagiarism suit. He could often convince himself to be certain that it might, one day, be dismissed or disproved, collapsing from the weight of its lies. They were clumsy lies, and Claire's reputation as a writer of television films was strong. But the winter had nearly undone them. It had been a season of heavy snows, quick thaws, and then, in late March, two- and three-day ice storms, with trees around their house in Putnam County snapping at the stem or exploding at the crown. The landscape of drooping or shattered trees and withered hedges turned the color of dirty ice, and the metallic sky pressed hard on them. They would have to wait for the slow convulsions of the legal process, he thought, but Claire's network was willing to protect her, and its insurance firm had named a bright attorney to represent them, and they would come through, Richard thought. He wondered what they would carry with them at the end of the passage if they did.

"So," he said, "let's clean up and put on the rain jackets and borrow the big umbrella in the vestibule and walk along the Liffey."

"I want fish and chips for dinner," Claire said. "I want to call our kid and buy fish and chips."

"Let's have them with Meursault and demonstrate how unbound we are by the long traditions of the way you're supposed to use the chardonnay grape."

While Richard, in the bathroom, was staring at the instruction manual for the water heater, he lost track of Claire. Then he found her at the front of the house, standing just inside the little vestibule. Still wearing her blanket, she was leaning her right side against the plaster wall they shared with the neighboring house. She crouched a little, he noticed. She moved her lips and he drew closer to hear her muttering. "This moron," she told him, "in this high-pitched voice, is having a conversation, as far as I can tell, with his radio. The International Voice is telling him about the weather and some kind of sports scores, and he's telling the Voice how he feels about the rain. And what's Weeta-Bix?"

"A kind of breakfast cereal," Richard said, pulling the blanket around her and knocking gently on top of her head to signify that he thought it might be filled with marbles rolling loose or twittering, tiny birds. "Sort of shredded wheat?"

"He says he eats it every day and his bowels are regular as clockwork."

"What a lucky man. So why are you snooping on him?"

"I heard the radio."

He pulled her from the wall and held her. "You went snooping so you *would* hear a radio. What are you looking for? Do you know?"

"To check the scores?"

He tugged her by the front of the clutched blanket and she followed him to the bathroom. The water was hot, and Richard washed her as she stood naked and rosy before him, spraying her with the handheld shower nozzle. What he felt now wasn't the earlier urgent flare, but a kind of sad admiration of her thick nipples and heavy breasts. She was like a child as she entrusted herself to him, ignoring the power of her body over him where he soaped and rinsed her, and exciting in him a gentleness next to pity. He toweled her back as if he were warming a victim of shipwreck.

As they dressed in clean clothing, Claire said, "You know, it's a cruel book."

"The *Gunman*? People talk about its gentleness."

"He makes his father gentle sometimes, and his mother was very quiet. She had to be, bearing all those children and almost dying of the last one."

"That was Bill."

"Yes. But I don't mean the IRA stuff. I mean the cruelty of the uncle—remember?—and just the matter-of-fact way he talks about all of that seasonal stuff. Chickens with their necks wrung and the dog with the leg lopped off by the scythe. He gets away with it."

"Oh," Richard said. "I know now."

"You know what I mean?"

"You're talking about the case."

"Only a little."

"You're talking about his reputation. So you're also talking about yours."

"Only a little," she said. "I mean, the son of a bitch litigious bastard never wrote for a TV magazine show. He never wrote a whole film, not news or documentary or dramatic. He came up writing half-hour sitcoms! He wrote for canned laughter! He wrote for stand-up comics who couldn't act! And he says *I* copied from *him*! So what's it supposed to mean in the industry about me? It means I'm a cheat. It means I steal. It means my brain's not good enough, my word's not good enough—my *name's* not good. It can't invent, it says. Your Bill Robinson can make things up or embellish them or, you know, *art* them a little but still tell them truly and people want to believe him. But *I* have to steal. It means I'm false, Richard."

He said, "You're true."

"I'm dying of lies," she said, looking down at the walking shoes she'd just put on. "They're strangling me, like the god-damned chickens on the goddamned farm."

In a familiar heavy silence, they shared out euros, they took up the guidebook and map, they found the keys, and they went downstairs to the door. He was thinking of what he would say at the symposium about his pride in publishing a writer who cre-ated evocative language about domestic life and the death throes of the Church, and of course the waning, though no one would have thought it, of the IRA. Careful with that, he thought, though Claire would tell him to say it and to hell with anyone. He would characterize Robinson as a creator of language you might describe as harshly beautiful, he decided. It wasn't puffery, and he believed that even Robinson himself might agree, though not readily, and never in public. The heavy, long key turned easily this time, but the second one stuck. He withdrew the short, brass key, inserted it again, jiggled it, and then was unable to either turn the lock or retrieve the key.

Claire, behind him, said, "What?"

"It won't open."

"How can it not open?"

"Because it's stuck?"

"We can go out the window if we have to," she said.

"Don't get claustrophobic."

"You don't *get* claustrophobic. You *are* claustrophobic."

He heard the hiss of the cloth of her waterproof jacket as she left the vestibule. He knelt and tried to move the key delicately, but it felt soldered into place. He tried the doorknob, and it moved a little but didn't turn. He tried the key once more, tipping it up against its impediment not because he was clever but because he was desperate. The key fell back into place. He gently pulled, and it came out into his hand. "I don't think it's opening," he said. "I've got the key, but I don't dare stick it into the lock again."

"The window's painted shut," Claire called from the sitting room. "Or nailed shut. Or screwed shut and painted over and then nailed shut. It isn't opening, either."

"Don't hurt your back pushing."

She said, "We can knock on this window or go upstairs and knock from the bedroom. Somebody walking past can call a locksmith," she said, "or the police."

"I think the rain's knocking louder than we could—you know, without breaking the glass."

"All right," she said, "I'm game. Let's break the glass. And I'm not panicking. I'm not hysterical. I'm just an American plagiarist who's breaking some glass."

"There's an alley," he said.

"Behind the house?"

"That's where they keep the alleys."

"Please do *not* act lighthearted with me. Everybody knows where they keep the alleys in Ireland. Which way would you say is behind. At the back?"

"Come here."

"No comfort is necessary, thank you. I am not panicky. We'll get carried out of here, someday, and then we can laugh our spectral laugh about all the months we were locked in one of the quainter artisans' houses on the old cobbled streets, dying. And how they discovered our corpses at the foot of the refrigerator, down among the empties of the first-growth Burgundy wines."

Richard went through the kitchen and Claire followed. Where they had turned left to go to the bathroom he pointed at the white-painted wooden door set in the white plaster wall. The latch slid to, and the door swung in from into the wet, littered, narrow alley. The joined houses on the next street backed onto this alley and so did the neighboring houses on their street. Richard could see the wooden back doors. Each end of the alley was walled.

He said to Claire, "I'll knock on every one of them. Somebody has to be home. Somebody will open up, and I'll tell them we're locked in."

"And they'll believe you because you have an honest face? You're a *publisher*. They'll slam it and start screaming."

"You close the door so you don't get wet. But don't lock it. Jesus, don't get yourself completely locked in and me locked out."

He knew what she thought. She was seeing them that way, herself unable to leave and him unable to return to her, each locked away from the other one, three thousand miles from their grown child at home. It was the being alone. He felt it, too. They were each the one who kept the other from being alone. He embraced her, their rain jackets scraping harshly, as if they were to be separated for months and possibly for life. The chill of the rain reminded him of the ice-colored skies that had settled onto the trees at home which had become so heavy with their coating of ice. This is a world, he thought, where the lawsuits of strangers, these whimsical, implausible constructions, can fall upon you with such speed and weight. He marveled, each time he thought of the phrasing of the allegations, how something so very imagined could crush you into the frozen ground.

"Come back," she said. "I mean it. Come back."

"I will," he said, wondering as he did at his and Claire's fright, and moved by how tenderly he regarded them.

He stepped out and to his left and at once confronted a leaning stack of lumber, six-foot-long supports that looked slightly larger than two-by-fours, turning from brown to silver as they weathered. He had to ride them, rolling first his left thigh and then the right, along their rough, soaked surface to get over them. His trousers were wet, then, and his legs and loins were cold. As he pushed himself away from the wood, his palm tore on a nail or wood screw, and he licked at himself and shook his hand. Then there was a barrier of green plastic rubbish bins that were broader than he was. He sat on the first, which rocked as he moved, and pulled himself with his heels to get his rump across the four bins so he could slide to stand on their other side. Now his pants were as wet as his hair, which dripped into his eyes and onto his nose. Moving sideways, since the alley was too narrow to permit him to walk on its weeds and gravel and bits of coal without sidling, he arrived at the closest door, which was to his left, at the back of a house from the next street over. It seemed made of black, rusted iron. He pounded his fist against it but made little noise. He put his palms against it, though he wasn't sure why, and he pushed. The torn skin of his hand hurt, and he thought he could feel the heavy engines of trucks and taxis vibrating in the metal.

He leaned his head against it, then moved crabwise toward the next door, also belonging to a building behind theirs, made of dark, unpainted wood. A low wall of brown cardboard cartons stood against the door. The boxes seemed to contain newspapers and magazines disintegrating slowly in the rain. He moved one, then pulled at the side of another and tore it, spilling out glossy pages bright with bath and beauty products. He heard his breathing, harsh and rapid, the sound of panic. He thought, as he tugged and hefted the cartons, of Claire in their borrowed house. She would be picking up the dead telephone and slamming it down, trying the key again and again, then walking rapidly upstairs, breathing as harshly and quickly as he was. She would shove at the window sash, place her palms against the pane, shout at the street. He couldn't help thinking of her flights upstairs and then her descents, of her twisting at the jammed key and cursing it and everyone. He thought of birds that flew down chimneys and got entrapped in homes, their frantic juddering at windows, the slapping of their wings at walls. If one of his young authors had offered him such a bird, he thought, he would snarl at the manuscript and find a way to exile the image. Though sometimes, he thought, you have to permit it if it's true. Claire at the windows and the front door lock: true.

He had exposed the door, and he knocked, calling, "Hello! Hello?"

No one answered, and he turned awkwardly, in a few motions,

to place his back against the doorway now littered with torn, wet cardboard and a year's-worth of spent pages. He was facing the door of the house that neighbored theirs, where the occupant, according to Claire, had conversations with his radio. This door seemed to be set not into the house itself but into a wall only slightly taller than an average man where perhaps there was a small garden, he thought, and where the neighbor perhaps grew squashes and conversed, as well, with them. He wondered if he would have to climb over this wall. He wondered if he would attempt to, using the heap he confronted of terra-cotta tiles and empty plaster pails and chicken wire tied in large, loose rolls. He moved the tiles a few at a time, stacking them to his right. He was out of breath now, and his hands were so cold, he thought of winter at home. He forced himself to move the tiles, move the tiles, because Claire moved ceaselessly in his thinking, and his harsh breaths sounded to him like sounds she made in turmoil. If no one answered, he thought, he would move the tiles back before the door and then stand on them, then lift himself up and over, then hammer at some available door or window until he was admitted to the neighbor's house. He would come running, then, from the neighbor's front door and he would release his wife from her imprisonment.

He hammered at the wood with his sore hand. He looked up into the rain to see if it was turning to snow.

"Hello, the house!" he shouted, feeling ridiculous.

A man's tenor voice called back, "Hello *from* the house."

Richard called, "Hello?"

"Here I am," someone called, "here I come. I'll be a moment, as I move rather slowly."

Richard called, absurdly, he thought, "Please don't hurry yourself." Under his waterproof jacket, his heaving chest and upper arms were dry. Everything else—face and neck and hands and forearms, his legs from buttocks and balls to his feet—was as wet as if he had swum from their house. In a couple of minutes, a cheerful voice said, "Who's that, then?"

Richard said, "I'm Richard Pottinger. I'm staying next door. In Mr. Robinson's house."

"He's very famous at the moment," the neighbor said.

"Yes. We're friends of his. The door's stuck. The lock? And we can't get out, onto, you know, the street. We're locked in, my wife and I."

"Well, I'm very pleased to meet you," the voice said. "And I'm James Connell. It's happened twice before that I recall, with Mr. Robinson's latch. You know, I actually think it was Americans the last time as well. It's what I would call 'crotchety,' that door next door. It's like a punishment for evading the progress of the neighborhood, isn't it? Doors that won't open and roofing that leaks. We all ought to know better, the developers say, and sell up and let them tear the old dears down, then replace them with a block of flats. Well. I'll soon have this open, and then we . . ."

Richard waited, shivering. Then the voice came again: "Do you know, I can't seem to get this bolt to slide back. It sounds as though you're still locked out. Well. No, locked *in* is what I suppose I mean. You're locked somewhere, all right, aren't you? I'll—no, it won't do any good, I'm afraid. I'll tell you what, Richard. Do you think you can pass the key over the door and trust me to run round—slowly, mind you—and unlock your wife, while you come in through your back door and join us at the street?"

Richard stood on his toes and held the key up. A pale, slender hand that was strangely knotted appeared above the wooden door. The fingers were twisted with arthritis, he thought, and the joints were badly swollen. Richard pushed the key into the ivory flower of knuckles and somehow it took hold.

"That's the ticket," James Connell said. "I will meet you at your own front door."

Richard worked around the exploded cartons and heavy, soaked newspapers, he climbed across the bins and crawled around the leaning lumber, walking sideways back to Robinson's, where he went through the kitchen and past the dining table to Claire, who was pulling at the little man to get him in from the rain. She hugged James Connell and Richard watched him tighten at the intimacy. "Thank God," she said to him. He smiled weakly in return.

Connell wore a white shirt with a red tie under a navy blue sleeveless sweater that matched his navy trousers. His tan shoes were shined, and his thin, white hair was brushed over. He was dressed, Richard thought, to eat his cereal, have a chat with the radio, then leave with his umbrella to shop for something to prepare for a pensioner's lean tea. Richard took hold of James's knotty right hand and gently shook it. With his left, James held up the key and deposited it on Richard's left palm.

"The last people locked in here," he said, "had one of those portable telephones. They rang for the gardai. It gave us a great show on the street."

The door was still open, and Richard found himself afraid to close it. He imagined the three of them locked in together, and what Claire might cry out about Connell and his radio. Claire had one hand on the edge of the door, and he knew she was thinking the same.

He said, "Aren't you chilly, James? Could we make you some

hot tea? Can we give you a drink?" He looked at the thin, smiling old face and then—he couldn't help himself—down at the knotted fingers with which he had worked to release them. *I'll be a moment, as I move rather slowly.*

Claire's face, he saw, was streaked by tears.

James said, "Thank you just the same, but I think I'll leave you to your excursion. Do you need directions?"

"We just wanted to get out," Claire said.

Sometimes, Richard thought, shaking with cold, what it takes is a slow-moving small person with crooked hands who talks to his radio.

James said, "Well, there you are, then."

Claire said, "There we are."

MANHATTANS

He drove though he wasn't supposed to. According to the tiny print of the pamphlet that came with his medications, he wasn't supposed to operate heavy machinery or drive a car. He steered into the passing lane before his courage failed and he wobbled back to the right and slowed to forty-five.

"I'll get better," he had promised his wife, sick with his conviction that his sickness was the only truth and health was a lie.

"But I might not," she'd said. She had said it flatly and evenly, as if she were telling the time.

He understood her anger, he thought. She had spoken to him, before leaving, in the sorrow of her understanding that nothing was left for her but leaving him. If she didn't, she would have to face him during all the hours of every day of the weeks of his medical leave of absence—it would never be long enough—and even Green himself knew the bleakness of the prospect of living with him. He found it impossible to live with himself, he thought, speeding up, then slowing down, blinking in the bright, watery light that poured around trees and over the face of an iron-stained high, white cliff at the side of Route 17, a hundred miles from his city, New York. Was that thought, about not being able to live with himself, a thought about not living at all? Was he talking to himself about suicide? He didn't much care, he thought, and he knew that such considerations might be called ominous, though disguised in something like *unpleasant*, or *a warning shot, let's call it*, by Marcy Bellochio, his therapist. Dr. Xin, who wrote his prescriptions, didn't speak English well enough to suggest synonyms. He would call a suicide just that.

Bess, his wife, was angry at his disorderly disease—angry at him for giving in to the illness and angry at herself for failing to understand that he hadn't chosen to suffer it. And she knew it, he knew. Still, something in her fury at him, which left her trembling at times as hard as he always did, suggested to him that maybe a broken segment of his character *had* made him get sick, or had kept him entangled in what he thought of as its thousands of tiny branches that grew through his body and couldn't be torn away unless the body was torn apart.

They'd been right to marry, he thought, speeding up. They'd always understood each other, even now, while her energy for sustaining the knowledge, the plain bad news, ran out.

Tearing the body apart to root it out would be classified by Marcy Bellochio, he knew, as a suicidal ideation.

"We'll have none of that," he instructed the car, slowing it at an exit that he thought he remembered and driving, according to the rental-car dashboard compass, due north. "Let's really try and have none of that."

He passed a diner and thought of hot coffee with a lot of sugar and milk. He saw his hands shake as he gripped the cup with both of them. He saw the coffee spill, the mess of sugar crystals and milk drops and dark tan coffee stains on the napkins he would wetly wad as he scrubbed at his paper place mat.

He said, "Let's try having none."

At first, Bess called them The Shakes. Then, when she understood that calling it A Case of The Shakes suggested that sometimes he didn't suffer them, she stopped referring to them at all. "It's a side effect," he'd told her, although she knew it was, and he knew that she did. "Pharmacological side effects may include sexual dysfunction, palsied trembling, and being unable to gauge the distance between the self and the world or the pain inflicted on the world by the presence of the self. It's the price one pays for ingesting psychotropics in what I think we could call large quantities."

"I think we could call them frighteningly large quanities," she said. "It's part of the treatment, though. I say treatment because I suppose we shouldn't call it the cure, there apparently not being one."

"My trembles and the little dysfunction business and your tears."

"Never mind my tears, thank you."

"And never mind my trembles or the other," he said.

She smiled a broad, false smile that made her lean, patrician face look cruel, and she said, "There. Haven't we managed our little crisis?"

He remembered that while they parried, he had very powerfully felt that he might start to cry. It wasn't until she had left the room, turning to walk away as if she'd suddenly been frightened, that he wiped at his cheeks and felt the moisture of his tears.

It would be best to be strong and resolute and comforting by the time he got there, he thought. Jerry and Nancy Stradling were old people in a cul-de-sac of distress, whereas Green was only middle-aged, merely rocked breathless, from time to time, by sorrow. Everyone in the world gets sorrow, he knew. You hadn't a right to complain when you did. But distress, he thought, was another matter. Distress was a complaint of a higher order. The Stradlings were very old people alone in the world except for others like themselves in their circle. By now, it had to be the smallest of circles. He imagined drawing it on the sand of a hot Rhode Island beach, or in chalk on the cloudy, gray board of a Fordham Law School classroom, or with a brush dipped in whitewash on the liver-colored stone of a three-story town house around the corner from lower Fifth Avenue. It would be closer to a big dot than a circle. The old couple's son lived in Europe, and he flew from Brussels to New York and drove this same route up to them in a rented car whenever he could. Jerry Stradling's partners were dead, and his remaining associates in the Syracuse firm conducted a cold, lucrative legal practice that had nothing to do with his former clients or him; at Christmastime, the firm sent a basket of cheeses out in a van, Nancy had told him. She had also told him that her sister sometimes visited, but she was as old as Nancy and Jerry, and she had to be driven from Concord, Massachusetts, by her daughter, who seemed not to have too much time for her mother, much less her ancient uncle and aunt.

That apparently left Green as the one to call, and as he drove under the dwindling flare of dusk he imagined a little circle inside of which was a doodle resembling his face. He had been a summer intern for Jerome Stradling several decades before, and then for nearly six years he had practiced law as a junior colleague while learning what Jerry could teach him about pleading in the Second District of the federal bench and the New York State Supreme Court. Jerry was a gent, a cordial maverick, a slick litigator, and an accomplished scholar of the law. In the office, he'd worn excellent Donegal tweed sport coats with slacks of bright primary colors such as golfers wore on the links. In court, he wore rich sharkskin suits with muted stripes and neckties that cost a hundred dollars each. His little moustache had sat heavily on a mouth that frowned more often than it smiled, and that rarely was still. His nose was hawkish, his forehead high, his body broad. He was a decorated naval officer who had served on destroyers in World War II, and in the long winters so common to this part of the state, he liked to talk about some weather making, and how they might see a little action on the deck. Now, backed into the last available corner of his old age, Jerry was alone with Nancy, once a great giver of dinner parties and cocktail parties and even high teas—cucumber sandwiches on homemade bread, Green remembered, and slices of salty Southern ham, and real scones, buttercream layer cakes. She had been rumored to have been a debutante in Rochester, New York. She had been a fine skier, trained by professionals after World War II. She could sit much of the day without complaint in a duck blind and bring down more than most of the men who shot with her. It was Nancy who had telephoned after so many years of silence between them to say, "Can you come for a weekend visit, Jim? Well. It's actually—could you come up here and lend us a hand?"

The Stradlings' house was two hundred miles from New York City. He felt as if he'd come a thousand. He was probably the fifth or even tenth she had called, Green thought. He could imagine her sitting with their very old book of telephone numbers and addresses, many of them perhaps crossed out. He couldn't bring himself to efface the names and numbers of the dead who had begun to accumulate in his life. He saw it as a coming on, a kind of dusk, an ashen light that would grow dull and then dim and then dark. As if he were not giving in to the failing light, he kept the names of friends and acquaintances who had died. Their telephone numbers were there to consult among the numbers of those who had greeted him with pleasure when he called. But he didn't call them anymore, and he suspected that they wouldn't be smiling at the sound of his voice if he did. And Nancy, hearing reason after reason for the failure of their past to assist them, had at last come upon his name and had called him for help.

They had exchanged holiday greetings every year. They hadn't spoken since he'd left to practice in New York City. But you have to say yes when they call, Green thought, because when you stop responding to something like that, you're controlled by the darkness. It owns you. All you have a right to expect, after not saying yes when they call, is the purchase of a newspaper every day, and a meal if you can keep it down, and the medication, and then television with everyone laughing, and nights of not sleeping followed by what is sometimes called the light of day but which Green and others knew was darkness with its name changed.

Although it was spring, the low-ceilinged Colonial house was cold. Nancy Stradling wore a man's bulky gray cardigan over a dark blue polka-dotted dress. She greeted him with a smile that appeared to raise each crease of her seamed, small face. Her hair was thick and silky, purely white and twisted into a bun. He remembered it as a shade of light chestnut, or maybe even a honey blond. She was proud of it, he could tell, because she drew the eye to it with a filigreed silver pin bearing small garnets that protruded from the bun and caught the light. As soon as she let

go of his hands, he stuck them in his trouser pockets and followed her to the kitchen, where she insisted on his drinking a
cup of coffee.

"I forget how you take your coffee," she said. "Of course, some
days, I forget how I take *mine*."

"It's been a good many years, Mrs. Stradling."

"Oh, you call me *Nancy*, for heaven's sake, Bill."

"It's Jim."

"Jim. God. Jim! Of course. Forgive me. Tell me the truth, now.
Do you think the house has grown shabby after all these years?"

"Well, no, actually. No. It's always been lovely. I remember
wanting to live in a house like yours—when I was working for
Jerry, in the early days. I even insisted that we buy a table like this
one. Curly maple, right? I remember you telling me it was curly
maple at, I think it was, one of your parties. Maybe at some
Christmastime."

"And did your wife agree when you insisted? She's called . . ."

"Bess."

"Perhaps next time she can come with you."

He smiled. He had to look away from what her face did when
he tried to smile. "Maybe so," he said. "Jerry's pretty low these
days?"

"If he were any lower," she said, carrying the coffee to him in
the dim chilliness of the narrow kitchen with its unlighted
woodstove and windows with crazed panes that made the day-
light look smeared, "he'd be flat on his back." She set the coffee
before him. "Of course, he *is* on his back. Oh, he's very pleased
that you're coming. He'll be up and about later. I wouldn't be
able to keep him from dressing smartly and greeting you. Later
on, he'll be out."

"Nancy, you said you needed a hand."

"I did?"

"Over the phone. You asked if I could come here and give you a hand. Is there a specific problem? You know, something concrete I could tackle for you?"

Sitting in the junction made by the side of the table and the kitchen wall, she opened her hand to reveal some small silver spoons that were tarnished nearly black. "You must remember these," she said.

He didn't. He nodded and smiled, and Nancy looked away.

"Would you like the one celebrating the Erie Canal, the lovely Stuttgart, the—ah!—the Cipriani in Venice, and this is Mexico, this is Taos, and here's Niagara-by-the-Lake. We've collected dozens. Pick whichever one you want."

Suddenly, he did remember them, from an evening's cocktails, with Jerry very carefully measuring out small shots of bourbon for what he called highballs, though he served them in low glasses, and excessive portions of vermouth for weak martinis on the rocks. He recalled candles scented with vanilla and someone playing "Moonlight in Vermont" on the huge, Victorian upright piano in the front sitting room, as he now remembered their calling it. He remembered his broad pleasure, Green recalled, as he'd thought that night of the woman who was flying in to wait for him at the Hotel Syracuse: Bess, he said to himself as his stomach twisted and his face felt filled by a surging of blood. It had been their first hotel together at the start of what was a very short courtship and a marriage that had lasted at least a year too long for her. And he had come to the senior partner's party without her because her plane was arriving late and because he knew how little she would want to be among the braided rugs and old, dark furniture inherited by Jerry from his mother in Kansas, and the worried junior lawyers, and of course the polished commemorative spoons arrayed beside the glasses for stirring drinks. He remembered how Stradling and his wife had made them select a souvenir spoon that then was served protruding from their drink. Perhaps he was inventing it, he thought, his recollection of the young lawyers standing and sipping with one hand while holding with the other a purposeless, shiny, small spoon.

He paddled tiny circles through his coffee with Niagara-by-the-Lake and lifted his cup with both hands. She had the grace to turn her attention to her cup while he tried to drink from his.

"The firm frowned on our living here, you know."

"No, I never did. Of course, the junior associates only speculated about the senior partners. We called them The Gods."

"I had heard that," she said. "Look at us. Some gods."

"But why? The frowning, I mean."

"They wanted all of him they could get, and that included time spent in commuting. The partners found it difficult to understand that it was his therapy—the cars, I mean, and the drive. It cleared his mind."

"Good cars," he said. "I remember that now: excellent machines."

"The Studebaker Silver Hawk," she said. "And the little Spitfire. And the Jaguar, of course. He always complained about the carburetion in the Jag. But he adored the Hawk. And now we aren't allowed to drive. We can't. But we kept a little white Ford, very bland, and I can get us around by going slowly. It's not so easy in winter, you remember our icy roads. I'm not supposed to operate a car. But you have to live."

He felt himself about to argue with the proposition that living was imperative, and he said, "But Jerry would let himself relax when he drove, you're saying? It would clear his mind?"

"Exactly. He remembered you as being sympathetic, he said. And there you are. You can put yourself in the other fellow's shoes."

"Shoes are easy," he said. "But about my being useful to Jerry and you . . ."

She cocked her head and took a noisy breath. She said, "It gets *very* hard."

"Yes."

"Aging. Illness. He's quite ill."

"Yes."

"And that gets hard."

"Yes, it must."

"I'm as healthy as a dray horse," she said, laughing without any apparent pleasure. "I have normal cholesterol and my blood pressure's rather good for someone my age. All my tests are always rather good. And poor Jerry, the military hero. He's the one who crossed the North Atlantic four times on a World War I–vintage tin can. He's the one who was always splitting wood and mowing the lawn, for gosh sakes, with a hand-powered mower. He's the one people used to call on to help them take up tree stumps in the town, or put together a pipework scaffolding to lay down a roof. He hasn't barely got a pulse some days, Jim. His blood pressure's so low. It's affecting the—well—"

She turned away as if to look at someone seated beside her. She shook her head, then faced him again.

"All that's left is indignity," she said. "The best of it's frustrating, or embarrassing, and the worst of it's as bad a humiliation—

an affliction, I'm tempted to call it—as you could imagine. He can't see very much at all. He can't read anymore. It affects his brain, I think. I don't mean the memory. That's gone most days, or going, though he still remembers events from the office or the courtroom. So that's that. But his *reasoning.* He was the most sensible man, wasn't he?"

"A good lawyer's as analytic as a chemist—as an accountant. Even his feelings have to be mostly cold thought. Or so his wife would say." He barked a laugh too loudly, and she recoiled.

She moved her cup away and clasped her hands on the table before her. She said, "He isn't thinking well. I wondered if someone from the old days, coming into the house, into his mind, I suppose I mean, might jolt him. Do you know? That kind of *jolt* you sometimes can get from the past? Even when you might not be remembering well? Do you and your Bess have children, Jim? I should have asked you right away."

"We have a son and a daughter, yes."

"And where are they?"

"One's in the army and the other is either a partner in a dot-com in Eugene, Oregon, or he's on unemployment, we aren't sure which because neither is he."

"So your *girl's* the soldier. It's a new world."

"Sarabeth is a captain. She flies helicopters in frightening places. Like her mother, she is very brave."

"How wonderful for you."

"Yes," he said, "it's wonderful."

"And do you think I was right to ask you all the way up here from Manhattan?"

"Right?"

"The jolt," she said. "Like the—you know. Oh, what's it called?

Electric shock, for crazy people? It's supposed to bring them to their senses, or something. Do you know?"

"Electroconvulsive therapy," he said. "It's called ECT."

"The little jolt," she said.

"The little jolt. I believe it's thought of as the last resort for certain patients."

"Is it really? I'm afraid I know nothing about it."

He said. "I know about the jolt is all."

"Yes," she said. "And do you think we might try that with Jerry?"

He saw himself leaping from behind a curtain with his arms outspread, providing the sudden little jolt. He saw Jerry, in liver-colored Donegal tweed jacket paired up with lime green golf slacks, standing still, paralyzed with terror, then going pale, then falling to the hardwood floor with his heart stopped.

"Maybe telling him first that I'm here."

"Yes," she said. "Of course. He knows that already."

"Then maybe a gentle, small prod more than a jolt."

"I knew you'd know what's best," she said.

"You did?"

"Well, of course, Jim." They nodded like the little figures on an old German clock who spring out to chase each other when the hour tolls. "That's why I called you up," she said. And then, as if it had been the topic of conversation all along, Nancy asked him, "Do you have photographs of you and your Bess at your wedding?"

"I think we do," he said. "Yes. I think we have a scrapbook's-worth, a lot of them. We never look at them," he said. "Like most people, I suppose."

"Not us," she said in a flat, hard voice. "Not us. We were married by one of Jerry's professors, a philosophy teacher at Lehigh. He was a Lutheran pastor and because I was Catholic and Jerry was a rather exotic species of Baptist, the teacher was our way of bridging the gap. A Christian, but not a sectarian, marriage, I suppose you would call it. We were very independent, and no one in his family knew about marriages. That is, the planning, you know, and catering and all of that. My people, if we'd have let them, they'd have taken it over and staged a quiet little affair with the Rockettes and the Notre Dame marching band. So we just drove out to the professor's farmhouse, near Easton, and we got married. Well, we had set the *date*, mind you. We had an appointment with the professor, we didn't just show up. But it was more or less 'Hello, let's have the wedding, now you're married, congratulations, goodbye.' His wife was very unhappy. She was our witness. I mean, I think they were unhappy together. At first, I was frightened that it was an omen for us. But we did pretty well for a very long time. I can't complain about that. It's the pictures."

"Pictures of you and Jerry at your wedding."

"We don't have any. The unhappy wife never thought to take them. I never thought to ask for them. Maybe she enjoyed knowing that someday we'd want them and there wouldn't *be* any. Maybe that was the omen part of the ominousness that I felt. She was all pale and doughy and slope-shouldered and quiet, and she frightened me. She had a wen or some sort of thick, fleshy protrusion under her lower lip. She never said a word. She didn't even say 'Congratulations.' She never hugged either of us. She shook my hand. Her hand was as cold as a stone from the river. And now there isn't a picture of us from the day we were married. It's as if the day didn't happen. Of course, it did, and I know it. But I would love a little proof. You and Jerry understand proof. It's what you deal in."

"You make me want to drive home and look at our photos and feel lucky," he lied.

"You do that. Don't rush off, of course. But count your blessings."

"I will," he said. "I do."

"Good," she said, "because you've a sad expression etched into your face, Jim."

"That's what my mother always warned me," he said.

She laughed, and she was a little bit of a pretty girl. "'Make that face too much, and your face will freeze that way.' God. Didn't they all tell all of us that?"

"And all of them were right," he said.

She nodded, and he nodded back. He thought again of the dark, high wooden clocks in Europe when, as the hour was struck, the figures chased other figures in jerky motions across the base of the broad, white dial. It was often someone wielding a scythe in pursuit of maidens, he thought he recalled.

While Nancy went in to Jerry, Green walked, on his toes, like an intruder, through the front of the house—the living room that led to the foyer that led to the sitting room with its piano and its broad bureau that they used as the sideboard for drinks. The living room was furnished with comfortable chairs and deep sofas, and the walls were dressed with paintings by artists Green had never heard of. The pictures were mostly of snowy scenes, although there was one portrait that bore a likeness to what Jerry looked like thirty years before. In the sitting room the furniture was dense, more black than brown, heavily worked—the worst of proud Victorian decoration—and the walls were hung with murky prints. On the sideboard were bottles and glasses and, of course, more small commemorative spoons. In the back of the sitting room on the wall was hung a plaque that celebrated Jerome Stradling for his selfless service to the Bar Association of Central New York. Beside it was a photo, in a hardware-store frame, of a smiling, athletic young Nancy Stradling in a strapless gown who held the arm of Jerry, in his late twenties, who was wearing a dress shirt and cummerbund with his tie undone, his eyes a little glazed with drink, Green assumed, and the two of them about to take possession of a lot of the known world.

He went quietly back to the kitchen to drink cooled coffee. He slopped some over the side of the cup and onto the floor. He was mopping it with a paper napkin when she brought Jerry in. He had shrunk in height and breadth and had become her size, Green thought, and he wobbled a little from side to side as he moved forward. His face was bony and pale, and his nose seemed all the more like a beak. It was naked-looking, and Green took a minute to understand that the bristly moustache was gone. The waxy skin around the nose was blooming small suppurations, some of which had formed red-and-white scabs. His light blue eyes looked clear, though his vision was nearly gone. He gripped Nancy's upper arm and appeared, at first, to be looking directly at Green. But he didn't see much, Green thought, because he focused on the space between them, no matter how close he came, until they were nearly toe-to-toe.

Jerry stuck his small hand before him and said, in a slightly hoarse voice that had little of the baritone resonance Green remembered, "Bill!"

"It's Jim," Nancy said.

Stradling leaned his head back, as if trying to remember

something. Then he said, "Of course. Of course, it's Jim. You must forgive me."

"I'm happy to see you, Jerry. Any name you want to use is fine."

"You're as elegant as ever," Stradling said, smiling uncertainly.

He looked like an ancient child who made an appearance at the grown-ups' party. He was dressed in pale yellow golf slacks tightened high on the waist by a brown leather belt. The pants hung loosely about his legs and broke in a puddle over his black-and-red-checked cloth bedroom slippers. His corduroy shirt was a dark olive green worn with a loosely knotted golden silk tie such as Jerry might have worn to court forty years before. Green felt a surge of affection for her effort to dress Jerry as he might have dressed himself.

They sat in the kitchen, Jerry at the head of the maple table, where Nancy served him Postum while she reheated their coffee. "Perhaps you'd care to tell us about your practice," Jerry said, looking to Green's left. Green moved in that direction and Jerry said, "My eyes, as you can tell, have suffered. I'm not blind. I *am* debilitated. But of course you can see just fine, so you see that for yourself. Jim, why is it that I am tempted, steadily, to call you Bill?"

Green knew. It was because Nancy must have told him that she was phoning up Billy Grossman, who overlapped with Green for three or four years before Green left to work at the firm on Pine Street in lower Manhattan.

"A lot of people have told me I look like a Bill."

Nancy said, "But not a counterfeit bill. Nor a two-dollar bill. Nor a bill of lading?"

"You do crossword puzzles," Green said.

"I do," she said with pleasure. "You're a canny lawyer, aren't you?"

"I do them, too," he said. "On the subway, coming down from our apartment, going to work."

"'Six-letter word for a sixteenth-century lunatic Spanish ruler?'" she said, giggling. "Joanna. She was known as Joanna the Mad. I love any kind of game."

"It's the word part that I like," Green said, or would have, when Jerry cut in by saying angrily, "I enjoyed the billing letters. I itemized everything to the tenth of an hour. I included the sharpening of pencils, the steeping of a pot of tea. I dared them to object. And there was somebody, always, who did. *Those* were the conversations I enjoyed. 'I just kept you from a whopping fine for tortious interference, you maladroit boat jumper, and you quibble with me over *tea* leaves?' I used to have the girl make them with an infuser. We brewed first-rate tea that I sent her to buy over on Townsend Street. She had to scald the pot and use a cozy that Nancy purchased in Harrod's. And they paid for the leaves, for the water to pour on them, and for the breath the girl expelled when she poured it into good china cups."

They sat in silence.

"That was an outburst, I'd say," Nancy announced. "What got into *you*, Jerome Stradling?"

"Some things need to be said," he told her.

She looked at Green. "But what I really want to know," she said, "is what in heaven's name is a—what was it? A boat jumper. What's that?"

Jerry raised the fingers of each hand, one after the other, and held them against the table. "What's that? Ten? A ten-letter word for an illegal immigrant," he said. "You're welcome to make whatever use of it you wish."

Green noted how steady Stradling's hands and fingers seemed, and how he did not spill his Postum when he sipped it. The table in front of Green was spotted with sugar and coffee and milk. He saw Nancy notice it and he placed his hands in his lap.

"His wife's name is Bess," Nancy said to Jerry. "Did you ever meet her?"

"I regret that I did not," he said. "Not having met Bill, I could hardly have encountered his wife, given the unfolding of circumstances."

"Jim," she reminded him.

Stradling nodded and stared off. Green suspected that Nancy would be thinking that now, as Jerry wore out after a few minutes of conversation, now Green ought to deliver the little jolt for which she had made him responsible. It was almost five o'clock, and he thought of taking his medication while they watched and then excusing himself to go upstairs to nap. He hadn't slept for many hours of the past three days. When you've spent a good number of hours of the night in not sleeping, and you walk without purpose through your apartment to pause, finally, at a window, and you look at the city at night from eight stories up, and you wait—you're waiting, by then, for anything at all to approach through the thick nothing that wraps you—you begin to feel the pressure one remove from you in the air above New York. You sense the chill, you hear engine noises thinned to tinny rattles, and you see the lighted windows of office suites and apartments, the dampered intensity of distant lives nearby.

Then, let's say, you lie down again to close your eyes again and try. Your head is filled with the lights you saw against the nighttime sky, but now it's a different New York City that's inside you. After a while, instead of seeing bright, rectangular windows pulsing on the dark buildings framed against the dark sky, you're teeming with fragments of conversation and scraps of ideas and small shreds of image you can barely identify before they leave your head to be replaced by frightening pictures, whole sentences spoken to you years before by forgotten speakers. For people who cannot sleep at night for many nights, this other city is what you have instead of nightmares.

Even now, at this table in the kitchen lit by smeared, declining light, he heard his wife say as he had heard her say during so many of his hours of not sleeping, "Sure, it could be your mother's death. It could be your father dying eight years before her. It could be *my* father, or because we never got a dog and the—the *undogginess* just hit home. Maybe it's our daughter living like a man and our son is living like some overprivileged boy. Just because you give it a name, just because you *name* something, doesn't mean you know it. I don't *care* what it is. Call it whatever you want to, you know? But how selfish can I be? How unfeeling can I *be* after you've been living in hell for a year, for more than a year? Right? I am so sorry. I am. I really am. But I want you to just not *be* like this. Jimmy, get us back our *life!*"

"Jim," Stradling said.

"Sir?" he said.

"You argued the Oneida Board of Education matter, didn't you? Before the state appellate?"

"What an excellent memory you have," Green said. "Yes. I did. I won."

"I remember the victory. The head of the board actually kissed me on the cheek. He was that relieved. He smelled, I remember, of cheap deodorant. I ordered in chilled champagne from Liquor Square. It cost us a pretty penny. But then we delivered the bill. And they paid, of course. And we had our pretty penny back. So you can see that my mind is unaffected by the advance of—what would you call it?"

"I wouldn't," he said, waiting for Nancy to rescue him.

"Your complaint," she said.

"My complaint," Stradling said. "My broken-down heart. The heart isn't sad," he said, "but it doesn't pound away as sturdily as it used to. And of course there's the eyesight problem."

"But he sees well in his *mind*," Nancy said to Green.

"Try a . . ." Stradling counted his fingers. "Try a nine-letter word for hectoring blabbermouth," he said.

"Jerry!"

"Termagant," he said. "Seeing well in the mind, my Irish ass."

And so much for the little jolt, Green thought.

"I'm going to put the stew on," Nancy. "It's a *daube*, actually, a stew of lamb that's been flavored with white wine, although one would drink some light-bodied red with the meal. We'll have to see what bottles are out in the pantry. I always prepare this meal in advance to let the flavors marry. It's a jolly springtime dish. I'm going to add some green peas, and it already has pearl onions and carrots. So I'll get to that, Jim, if you'll make us our highballs? Do you remember where the liquor is?"

Stradling said, "How many guests did you *invite*?" His nostrils were white and flared. The eruptions around his nose seemed to darken. His bony face seemed even more drawn. He said, "Gatherings and gatherings, with our backs still against the wall from the *last* time you invited so many strangers in."

"Jerry Stradling, you will lie down before dinner, even if it's only for a minute or two," Nancy said.

"I suppose I ought to. I suppose I will. Otherwise she'll knock me down is what she'll be telling me next. You remember." Then he said to Nancy, "Does he remember what drinks we want?"

She said, "I'm sure he does. He *knows* us, Jerry."

She looked at Green as if now, at last, he could deliver the necessary jolt. But then she turned to Stradling and moved him out of the kitchen. He went obediently, wobbling. Green took a tray of ice cubes from the freezer compartment of the refrigerator and went along to the sitting room to make them their drinks.

He remembered the care, the miserliness, with which Stradling at that party given so many years before had measured the shot of liquor he'd put in each drink. As if retaliating, Green dropped ice cubes into heavy, cut-crystal glasses and carelessly poured plenty of bar-whiskey bourbon into cheap sweet vermouth that looked and smelled like Merchurochrome. Green doubted that Jerry Stradling was supposed to drink liquor any more than he was. He used the same spoon—from a hotel in British Columbia—to stir each drink. Then he worked at opening a crusted, small bottle of maraschino cherries. He used the British Columbia spoon to place a cherry in every drink. He had to use his fingers to pick up two that his shaking spoon had let fall to the surface of the sideboard. He ate them both and then found purple-and-gold paper cocktail napkins in the first drawer he opened. He used a napkin to wipe his fingers and then to scrub the cherry syrup from the sideboard. He wanted to telephone his wife. He knew he made her sad. But he wondered whether she was as miserable without him as she'd been in their life together. He was afraid that she felt too much better away from him. He had a real malady, he knew, but to his wife *he* was the disease. He would have loved her to tell him otherwise, but he wouldn't ask. Even he, because he loved her and sometimes could remember that he did, would prescribe for her a life without him. He sucked at his sticky fingers like a child.

"Ladies and gentlemen," Jerry Stradling said.

He stood in the doorway of the sitting room. He moved his head as if surveying a crowd of guests. He smiled with the taut confidence of a capable attorney about to deliver his opening argument. "I want to thank you very much for coming tonight, and I apologize for the delay. If you will be patient a moment longer, my junior colleague will see to your drinks. And I will return to join you shortly." He smiled with no sincerity and said, "If you'll take over from here, Bill?"

Stradling nodded to no one with great courtesy, then turned in the doorway and, pushing at the doorframe as if to launch himself, he lurched lightly down the corridor and out of sight.

Green looked at the empty doorway for a while. Then he took a small oval metal tray from the sideboard. It was decorated with the faded head of a terrier, painted in white and black on a red background. He put the Manhattans on the tray, and then he selected for each drink a spoon that was a forgotten commemoration—the British Columbia for one, an Allentown Fair for another, and a Red Lion in Salisbury, England, for the last. Two of the tarnished spoons were stubby and broad, and the third was longer, slimmer, with a narrow, dull brass band around the handle, souvenirs stolen by a healthy, confident young couple who were starting to take their ease in the world. He folded three napkins and set them on the tray, and then he squeezed his trembling fingers around and under its edge. He lifted and wheeled and set off to follow Jerry Stradling down the dark corridor. He knew that he must not spill a drop.

THE HAY BEHIND THE HOUSE

This would be the time in my life, I often thought while it went on, that I would remember as the year, or half a year, or fiscal quarter—there was really no telling—when I lived with Martin Gold on Central Park West in Manhattan, and cooked in copper pots and ate on Spode that was figured in blue and maroon, lifting flatware as heavy as fire irons.

I said, "I am taking my walking shoes, but you don't really need to read anything into that. If you did, it would be more about you than me."

Naturally, he couldn't let the statement pass. I knew it when I said it. He would have to answer, and it would tell me more about him. And what he said was, "You can't legislate what I understand when you do something, Cara. You take your most important pair of shoes with you when you take off for the weekend, or conceivably for the rest of your life—'We'll know more in a few days' is what you said ten minutes ago—and it means something. It means something if you go. It means something if you come back pretty soon, and it means something else if you stay there longer. And it means something if you take your brown, ugly, scuffed-up, broken-down, walked-out walking shoes with the extra-wide toe box and the fat yellow trail boot laces."

One of the reasons I was drawn to Martin was his ability to sometimes talk his way out of trouble and, almost as often, back into it, and then to deny that there had been trouble in the first place. He was a short-order orator, with a limited but interesting menu. He could whip it up and dish it out: nasty sentences, or elegant and generous paragraphs, and, not infrequently, small, desperately seasoned speeches of uncertain intent. It was possible, I thought, that we had lived together in his Aunt Susan's vacant apartment too long. We had lived together for five weeks. And that was too short a time to think of as so long. On the other hand, we had lived together, as he had put it, *only* a little more than a month, not long enough to know how we felt, and anyway it was my parents' dilemma more than my own, he suspected, that drew me to leave behind what mattered most, or ought to: him.

I had started walking in college and I'd kept on after school. Often, on an afternoon, I hiked up the Upper West Side, for example, toward the northern border of Central Park and then across, in Spanish Harlem, over to Fifth and down Embassy Row to the fountain at the Plaza, then along Fifty-ninth to Broadway, then over to a place near John Jay where cops who went to school would sit around with coffee and open notebooks; I found them touching because they were as worried as they were tough, it seemed, and so, I think I fancied, was I. For walks like this, I wore the same shoes I had worn in college a dozen years before, the welts of which had been restitched, the lugs replaced once, the laces three times. The walking kept my weight down, my eyes open, and my endorphins up. I worked alone, in other words, at turning myself on. Why, Marty wondered, did I need to?

"And you might ask yourself," he said next, after commenting on the aesthetic disgrace of my walking shoes, "why you need to walk so much. Charles Dickens sometimes walked twenty-five miles a night. But that was in London. And he was neurotic. It's *crazy* to walk so much. And, anyway, he was a genius."

"'It's a dark and stormy night,'" I said accurately, if weather were the subject.

"Disraeli," he said.

I raised my brows and said nothing. He loved it when I did that.

"A different writer," he said, "who is never, *ever*, confused with Dickens."

"I never read either of them. The stormy night's from a Peanuts cartoon."

He slowly shook his head, expressing pity with his wide, astonished eyes, and then disgust with his very terrific broad mouth. "Not even *A Tale of Two Cities*? Come on, Cara."

"No," I said. "We were supposed to read it for English in high school, but I saw the movie on TV. It was a far better thing than reading it."

"Far, *far* better thing. Come to think of it, there's a hell of a lot of walking in that book."

"And there's probably an even chance that whoever lived with Dickens didn't give him grief about his shoes. Or even his walking, maybe."

"I don't know," he said. "I don't know."

"That's a good start. It's the third thing you admitted to not knowing since I moved into Aunt Susie's place." He was going to ask me what the other two were, but I was already there, bending back the upraised fingers of my left hand with my right forefinger. "One: 'Marty, are you *sure* the F train doesn't stop at Bergen Street?' Two: 'I can really take these Percodan with a bottle and a half of wine?'"

"Your heart did not stop beating," he said. "You felt like it stopped, but it didn't. You fainted because you hadn't eaten. And your tooth was abscessed. And you were tired."

"And my heart stopped beating," I said. "You think I wouldn't notice a little absence like that? My own heartbeat? Marty: my *own.*"

"That is so pedagogical," he said.

"I'll be back in a couple of days. Or maybe a little more. I'll let you know."

"You're driving on a night like this?"

"Say it, Marty."

"A fucking dark and stormy fucking night, Cara."

"It is three-fifteen of a sour Saturday afternoon," I said. "It'll hardly be night when I get there. And don't read so much into the walking shoes. I was afraid you would."

"You were hoping I would," he said, beginning to look like a sulky, adolescent version of a thirty-four-year old Legal Aid attorney with no parents, a generous, wealthy aunt who traveled most of every year, and a girlfriend with exceptional leg muscles who wrote cooking columns for newspapers, magazines, and a site on the World Wide Web.

I kissed him on the cheek beside his mouth. I kissed him on the upper lip and nibbled it. I nibbled on the lower lip. I squeezed his not entirely firm belly. "Thank you for letting me take her car," I said.

"And thanks for sitting around to wait and see if you come back?"

"I have to come back," I said. "I'm leaving my stuff here as hostage. And, since you live here, you're naturally going to be around to see what I do." I couldn't say the part about coming back or not.

"Great," he said, "consider me consoled." Then he said, "You're not leaving your terrible shoes here, though. I'm going to think about them."

His next words would be, "Day and night."

He opened his mouth, but I was out the door, down in the elevator, then walking with my chin at an absurdly high angle as I passed the doorman who thought of us, I knew, as Ms. Susan Stern's poor relations, which we were—which one of us was; one of us had her own relations to worry about.

Mine lived upstate, two hundred miles north of the city, and that was where I was headed in Aunt Susan's large, old, shiny, dark-green Mercury. It waddled softly, and you aimed it more than drove. All I could tune with clarity on FM was a station that played Hispanic love songs, the only word of which I understood was *corazón*—they made me feel sad and solitary— or WNYC, on which a books jockey was interviewing a man who cared for abandoned house pets, or WQXR, on which a soprano was singing in Italian about love, I guessed, just prior to killing herself. I opted for AM and I listened to a Pink Floyd retrospective until I was on the Palisades Parkway, still for much of its length a road that was narrow, with handsome, tended roadside plantings that always made me think of 1940, a year I knew next to nothing about except that both my parents had been born in it. Then I listened to a show on which a woman who seemed to be a psychologist made cruel comments to everyone who called her.

Hi, Doctor. My name is Caroline Terranova. I believe that my parents are falling apart. My own emotional life is a little tattered. Do you think these circumstances are related? Does that strike you as healthy? And what do you think about people who demonstrate a powerful need to walk?

Hello, Cara, she'd say with that slightly offended, cigarettes-and-whiskey voice. Then she'd say, *Goodbye, Cara. Take a hike.*

MY MOTHER WAS trying to tell me a funny story. I knew that I was drifting, very slowly, around the kitchen—*her* kitchen, I kept reminding myself—to look through heaps of mail and magazines and bills, to examine recipes on her corkboard over one of the counters, to sweep salt or bread crumbs or garlic skins off a cutting board and into my palm. I should be looking at her face, I thought, to memorize it, or to understand its expression. I ought to be communicating, with my own expression, so that I was not the neurotic daughter descending with her infamous rigidity into their—could you still call it middle age? Was sixty-one the middle of *anything*? Were they old enough for me to call them— at least behind their backs—old?

"Wait, Mom. Wait. What did you say?" I said. "He left you what?"

"It was a note. Thumbtacked to the whatever you call it that's the wood at the top of a door. The jamb."

"Isn't that the wood at the side?"

"I think maybe it's also at the top. Anyway—sweetie, *listen*—at the top of the door to our bedroom, there was a note from your father. It was hanging there."

"On the jamb, if that's what it's called. Is lintel a better word for it? Or: could it be the architrave?"

"Sweetie, don't be ridiculous. This is about something funny. And it *was* very funny. When I told him so—this was later on. When I told him, he said, 'What did I call myself? The Rememberer?' In fact," my mother said, "he'd printed out, 'This is The Reminder Reminding You.' It was about something to pick up when I went to town for the newspapers and groceries. And I told him, 'Oh. I don't remember. I didn't see it that clearly. I didn't have my glasses on.' And we looked at each other, in this mutual silly fog of forgetting and nearsightedness, and we both began to laugh. I'm going to remember it, if I *do* remember it, as our first joint joke about getting . . . on."

I smiled and nodded, but I wanted to cry. I'm afraid my expression said so.

"What, sweetie? What's wrong?"

I shook my head and smiled what Marty once described as my black-and-white movie heroine's smile: she knows that the last chance is gone, but the hero hasn't seen that yet.

"Are you having a bad time with your Marty?"

I shrugged. My mother came across the kitchen to me and opened her arms and I, who had come to be her harbor, headed in and docked, face in her shoulder and arms around her waist so she could wrap her own around my back and hug.

Her tending made me brave. I said, "How is it with Daddy and you?"

"We're okay," she said. "His health could be better. I guess everyone's could be. Not that he takes it easy."

"Not the splitting wood thing?"

"He bought a new axe by mail from some company in New

York. He cuts a lot of kindling, but he doesn't do much cord-wood splitting anymore."

We stepped back from each other, which meant that we released each other, as if care were a kind of shackling. She removed her glasses, wiped her eyes, smiled, shook her head, and put her glasses back on. They magnified her very dark eyes and they made her seem frail. She raised her brows and I felt my own go up in response. She was pretty, and, except from some white streaks, her hair was still the light brown it had been in my child-hood. She was half an inch taller than I, and she looked slender and strong in my father's Black Watch plaid flannel shirt worn with the tails out and the baggy sleeves rolled up. Her neck was a mess of cords and wrinkled skin; it was where she looked oldest, and she saw me study it. She lifted her chin, an instant, as if dar-ing me to comment.

I said, "Daddy sounds . . . upset. Sometimes, on the phone, he sounds sad. Would that be a fair way to say it?"

She was pouring coffee beans into the little grinder, then fill-ing the kettle, taking a filter from the drawer she had always kept them in, and I suspected that all the motions of this routine pro-vided her with someplace to hide. When she was done, she turned to me. She said, "Yes."

"Yes?"

"A fair way to say it, as long as you aren't saying it to him. All right? He noticed, suddenly, that he's a good distance from young. He did this before."

"I remember. Forty."

"No. That wouldn't be your father. He did it his own way, which was to not even *care* about turning forty. Or he pretended not to care. If he did, he completely fooled me. But when he turned forty-one, he went down low, into his shoes. He was miserable for months."

"He tortured you," I said.

"He did not torture me. He was unhappy."

"He snarled. He growled at you. I remember, Mom. It was unbearable."

"It was not unbearable. I bore it. Do you say 'bore' for that? I think so. I handled it. I dealt with it. It became all right. You know, I sometimes still want a cigarette. If I could have a cigarette with this cup of coffee, when it's ready, I think I would really enjoy it. Do not, Cara, open your mouth and tell me not to smoke. Don't."

"I'm becoming a pain in the ass again."

"Not you. But don't manage me right now, sweetie, is all."

"Not me," I said. I know that I blushed. She was able to make me blush more than men. She was the smartest person I knew, and Marty Gold was brilliant. Nor was my father the kind of person who had to move his lips when he read. And my brother, Douglas, was in charge of his own particle accelerator in Seattle. But Jessica Terranova was the champion at understanding directions that came with complex machines and at puzzling people out. She had been a social worker in Utica, but she could also, if she wanted, have been the head, say, of the Food and Drug Administration.

"And don't, please, give me a tip about placing eggshells in the bottom of the coffeepot or anything."

"That's a household management tip from a hundred years ago, Mom. I write about *cooking*. I am being a pain in the ass, though."

"You might become one, let's say. You came up here with

either saving me or saving Daddy in mind. Or getting saved. I'm all right about saving. I'm the lifeguard type. Parents get trained to do that. But I have to admit how terrible I am at getting saved. And you've got a saving-people gene loose inside you. It's from your father's father. He was a lifeguard at Coney Island. The oldest, sexiest lifeguard of his time, according to Daddy. Until he was fired for playing house while someone almost drowned."

"'Playing *house*'?"

"I think you know what I mean."

"Well. Making out? Screwing teenage girls? Feeling up the over-fifty set? Was Queen Victoria still alive?"

"That would be in England, Cara."

"'It was a dark and stormy night,'" I recited.

We drank coffee and talked about bone mass in middle-aged women, and then, just a little, about living with someone as a way of figuring out whether or not to live with them. The family eyebrows rose and fell, and we moved on from coffee to chilled vermouth. I made a marinade of white wine, olive oil, marjoram, and red pepper flakes for the swordfish my mother had defrosted, and I was cooking us a potato galette with scallions and grated parmesan when my father came home from his hospital.

"What kind of job gets you home at nine at night?" he asked. "The younger doctors get home on time. To hell with it. I'm going to retire."

"Good," I said, "you're getting old."

"You sound like Mom," he said, hugging me, kissing me on the mouth and once on each cheek, and then hugging me again. "I'm glad you're here."

"Is something wrong?"

"Yes. My daughter grew up, my son moved to a different time

zone, my wife doesn't treat me with respect, and my physicians' patients consistently refuse to send in their stool sample cards."

"No bowel jokes," my mother warned.

His five o'clock shadow was gray-white, and his skin seemed pale. I thought I could smell hospital soap on him, and ink, both of which I probably imagined. He spent most of his day with paper and verbal complaints. "Sorry to be late," he said. "Half the staff's been sick or on vacation. A nurse retired and another went into private service. And we have a genuine money hemorrhage. Do I have time for a drink?"

My mother pointed to the glass of red wine she'd set on the table.

He pointed to his mouth and she walked over to kiss him. He hugged her and patted her bottom. They stayed like that, and I turned away to work the galette onto a dinner plate so I could flip it over back into the pan. The swordfish steaks were in the broiler, and I instructed myself to remember to buy them a non-stick pan with ridges so they could grill on top of the stove.

"Cara," my father said, after drinking a little of his wine, "what brings our far-flung correspondent home?"

"It's been a while, Daddy."

"True. But?"

"Why now?"

"All right. Why now? Martin Gold, Esquire, Attorney-at-Law? Is he a reason?"

"Marty's a reason."

"It's not working out for you down there, up in the aunt's penthouse?"

"Not a penthouse, Daddy. Just a big apartment. Very big. God. You could have an overnight for a Girl Scout troop in the living room. The piano is long enough to use as a tugboat. I will never live like that again in my life."

I turned to see him looking into his wine. I'd have bet that he was imagining me in a bathrobe, walking down a long, carpeted hall from the shower to a vast and opulent bedroom. He slowly shook his head.

"And Lawyer Gold?"

"He's a sweetheart," I said. "Otherwise, I wouldn't have moved in with him. Otherwise, I wouldn't stay."

"I'm sure that's true," he said. "Of course, since it's you, the fact of your having decided to move in with him could be enough to *force* you to stay. If anyone were to try to analyze anyone else, or understand their motivations, et cetera. Instead of shutting up and drinking their wine." He took a sip.

Because my mother hadn't shut him up while she was making the salad, I knew that she was thinking something similar. So, of course, was I. We drank the jug wine that tasted like mothballs in vinegar and we ate swordfish, galette, and green salad, and there was a lot of banter I was happy to hear again from my parents. My father looked weary but undefeated, and, as he stood, he seemed powerful again. I became so tired from the drive, and, I suppose, from what had set me traveling, and, more than likely, from being there and with them and feeling—there was no other word for it—safe, that I thought I would sleep where I sat. You came home, at my age, to work on behalf of your parents or to let go of what you gripped and steered while you were away from them. Not knowing precisely what had really brought me, I closed my eyes and let my hands go loose, and they acted as if it were twenty years before, marching me to the stairs so I would go to bed.

I don't remember dreams, though I did waken several times and, each time, I thought I heard them whispering, downstairs at first and then in their bedroom at the other end of the hall. I heard no specific words, but I woke on Sunday morning to remember with certainty that their conversations had been about me.

What woke me was the high, loud, ragged voice of Stanley Sobriski—I knew it at once—as he called to my father, who probably stood two feet away from him, as if they were separated by half of the hay field back behind the house that Sobriski paid my parents in order to cut and bale for his dairy farm. "Honest ta God, Docta Terranova, I'm gonna pay every penny. Honest ta *God!*"

I was glad for the hubbub, because it kept me from reexamining my childhood room and permitting or even requiring a sentimentality I had no patience for. I was too old for it, and so were my patents. And Stanley Sobriski, I knew, was behind in his payments again. They rented him the right to cut hay for his dairy farm, five or six miles down the road and across a county highway and up to where, on a steep hillside, he kept what my father had described as a tilted farm on which the cattle stood crookedly to graze and where the mire and stink of the barnyard had entered the battered, small farmhouse where his tiny wife and illiterate son—he somehow had kept him from school and raised him as an agricultural laborer—lived in the familiar cycle of debt and failure that characterized so many little upstate farms.

When I had showered and dressed and come downstairs, my father and Stanley were gone from the house. A small bottle of Scotch stood on the kitchen table, where it caught the morning light and glowed amber. There was a green-and-red-striped ribbon tied at its neck. I thought of Stanley Sobriski's little wife, in a smelly, dark kitchen, tying the bow. My mother stared at it from where she stood, at the sink, with a spatula in her hand.

"Are you making pancakes?"

"No. Would you like some?"

"No. I'll get coffee for myself. What are you cooking?"

"Nothing," she said. "Why?"

I pointed at the spatula.

"Oh. Oh, I think I picked it up because it was the nearest weapon. I thought they were going to have a fight. Your father kept rubbing his arm, it got so bad between them."

"What's wrong with his arm?"

"It's where people his age rub themselves when their hearts— It's angina, sweetie. It radiates from the chest. You know."

"Daddy?"

"You push a hospital against the tide all day, that's what happens. The tension gets to your heart. His father had the same thing."

"I knew I was right to be worried."

"Well, of course it's right to be worried."

The structure of her face collapsed, then, into vertical lines, horizontal wrinkles, loose flesh, red skin, and those eyes that her glasses seemed at times to enlarge so grotesquely. I had absolutely not a word in mind with which to comfort her, or comfort myself, or simply break the silence that seemed to harden and to separate us. She was alone on her side of it, I imagined, sensing her loss of him and the beginning of a fierce, long loneliness. And then it all fell back into place, and she was my powerful mother. But I had seen who she was when she was in her privacy. She would be far from pleased that I had.

She shook her head. "He's lucky I didn't take him apart with my spatula," she said, tossing it into the sink.

"Stanley's not paying?" I asked her.

"He's bringing the half-a-bottle of Johnnie Walker Red. And honest-ta-God, Docta Terranova, this year he's going to pay. Just forgive him for not paying over the last three years and let him start cutting today. You know what he's like."

"He's a deadbeat," I said.

"He is."

"And Daddy's a pussycat."

"Until he told Stanley about sound business practices and Stanley said then how come he's driving the hospital into the ground and everybody who goes there gets sicker on account of Daddy not buying the necessary equipment and your father grabbed his arm and started that very low city-Italian muttering he does when he's crazy with anger."

"Is he having some kind of attack?"

"If he's dead next time we see him, then probably he was."

"You're so tough," I said, watching her keep her face composed.

"That's where you get it from, sweetie."

"I would like a fried egg sandwich, please," I said. "Just like the ones they make at a place called—really—Nick's, near Ninth Avenue. Pulpy white bread, please, and with ketchup."

"Shall I make more coffee?"

"I think chocolate milk," I said.

But she didn't go to the refrigerator for eggs. She wore dark clogs and her own faded jeans and a different one—Stewart, I think was the plaid—of his long-tailed flannel shirts that was open enough for me to see how the edges of her breasts had gone crepey. It was like old lovers, I thought, her exposed like that and me noticing. I remembered how smooth her chest had looked, how tight her breasts had seemed to me when I was trying, through prayer and manipulation, to coerce my own to grow. She leaned against the stove and yoked her hand's webbing, from thumb to forefinger, against her own throat, as if compelling herself to stand still. She said, "I worry about him every day. I don't think there are any hours anymore when I don't worry about him. And I know he's the same about me. It's so stupid. We're together so much, and you know what we do? We worry about each other dying and the other ending up alone. So we do that, and of course it creeps into the being together. Every time there's light, we make it dark. We admitted it one night. He got home on time, and we drank too much wine with dinner and we said things. These aren't things you and Marty Gold would be saying, I hope."

I shook my head. She didn't see me.

"This is precisely what I made myself promise I wouldn't say to you when you told us you were coming home."

"It's why I came."

"Sweetie, that's terrible. You shouldn't have to come home like we're dying and you need to comfort us and see to our medication. You ought to be able to come home because life is miserable for *you*." She put her hand on her mouth and then she laughed. It was real laughter, and I enjoyed hearing it.

"I'm a *little* miserable," I said.

"Good girl," she said. "Thank you."

I nodded, and then she did. "So I can't help," I said.

"You always help. Come be here with us once in a while. That's lovely. There's no real *helping* what I'm talking about. It's like the ocean, only slower. It comes in."

"We need Grandpa Terranova, if we could pry him away from the hotsie-totsie girls at Coney Island."

My father, coming into the kitchen, said, "Why?"

"Tide's up," my mother said. "How are the local relationships?"

"He didn't punch me out when I insulted him. So I'm still the lord of the manor."

"And he hates us," my mother said.

"That he does. But it's always like that if somebody depends on your favors for feeding his family. They always hate you if they need you to be good to them. And I was trying to be *bad*."

"Did you fire him, Daddy? Or whatever you do to tenant farmers. *Is* he a tenant farmer?"

He shook his big head. He wore an old crewneck sweater of a peculiar mud-green color that made the skin of his face and even his wrists and fingers look gray. I watched my mother's dark eyes on him. "Nothing that grand," he said. "He's supposed to pay us a few dollars a bale. Windrows, they call them now: those giant wheels of hay they wrap in white plastic and litter the world with after they unwrap them for the herd. He's supposed to make it grow"—he gestured toward the large field behind the house—"without putting toxic chemicals into the groundwater."

"He hasn't paid in years," my mother said. "So we decided, since we weren't making anything on the field anyway, we'd just as soon do without his tractor going back and forth all day on the way to and from the field. And God knows what kind of deadly stuff he's put into the ground. Let's have it quiet again, we thought. That's what Daddy told him this morning, when he came with his little bottle of whiskey and his excuses about paying."

My father sat to drink the coffee my mother offered, but he

only held the cup in the air, away from the saucer but also away from his mouth. "I told him he could take any bales he'd cut last year, but that I didn't want him cutting anymore."

"So he's gone?" I asked, sipping coffee I didn't want.

"No, he's up there, being sly. He'll take any bales he finds, for sure. And maybe he'll cut more. It's a fine summer day. I'm trying to decide whether I want to drive around and hike across from the access road just to catch him in the act."

"No," my mother said.

"No?" he said. "Why not?"

"Because it's Saturday, and Cara's home, and I'd just as soon you didn't throw an embolism or blow your heart through your chest and spoil her weekend with us."

"Medical talk," he said to me, jerking his thumb at her. "Ask her what an embolism is."

"Not me," I said. "I don't want to know. Anyway, if you kick off, I won't be able to solicit your advice."

He leaned back in his chair and put the coffee down.

My mother said, "Did you really want eggs?"

I shook my head.

"Because you do look very pale," she said.

"Mommy, I never get pale."

"Are you sick?" my father asked. "Are you . . ."

He waited for me to supply him with words: Loveless. Pregnant. Fettered by despair.

"I'm not sure," I said, "about living with Marty too much longer."

"Is that a dilemma?" my father asked.

"You mean a choice I can't make?"

He shrugged. "I don't know *what* I mean," he said. "I never lived with anybody except your mother. She didn't—" He looked up. "Yes, you did," he said.

She shook her head.

"You told me no, but I always wondered about the Frenchman. A hockey pro, a semiprofessional hockey player? In Utica. Before us. Le-something. Leblanc."

"Lafleur," she said.

"Mommy."

"We never lived together in the same apartment or house or anything." She looked pleased by her recollection. "I told you the truth."

He said, "But you need to tune it in a little?"

Her neck was red. She shook her head. "Don't be silly," she said. "His family had a camp up north, in the Adirondacks, near one of the lakes. We stayed there a couple of times." She turned to look out the kitchen window. My father and I were staring at her shoulders and buttocks and back. I wondered what he was thinking while I considered how she might have lain beneath a broad, tall hockey player who, even as they celebrated his power, was losing his career.

I thought of Marty as he sat in his plaid boxer shorts and knee-length businessman's socks to study the laws of New York State while he dressed to go to one of two courtrooms where he waited to be necessary to people who were poor and accused. He was a lovely man, and bright, and he had done his share of scuffling in the tougher precincts of the city. I was going to write a column, I thought, when I got back, about *pasta puttanesca*. It was a fall or winter dish, but it would have to do for early summer. I wanted, just then, to write only about the food of people who lived as close to the bone as Stanley Sobriski, and cooks consulting my column would learn Whore's Pasta—garlic and capers, tomatoes, Nicoise olives and anchovy fillets, oregano and red pepper flakes. With *puttanesca*, you think you're getting an everyday sauce, but then you're surprised.

The intensity of the silence between my parents increased. When my mother said, "He was a nice boy. He was gentle, which you wouldn't expect when you looked at him," and when my father turned toward her but said nothing, I excused myself and went upstairs for my walking shoes. I brushed my teeth and came down to an empty kitchen in which dishes left on the table, and chairs pulled away from it, suggested interruptions and necessities. I put a banana in the hip pocket of my jeans, and I went out the back door, past Wellingtons that leaned toward one another and rain jackets heavy on their hooks, to walk across the back field that had put Stanley Sobriski into debt and my father into such discomfort. I hadn't walked across this field for years—across the marshy ground on its way down into a creek and then up, across more marsh, and then higher, quite steeply, until the ground hardened and curved to a kind of plateau that went on for acres to the hedgerow that marked the end of my parents' holding.

It was wet walking, at first, but I didn't mind. My shoes were waterproofed, and because I was wearing them I felt canny and adequate. When I was a girl, I used to follow the stream down to a basin of land where, for no reason I understood at the time, I had dammed the flow and had created my own small lake. It was important to call it my own, and my father had agreed that I could, if I made a spillway with my fieldstone dam that would direct the slow trickle away from the lower edge of their gardens below the house. He had grown beans on a trellis of lashed, long branches, and I had been the keeper of the dam. Then I was across the marshland and walking against the steepness of the hill. I could hear my breaths, and I realized that I had forced my breathing into something of the familiar rhythm of Marty and me as we panted together on his generous aunt's walnut sleigh bed.

Well, didn't you get to me, I said as if to Marty.

And aren't you surprised, I heard as if in his voice.

The slope of the hill must have been interrupting the sound that I suddenly heard when I was walking almost on the level, forcing my way through the tall, tender grass that had grown higher than my elbows. I saw that a man—Stanley Sobriski, I was certain, hunched and round with muscle, taut with purpose, on top of his blue tractor—was cutting hay. The blades spun clean and powerfully, and the grass was flung behind him with a sure, organized heaviness. I thought of my father, rubbing his left arm as he and Stanley argued about the word given and the word broken. I thought of each man feeling the certainties that surpassed their words: Stanley the hungers of his bony cattle, and the land, growing unavailable, that was all that he in his debt could rely upon to lighten the debt; and my father feeling in his chest and arm the sense, I had read, of being crushed.

Stanley saw me as I stood in the tall, uncut grass, and he did something terrible. He had been cutting in rows that more or less followed the contours of the hill. Seeing me, he had slowed, and then he'd speeded up. He drove toward me against the grain of the hillside, violating the shape the swaths should have made. He tore the field apart as he drove to me. It was a defilement, a punishing of the order that emanated from the farmhouse to the owners' field. And it frightened me.

He stopped the tractor a safe—you could even say a polite—

distance from me, and he left the motor idling. He stayed that way awhile, his head back, as if he were smelling the stink of diesel fuel or something else in the air while I squinted into the late morning sun. Finally, he shut the tractor off and came down the slope through the grass, which came almost to his shoulders. He stood before me, his curly red hair stippled with bits of stem and leaf, his white teeth exposed in what he might have thought of as a smile.

"I ain't seen you for a long time," he shouted, although we were only a few feet apart. He wore a stained rust-colored cotton shirt, its sleeves rolled high. Bits of grass were tangled in the light hairs on his forearms. "Honest ta God, you grew up good."

I said, "Hi," and then said what I thought, and what I thought I perhaps shouldn't say. But I was thinking of my father and the pressure in his chest. I was thinking of my mother's face when it fell. I said, "Are you supposed to be cutting hay here anymore, Mr. Sobriski?"

"He sent you?"

I shook my head. Then I decided to say, "Never mind who sent me, please. *Are* you?"

"Am I what, Miss Landlord?"

"Supposed to be cutting?"

His eyes shifted from side to side, not engaging mine. They were cruel, like a clown's, when they finally fell upon my face and locked still and he smiled without pleasure. "Sure. He said, your old man said: 'Go up there and finish it off.' 'At's all I'm doin' here. I'll be outa here, a couple hours, you won't know you saw me. Whaddya say?"

"I think what I should say is no. So: no, Mr. Sobriski. My parents don't want you cutting on their property." I thought I sounded pompous. I thought I sounded arrogant. I thought of his wife in their dark kitchen.

"It's always money with you people," he said, finally looking at me. He didn't seem to me, anymore, to be a clown. He looked like a man who was going to punch someone. I was one of *you people*, and *you people* were the ones who needed a little smacking around, and that's why I jumped and gave a timid little hiccup of fear as his hands came out very quickly to seize my shoulders. I felt his fingers against the bone. "Payments. Installments. Due tomorrow, due today, kindly remit. *Kindly fucking remit.*"

He worked the right shoulder backward, then forward, then backward again. He did the same with the left. I tried to pull away from him, but of course I couldn't. He was powerful, and his bulk was immovable He was going to set me down in the tall grass, where we'd be invisible, and he was going to furrow and reap. Instead of practicing one of the veteran city woman's surefire maneuvers of self-defense—keys (back on my girlhood bureau) extended between the knuckles of the clenched hand; swift knee to the groin; finger in the eye and not relenting *no matter what* until the eyeball's out of its socket; knuckles of second and third finger, repeatedly, hard into the larynx; flight; high-pitched scream for assistance; stab at the heart with an unpeeled banana—I closed my eyes and I choked back my weeping.

He let go of my shoulders, and I heard the grass whisper against him, so I opened my eyes. It was my mother, of course, holding before her with both hands what seemed to be a smallish axe with a long steel head. That, I guessed, would be my father's new kindling axe.

She said, in what I suppose was the toughest voice of Utica,

New York, "You want to fight, Stanley? You want to try something with my kid?"

"Hi, Mommy."

"What *did* you think you were doing?"

"No," I said, "I was just walking."

"We'll talk about that," she said, as she had so many times in my childhood when I had trespassed or strayed and had needed her help.

"Hey, Missus," Stanley said, "honest ta God, I was just—I think I lost my composza. This morning with the doctor, that was bad for everybody. But no harm intended, unnerstand?"

"I'm going to the state police," my mother said. "We're going. We're filing a report on you. Attempted—" and she couldn't say the word. "I'll go the sheriff, too. I won't leave you alone after this." She lifted the axe, as if she expected him to jump and run.

He did neither. He looked at her and then at me. He lifted his face so that his nostrils were pointed toward us. He breathed in deeply, as if he could distinguish our scent, on the breezes in the field, from the smell of mowed hay or diesel fumes. He turned and walked through the grass, which closed behind him, and then he was on his blue tractor, and then he was driving—still mowing, tearing the field apart—as he went toward the access road at the far western edge.

I sat down where I'd stood. My mother sat beside me, her eyes closed, her head shaking a little, although she didn't weep.

"You were going to chop up weeds?"

"I took the axe with me because I thought maybe if he couldn't find his new toy, he'd skip cutting kindling we don't need. What we need is for him to rest."

"What was the *with me* part, though? What were you coming out here for?"

"I wanted to talk with you. You had that look you used to get as a kid, all taut lips and grim eyes: Cara moving towards something really not advisable. I wanted to talk to you before you got there."

"I didn't know you saw me," I said. "It was just a walk. I was trying to figure things out. That was all it was."

She let her breath out noisily. She fiddled with a leather thong attached to the handle of the axe. "Things with Marty Gold?"

"Him. Daddy. You. What kind of food stuff I should write about when I get back. I wasn't looking for trouble. God, he was so *angry*. I think he would have done it."

"I think he would have done it," she said. "That, and stealing hay, maybe watching Daddy have a heart attack: what else could he have done? But what *about* Daddy and me—what you were trying to figure out?"

"How to handle missing you."

"Come home more. Or we could visit you down there. It might be good if I could get him out of town more often."

"Not that kind of missing," I said. "The kind where you miss people sort of in advance. While they're still around."

She ran her finger along the pale wood of the axe handle. She shook her head and said, "That." She hefted the axe, then set it down on the crushed grass. "No," she said, "I don't know anything smart about that kind. No."

"No," I said, "I don't, either."

We sat in the clearing we'd made with our bodies, surrounded by high grass, while the sun rose to noon. Birdsong came in, and the hunting cry—that half-whispered menace—of a hawk too high to be seen. I felt the banana in my pocket and pulled it out.

"Want a bite?"

She shook her head.

I peeled it, but when I felt my lips around the curved, fleshy tube, I had to spit. I tossed the rest away from us and watched it sink into the tall, pale grass. It would lie in the unworked field and decompose.

"I'm betting that you didn't sublet your place," my mother said. "Am I right? So you'd have someplace to go back to?"

I smiled for her certainty.

"You'll leave him," she said. Her glasses were off, and she was rubbing her eyes. She looked up, and each of us knew she was exposed to the other.

"But we do stop leaving them," I said. I untied each yellow lace and then tied each knot again.

"Well, of course." She replaced her glasses.

"Of course."

She stood, a little stiffly, holding the axe at her side, and she reached down for my hand. I pulled against her to stand. Her grip was dry and powerful. "And then we get all the scaring we always were right to be scared of," she said.

I AM THE NEWS

"Nobody got left behind," my father liked to say. "Everyone came home," he'd say. He referred to Marines killed in combat. He was an old, but never a former, Marine, and even when he was dead, having outlived our mother by a dozen years, when my brother Scotty and I were working in his house to clean it up by throwing and selling most of its contents away, I continued to hear from my father about the Corps.

I ran into him two days after his death in the room he'd called his study. It was behind the living room, off the rearmost corridor in the house. I had been trying for hours, since I'd driven up from New York, to attend to my father's papers. And, for the second time, I put the cassette into the machine and listened again to the narrator's voice, resonant with theatrical manliness, suggestive of the courage in the face of what he called "withering fire," which "our boys" were about to confront without wavering. He spoke while orchestral strings and woodwinds drifted and wobbled, as did the narrator's voice, so that his words were a part of the off-key song of bravery I listened to in the room in which my father had paid bills, read letters including, I supposed, those that Scotty and I had sent him, napped on a daybed, and lain in to die.

The tape I watched had been made in black and white and it told the story of the United States Marine Corps' retreat from the Chosin Reservoir in North Korea, which was a famous moral victory for everyone in the Corps except the men who died of it. The images jumped and tightened, and there was my father. He stood in what seemed to be a hot, barren, rocky mountain pass with his suit coat held over his right shoulder by the crook of the forefinger of his right hand. I knew that he stood in South Korea while he spoke of their adventure in the north. He had been a burly, dapper man, with broad shoulders and chest and a heavy neck, a big, bald head. Here, in the scene shot as if for a family film—the big man in harsh light photographed by someone who didn't know how to work with sun and shade—he squinted as if the camera, or the gaze of onlookers, were painful to his eyes. He looked so pale, I thought he would faint. His expression was grave and his voice was hoarse as it scraped over his teeth from a tight throat. I had seen and heard him this way in the past, and not in Korea, but in his own living room, or on his screened-in porch, or in a restaurant in Salisbury, Connecticut, once, when he thought a fellow diner had made an anti-Semitic remark. Now, in the film I watched, he and several members of the Seventh Marines, First Marine Division, were talking about the time in 1950, pursuing North Korean troops almost into China, the force of 12,000 Marines was suddenly required to fight their way back south through 150,000 Chinese troops who made a surprise attack across the Yalu River into North Korea. Marines died of their wounds when the plasma froze. The injured, outnumbered, and harried survivors brought home their dead.

It was a hallmark of the Corps, he'd told us, that they carried back the killed Marines. They really didn't, always, he'd admitted. "Sometimes, you just can't. But you try. They insisted that we always try." When he said "we," he referred, we knew, to the enlisted men and noncommissioned officers such as he had been, a gunnery sergeant who, as he saw it, had worked with his men for the officers.

I'd been in college when he'd made the distinction between "we" and the others. "That's not very esprit de corps of you, Dad," I'd said.

He had stared with his light blue eyes. In our family of four, my brother and I and our long-dead mother were homely or, anyway, ordinary-looking, and we had unremarkable brown eyes. Our father's eyes set him apart from us, and so did his tall, athletic good looks. My brother and I used to joke that we had adopted him. But there wasn't a good deal of humor in the air after my comment about him and the Corps. I was a left-wing political science major, and possessed of not much knowledge as well as the ability to speak as if that were not the case.

"When your friend's reduced to a handful of leg bones and ribs glued together by blood," he said, staring out of those frightening, light eyes—they always seemed to know the truth denied to me—"then you try to get them home. Whether or not an officer has told you to. You don't stop until an officer tells you *not* to."

"So did you believe in that or didn't you? I don't get it."

He stared at me then as now he stared at me from Korea and from deep inside the world suggested by the film—a place that he and I knew I'd never go to. He looked worn down, and he seemed to be close to despair. I felt, now, that my heart was heaving about in its ribs like someone in a cell. I stopped the tape and looked at the floor. Of course it had been *his* heart jumping, when he spoke to me of the Marine Corps dead, and when he spoke—to me? to himself? to the men they never brought home?—from the harsh light on the cruel landscape in the film. When he'd died in the room in which I sat less than a dozen feet from the daybed on which he had chosen to lie, as far from everyone as he could drag himself, it was the tattered heart that killed him.

I would return to watching him, I told myself again. I would come back.

I'd gone to the attic, which was entered by a collapsible staircase that unfolded from the ceiling of a second-floor corridor, one of its panels opening out to make a kind of ladder that let me climb up and into a very large room containing several dozen cartons and two full-length mirrors, hundreds of stacked books, framed prints, and more toys than I could remember our playing with. It was lit by a single bare bulb in a shadeless sconce. I found myself squinting in the room's brown light.

The ceiling of the attic was too low for me to stand, so I squatted, like a soldier on bivouac, and I waited for sensations. There were, it turned out, too many of those, and I scuttled for the hatch to the stairs. Then, standing on the Persian runner that could have brought enough money to pay my daughter's tuition at Vassar for close to the entire school year, I pulled the cord that sent the staircase folding up and out of sight.

I returned to the study downstairs the way I had forced myself, in law school, to return to my apartment and memorize case law. But I folded my hands at the edge of the desk, and then I unfolded them and gripped the desktop, and then I sat with my hands, curled but open, in my lap. There was too much to get

hold of, I guess, and I guess that I had given up. Then I smelled
my brother. Scotty, who carried his makings in a tin in which
strong peppermint lozenges were sold, had rolled himself a death
house joint. He was nine years younger than I, so almost a distant
cousin more than kid brother or friend. But he looked enough
like me, and had aged rapidly enough, to appear to be my twin:
same hairline retreating around an island of stranded widow's
peak; same pointy jaw; same frowning mouth that was trapped
beneath a heavy upper lip and whiskers that needed shaving
twice a day; same long, clumsy legs; and, of course, the same
unspectacular bear-brown eyes. He wore dark-rimmed glasses
while I wore wire frames. He wore turtleneck sweaters even in
the warmth of spring while I wore open-necked shirts and rolled
the sleeves up. In what he called his leisure time—which, I might
have argued, lasted most of every day—he wore the draped,
dressy trousers of his suits; I wore cotton sweaters and unpressed
khakis to work unless I was appearing in court. But you would
know us as anything but unrelated. Each of us resembled our
father, even if each of us seemed less distinguished, and I suspected that he was made as uneasy as I, seeing the father in the
son. Scotty and I had to make conversation about a dead man
with someone who looked like his ghost.

He walked in smiling at a private joke. He lifted his hand to
offer me reefer, and I shook my head. He leaned against the wall
beside the door and said, "No end of it, is there?"

"Too much stuff," I said.

"And then there's what's in the room," he said.

My assignment for the morning had been to inspect the letters
and assorted financial papers our father had kept in his desk and
in the filing cabinets under the windows that looked over the

garden. I had found the tape, and a good deal of correspondence under A, for the alumni association of the Seventh Marines, and I had never got past it.

"I got sidetracked," I said, with what I thought might be a rueful smile. Scotty's expression suggested that I wasn't charming. "I'll come back up next weekend," I said. "This could take forever, roughly."

Scotty said, "He saved everything. All his letters from Mom before they got married, and while he was in Korea. All of the letters he wrote to her."

"You read them?"

He shook his head. "I couldn't."

"I couldn't have, either. There's paper in here"—I indicated the file cabinets—"nobody could ever have needed. Diners Club bills from the sixties. American Express from a restaurant in Paris where he had soup and wine and he gave the waiter a tip as big as the original bill."

"I thought you didn't give tips in France."

"Sometimes you do," I said, "if it doesn't say *servis compris.*"

"Nothing in my neighborhood says anything like that," Scotty said, maintaining his favorite fiction—that he was a street urchin from Hell's Kitchen instead of a Friends School alumnus who grew up on West End Avenue in Manhattan before his parents moved to this more genteel neighborhood. He had taken his lozenge tin out of his hip pocket.

"What it was, Scotty, was the bill was for two *potage*, two *ordinaire. Deux* of each."

"He was hungry," my brother said, his glance sliding from mine because he knew what I was telling him.

"He was with a woman," I said.

"The waiters in whatever *compree* make a note of that, do they?"

"You know he was."

"Well, good," Scotty said. "I'm glad the old man got laid."

"This was before Mom died."

"It could have been a client," Scotty said. "His business trips *were* for business, weren't they?"

I shrugged. "I don't know the first thing about him, Scotty."

He sat on the ottoman of our father's red club chair. "You know the first thing," he said. He was determined to protect himself with smoke. He had a paper out, and his long fingers were graceful as they doled and rolled his joint.

"You're right. I do," I said.

He raised his brows to offer me a hit. I shook my head. He snapped his butane lighter and made the usual toking-up noises—the inhale, the sigh, the gasp of exhalation—and then he said something like, "Mmm." He looked past me, at the television set atop the VCR on which nothing played. He said a few words I didn't catch, and then he lay back from the ottoman so that his head was on the club chair, his back arched and his face directed at the ceiling. "So what do you know?" he asked me.

"The first thing: he was the best-kept secret of the Korean War, and then the peacetime after it, and then the Vietnam War he tried to volunteer for, and that whole Dark Night of the Republican Head Case when he voted for Barry Goldwater and then Nixon. All the political stuff—his feeling of veterans being disenfranchised—that I can understand. But him? The actual person? *He* was the secret."

Scotty took in smoke and said with lassitude, almost drawling the words, "And that's what you know about our very father."

"Our very father, yes. That is approximately it. What would *you* like to add?"

Scotty seemed to tremble in place, but I couldn't see his face, so what I knew was that he struggled either not to weep or not to laugh. He held up his hand and inspected what he smoked. Then he began to speak, then was silent. Then he spoke. "He loved me," he said.

I couldn't keep myself—no: I *didn't* keep myself—from saying, "And wasn't that a great help."

"He didn't have to," Scotty said. "I was—it was—you were away. It was while you were on the coast."

"I was chasing Vanessa Braun, who worked for Greenpeace. There was pretty damned little environment involved, unless you count the ocean. We sailed little boats into oncoming oil tankers. She was crazy to die, as well as crazy in general. As well as finally very unfaithful to me because I was so reliable. Her word: reliable. I was *not*, I never have been, reliable. I was what I remain: boring."

Scotty nodded.

"Thank you."

"The point," he said, "this time around, the point is not you. This, what I was saying, is me. When you were out there, being doomed and faithful, I was in the city being a drunk. They were up here, she was getting ready to be dead in, like, overnight, and he was practicing the law on behalf of all the other rich folk of Salisbury and Lakeville. I was drinking everyplace on Broadway, between 85th and 116th, and in my apartment, and especially in International House on Riverside with this definitely, certifiably difficult woman from Minsk who was a graduate in something that had to do with peace—'piss,' she always called it—and justice. She was brilliant. She smelled a little sweaty, and she recited de Tocqueville to me on the subject of my young and primitive nation. And she got rid of me when the drinking kept me from performing well in the sack. From, actually, performing at all. 'With you,' she said, 'I will never hoff piss.'"

I heard this in the troubled, low tones of my father on the video. It seemed to me at that moment that Scotty and I might possibly be able to know each other once our father's ashes were scattered, when the house had been emptied and sold off, and when we would have to select a city, and a building within it, in which we could meet; for this was the last of anything approaching home that we could share. Once this house was gone, we had no place to go but into our separate lives. My chest felt constricted by the weight of the absolute fact.

"I came up here," he said. "Took the train, got a cab in from the station, showed up mellow and affectionate—"

"Drunk," I said.

"Drunk. Undeniably drunk. Mom was already getting sick. Dad was happy to see me, I thought."

"No, Scotty, he *was*. He liked us coming around."

"I think he did. Or he didn't hate it. Or he didn't care."

"But otherwise," I said, "we knew and understood him completely."

"And he sat me down in the kitchen and he made me a drink. He talked about the retreat for some time that night."

"You always reminded him of men in the outfit, the guys he called boys. He told me how many of them he knew who drank too much. He looked after them all he could. That's why he wasn't worried about you and booze, he said. Because of the boys he had known in the Seventh. They got straightened out after a while, he said, and so would you."

Scotty nodded. "I figured that out, after a while of not drinking. Incidentally, if you want a drink, please go ahead. I'm fine with it."

I shook my head.

"I am," he said. "Really."

"No," I said, "I'm not . . . thirsty for it. I'm okay. Thank you."

"Okay," he said. "Okay. So, we're at the table in the kitchen, I'm drinking Jack Daniel's Green Label and he's making himself a cup of decaffeinated coffee and tea for Mom and I'm rattling the old ice cubes pretty well when Mom says—you can imagine. Tell me. What's she say?"

I said, "Mom tells you either about a tragedy involving local flora or fauna—"

"Which," he asked me, "is which?"

I shook my head. "Couldn't help you—well, flora must mean flowers, right? So fauna has to be the animals. And either she tells you something about some very bad ecology event, or she offers up a little item from the news involving dead babies and maimed nuns or murdered Jewish doctors."

"News," Scotty said. "Dreadful events in the Deep South. Dad kind of looks at me, the way other fathers would look before they wink at you, except I never, ever, saw him wink on purpose. But he's looking at me, and I am suddenly completely clear on how he really wants me to be all right. He wants me to come through all right so the drinking thing is in the past, the way it is with his delinquent boys in the Seventh. And there I am, having never had anything to do with a military uniform, or military service, or even a minor act of courage with water back."

"Scotty, you remember the fights I used to have with him about his beloved tough-on-Communism politicians, or the CIA destabilizing some pathetic little government in Latin America? We used to shout and slam the table until the time his heart got worse. Then, after it was really bad, and he couldn't jump and thump, he'd sit there and stick nitroglycerin tablets under his tongue and do an imitation of a man who looked calm, but he still hated my ass for not believing. Don't be hard on yourself. He was plenty hard on both of us and maybe he loved us anyway. If that would be useful to know."

"It's possible he was right, some of the time. That's where I've gotten to in what seems to pass for my thinking. And that's how it was with him and me that night, I imagine, only I was too drunk to know too much too quickly—things kind of dawned on me very slowly in those days," Scotty said. "And after a while, all of a sudden, there's this little insight expanding inside of all the booze: he was really hoping for me, I thought. And he looked . . . *nice*." He was sitting upright on the ottoman now, and he swallowed and looked away from me. "He looked like a pleasant, aging man. And I kept thinking—Mom's hammering away at bodies discovered in a church basement, or skulls inside a feed store or something—I kept thinking: she's worrying about bad news. But *I'm* the news. I always blew into the house like some kind of a storm. And they must have gone so *tight*, so unhappy, when they thought of my coming there. Coming here. It was here, wasn't it, after all? Only, instead of wet and wind and all of that, there's my goofy smile because I can't see straight, and he's smiling right back at me, wishing I'd get better and figuring probably I will, maybe I will, God it'll be very nice if someday I will. There's bad news all over, and, when you think of it, in terms of how they must have felt, I *am* the news."

I received the news about our father's dying in my office

downtown, relayed from his night-shift nurse—ever vigilant, she
had wakened to note that he was no longer alive—to his attorney
in Lakeville, to one of the staffers, to me. I was putting together
notes for a report on thievery by school janitors for my boss, who
reported to the New York City Board of Education. We inter-
viewed and investigated and then issued detailed statements
about malfeasances involving huge budgets and children who
were born, it often seemed, to be the victims of predatory princi-
pals and teachers and teachers' aides. The sheet was from a yellow
legal pad, and the note, which I found late in the afternoon, said
that the call had come a little after ten A.M. There was the lawyer's
name and the Connecticut area code and three words: *About your
father.* So I knew, because—Scotty's sense of guilty importance
notwithstanding—the only real news it was reasonable to expect
about my father was that he had died. The lawyer, a pleasant man
named Flanagan, spoke to me about details he had taken care
of—dismissing the around-the-clock private nurses, notifying a
doctor to come and verify the death, calling the local mortician,
and suggesting to the bank that they meet with Flanagan for the
winding-up of my father's trust.

I read the note and reached for the phone so I could talk to
Brady, my wife, who had flown to London to research a story
comparing the journalist gadflies of the English Prime Minister
to those of the American President—a matter of transatlantic
boredom, I'd told her when she started the piece. But Brady
never listened to me about her work. I was a fair-weather lib-
eral, she said, willing to bitch about politics but unwilling to
suffer for the pleasure of using naughty words about people in
high office.

She was half asleep when she took the call, but instead of

complaining about the hour, or asking me how I felt, she said, "You didn't call Ella."

"No," I said. "Of course not."

"You'll have to be with her when you say it."

"I will. I promise."

"No, I know you will. Of course you will. And Scotty? Did you—"

"Not yet. First I had to talk to you."

"Good. That's right. But then you have to talk to Scotty."

"Sure."

"Well, you *do*."

"Well, I will."

"How do you feel about it? About him?"

"Brady, I've missed my father for something like forty years. It feels like it, anyway. Twenty, I'd say, for sure. So now I miss him, too, but nothing more."

"There will be," she said. "You remember how smooth and cool I was about my mother, and then you found me howling at myself in the cellar, sitting in a puddle of old letters she sent when I was at Girl Scout camp. It's tough, baby. I think I ought to come home."

I didn't tell her not to.

"I'll come home soon," she said.

"If I call your bluff and ask you how soon, will you hate me?"

"Will *you* hate *me* if I don't come home tomorrow?"

I said, "I'm not telling Ella yet."

"Christ," she said, "but her grandfather. I hate it that you have to tell her at all."

"I'll drive over to Poughkeepsie from the house. I'll take her out to dinner. No: we'll walk around the campus. I don't know. We'll probably end up sitting in the parked car and I'll just tell her."

Brady said, "I was hoping, with the medication and the therapist and this run of good luck at school—I was hoping she could have a good semester. And it would feed into the next one."

"She can."

"I'm worried she'll go to pieces."

"Me, too. But she could still get through this."

I was wrong, I thought, and Brady thought so, too.

I remembered our weekend visit, just before we dropped her off at college for her first semester, when we stayed over in Lakeville. Ella, who had been looking waxy and haggard from lack of sleep, struck us as a little less pale, a little more animated. At that time, my father could sit up to read in his study or stay with us in the kitchen for a little while. It was a year before he began to live—began to die—in the study. This was a hot August afternoon, near dusk, and Ella, in high-rolled blue jean shorts and no shoes, in a halter that Brady permitted but about which I had doubts, was explaining to her grandfather about Vassar's lack of a core curriculum or, so far as I could see, any other required course.

"So I take what I deem important," she said gravely, sitting at the refectory table in the kitchen and holding his hand in both of hers. She looked at the back of his hand as she gently pinched it, and I watched the bloodless ridge of plucked skin remain in place. He watched it, too.

"So you're responsible for your fate," he said.

Her skin darkened as she flushed upward, chest to throat to cheeks and forehead. Soon enough, though, she'd grown pale again.

"I like the idea," he said. "And you can do a good job."

"I don't know," she said.

"I know."

She picked his hand up in both of hers and banged it against her forehead. The force with which she wielded his hand surprised him, I saw, and it worried me. Brady closed her eyes. Ella struck herself with him again, then gently returned his hand to the table's surface. She patted his broad, long hand as if to keep it calm.

"I could make a real mess of the whole thing," she said. "I might sleep through classes, due to being tired all of the time. I'm always tired, Grandpa, you know? Like, even when I'm sleeping"—and here she started to giggle, as if something unknown in her had escaped—"I get tired in my sleep." She covered her mouth with the fingers of her right hand, but still she held his crepe-skinned hand with her left. She shook her head. "Never mind," she said. "Forget *her*."

He slowly sat forward, and he moved Ella's hand, now enclosed in his, up to his face.

He kissed the back, then turned it so he could kiss her palm.

"Her," he said. "You." He kissed her hand again and said, "I refuse to forget. It's what I want you to remember I remember: you."

I don't know how long we sat in the kitchen I had hated since my mother died, because it had been hers—it had been her—and now it seemed like no one's. I saw Brady bite her lip while her eyes filled. I can't imagine what I looked like—someone stricken, I suppose. And Ella and my father, in their matching pallor, sat in the silence and held on to each other. It was what you meant when you said for dear life.

On the phone, from London to my office, Brady said, "You'll tell her carefully and straight. That's you."

"That's me."

"And that's all. I mean, that's all you can do. And hug her. Hold her," Brady said, her throat tightening, "the way your father did."

"I was thinking of that time, too. I'll go to his house and pretend to be competent, and then I'll drive over to Poughkeepsie."

"Tell her I love her. And I'm starting for home very soon."

"I'll see you when you get here."

"And maybe let yourself cry or something, why don't you. Shout at someone. Pick a fight in a bar."

"Same to you, sweet pea."

"I'll slug somebody in the Bunch of Grapes who's wearing a tight, striped suit and those sideburns you hate. All the press are about seventeen with bad complexions and dirty hair. Except for the old guys in gray suits with sideburns and red faces from the double Scotch. And good luck with Scotty. Tell him you love him," she said, "he needs some of that."

In my father's study, I watched Scotty stand and deposit the roach in his tin. He moved about the study, the sickroom, the death room. I watched his slow, splay-footed walk that was almost a waddle. He was slump-shouldered and soft-looking, beaten by our father's dying and by a bad run of events. He had lived with Camilla Ten Eyck for a dozen years until, during an argument, he had tried to talk over her scolding by hushing her with his fingers around her throat—"Purely demonstrative, *no* intentionality," he'd assured me when he telephoned from a Hoboken police station to ask my help in arranging bail—and then he had lived an average of four months with each of six women who looked or sounded or acted like Camilla Ten Eyck. His latest effort to make a living had consisted of day trading. I called it gambling, only with stocks instead of cards, and with a computer instead of a green felt table. He had lost or left the women, though with no further demonstration in place of intention, and he had lost a great deal of money. And he had just lost his father. And with him had gone Scotty's opportunity to show his father that Scotty could be news that was good.

The room was a wreckage of file folders, notes, receipts, and good antique furniture that had been shoved around until whatever orderly arrangement my father had enjoyed was lost for good. On a fine, dark bentwood coat tree hung gray-and-white plaid pajama bottoms for his spindly legs and wasted shanks. A rich black felt homburg that he hadn't worn in ten years was on top of a three-drawer oak filing cabinet. Inside his closet hung a dozen Brooks Brothers suits, four of them in shades of dark blue. His English dress shoes, on the floor of the closet, were covered with dust. Blue boxes on a shelf in the back of the closet contained his Purple Heart and Navy Cross. The silver-framed picture of him as a gunnery sergeant in 1950—with a dozen or so men, all of them with what seemed a rind of skin that had been cured by cold and wind, all looking somehow shrunken in their layers of baggy, filthy uniform—was his souvenir of the retreat by his Seventh Marines, during five days and nights, through terrible terrain in subarctic conditions. They carried their corpses on jeeps, lashed to tanks, stacked in trucks, and, so he'd claimed, on wagons dragged by Marines taking turns. Fighting his way out with his men, he had discovered a self that no occasion had again, ever since, permitted him to become. There in the photo—the man who squinted and laughed a mouthful of teeth, whose left hand, leaning on the shoulder of a smaller man beside him, was extended as if to seize the molecules of the air of the occasion— there was his splendid moment. He and those Marines about him had come through a certainty of dying to be born all over again, and then they had lost the immediate feelings of that greatness. And all his life, for every subsequent day and night and sleepless hour toward morning—he groggily called it his dawn patrol when he came, unrested, to breakfast during the time of his later middle age and middling health—he mourned the loss, I think, as much as, and maybe more than, he finally mourned his wife.

I was happy to walk away over the wooden floors of the house: huge living room, cold conservatory, long, white-tiled kitchen, the baths and the guest room—what he had left open, over the years, after shutting off the second floor and then, gradually, neglecting rooms of the first until only the kitchen and one bathroom were used by the nurses, his study and its adjacent bath were used by him, and the rest of the house stayed dark, dusty, and stale.

Scotty said, "I need a nap."

"I need to pass out," I said.

"You mean you think that's what I need," he said.

We left that room and walked slowly through the house as if we had agreed to, though I think we had simply run out of the energy and will to speak. And we drifted up the stairs, as if there were something on the second floor for us. In the guest room he was using at the back of the house, upstairs, where he could look out over the garden where in spring a lawn service had mowed the grass and neglected the plantings, we stood before the bureau on which he had set a framed photograph of our mother wearing a peasant blouse and smiling past a large set of binoculars she seemed to offer to the photographer. The smile looked toothy and insincere, but she was young and busty and alive in the picture, and it must have satisfied Scotty's needs. Next to it he had set a duplicate of the Marine Corps photo taken when they had safely returned to Koto-ri, in a dark wooden frame. The air here was heavy with the pungent herbal smoke of his marijuana.

I said, "It's a little bit of a shrine, Scotty."

I hadn't intended to say it. Brady insists that you say what you mean to, and if you didn't intend to speak then you kept your peace. Probably she's right. In the same way, Scotty probably did intend to throttle Camilla, not merely to demonstrate to her the need for a momentary silence.

He said, "Shrine?"

I shrugged.

"Interesting choice of words," he said.

"Yes, I guess. I guess I could have said 'museum' or 'chapel' or something."

He said, "That would suggest I'm worshipping Mom and Dad, wouldn't it?"

"Or the kid who used to look up to them."

"I guess that's very insightful," he said, his face going stiff.

"Don't get pissed off, Scotty. And who the hell am I to comment on whatever you want to do about us becoming orphans?"

He cocked his head.

"There's nobody left to live here but us. And we won't."

He said, "I'm feeling mellow. No: I *want* to be feeling mellow, but now I'm not. You remember what I said when you called me? When the phone rang in my bedroom and you were on the other end, talking about Dad and dying and dead?"

I did remember, but I said, "No."

"You always remember what people say."

"Remind me."

"I asked you if he left us a lot of money. And you said something formal and full of lawyer and you figured all I cared about was the dough."

"No," I said. "I don't remember you talking about money. The description of the tight-ass lawyer sounds vaguely familiar, though. And in my experience, people ask all kinds of wild questions when people die. Remember what I asked Dad when Mom finally died?"

He nodded, and he couldn't help his smile. "You said, 'If you want to insist she went to heaven, I'll believe you.' Or something like that."

"It was stupid and chock-full of infantile need."

"If you insist," he said.

"So, anyway, I don't remember what you said when I called."

"I asked if he left us a lot of money."

I shrugged. "It's a reasonable question," I said.

This time, Scotty shrugged. "I don't know," he said. He looked at the photographs. "And you're the executor of the will?"

"I'm named the executor of the estate, and, along with the bank, as co-executor of whatever's left of his trust."

"What's the difference? Never mind. I don't want to know. Do I get any money?"

"Half."

"Half of everything?"

"The will is probated. We pay the bills. We sell the house. We wind up the trust, which means selling off the investments. The bank gets a fee. The lawyer gets a fee. The executor gets a fee, which I'm waiving. And you and I split all the proceeds down the middle."

"Unless I decide to live in the house," he said. "Did you ever think of living in the house?"

"Never."

"I did," he said.

"Bad idea, Scotty."

"Why?"

"You'd have to buy my share from me. You'd have upkeep on this terribly expensive place, which has a very, very old roof you'd have to replace as well as a furnace that's older than you are. And of course the ghosts."

"The place comes equipped with ghosts?"

"Wherever dead parents used to live is where their children see ghosts."

"You really believe in that."

"I do."

"You see them now?"

"I do."

"You mean the pictures I put up."

I shook my head. "I mean *you*. I see Dad's face inside of yours, and I'll bet you see it in mine. And Mom's here, too. Live here, and they'll be square-dancing in the hallways and yodeling off the tanks of all the toilets. It's a bad idea, Scotty."

We were silent, then, in the sweet stink of marijuana, and the sound of one of us breathing noisily, slowly, something like the snore of deep sleep.

Scotty looked at the metal box full of makings, and he said, "I'm just about broke, to tell you the truth. I had a run of luck that was so bad, you can't really call it any kind of luck at all. I had a run of falling down in flames, the past couple of months. I have to admit that. I was worrying about money. I mean, before he died, I was thinking of *when* he died, and the money that might come in." He licked his lips, then ran his hand over his face. I remembered our father using that gesture. Then I remembered that I used it, too.

"It didn't make him die any sooner," I said. "And he was in lousy shape. He was weak, he was hurting, he wasn't getting enough oxygen into his brain. Scotty," I said, "it was time."

He was up, a little unsteadily. From the bureau, where a carafe and two glasses sat on a pewter tray, he took a tumbler and walked resolutely toward the sliding doors of the closet, and he opened them and reached through extra blankets on the shelf to withdraw what I'd been afraid of seeing: a bottle of Green Label.

He poured two fingers and raised the glass in a toast. He stood in that posture and then he drank, and then he poured a refill. He blinked and blinked, and I could see his tears. He had stood like that, blinking, with a glass of Green Label in his hand, on a weekend, years before, that I spent there with him and our father—Brady had seen me off on what she called my actual guilt trip—while my father and I fought about the Hutu and the Tutsi in Rwanda. I had just finished pronouncing "genocide" as if it had a dozen syllables.

My father had made no effort to hide what he did. He'd reached for the initialed silver box of pills in the breast pocket of his red flannel shirt. He'd opened it and found a nitroglycerin tablet. He'd put it under his tongue. He'd sat back to wait for comfort. His face was gray-pale and lined. He'd looked as stricken in that moment, years before, as he now looked on the videotape I could not watch.

He didn't quite whisper on the late-autumn day of our argument, but his voice had been low and gruff. "When I hear people tossing 'genocide' around, whether it's about central Africa or someplace in Asia, it reminds me how many times they worked the word 'moral' into their petitions against the Vietnam War." He looked as though he had just stepped into something disgusting.

"Wonderful," I said, "I'm adoring this. Let me—I *tossed around* the word about the intentional eradication of a tribe, babies split open with long knives and old folks beaten to death with clubs and women raped to death. I *tossed it around*? And since when did the word 'moral' get legislated out of argumentation? Dad! You went and nearly got killed for people in a foreign country who were threatened by the North Koreans and the Chinese Communists. How can you argue against intervention *now*? And that was a dictatorship you were getting your ass shot for."

He folded his hands to imitate calm. "That line of reasoning ought to bring you, sometime before tomorrow rolls around, to the nasty dictators in South Vietnam. Or am I wrong?"

"Irrelevant, this minute, Dad."

"Am I wrong?" he asked hoarsely, still the gunny, still the ramrod, still on top no matter how his left arm pulsed, no matter the pain in his chest. He closed his eyes but quickly opened them. Then his head jerked, and he turned to face Scotty, who stood to his left, and my right, at the row of windows in the living room through which a cruel, bright November light came. Scotty, in turn, jerked his own head, as if to evade our glance. The movement brought the full, hard light against which he stood directly onto his face for an instant, and I could see his tears. He kept turning and, as if he looked out the windows, into the light, he raised his glass of Green Label and drank. Our father said, "I didn't hear that, Scotty."

Scotty turned back from the glare and, a silhouette, he repeated, "Mommy would have hated this."

I watched the hand move across my father's chest toward the

pocket of the flannel shirt. I shook my head to tell him it was too soon to take another, and my father regarded me, then nodded. He patted the pocket, then left his hand there, fingers splayed.

"Let's finish this later," I said.

"You're accusing me of racism," he said.

Scotty said to me, "Why not shut the hell up for a while? How about that for an idea?"

"It *is* racism," I said. "I'm not calling you anything."

My father had smiled as if I were a kid—though not, I thought, one of the boys he'd known in the Seventh—and he was about, I knew from his expression, to drop the heavy ordnance on me and wipe my argument out. That expression on anyone's face, that amused assurance, was still enough to worry me in court, and pitch me into anger in an elevator or on the street.

"It would have been *Mommy* crying if she could hear you," Scotty had said, looking down into his glass. "She hated this."

Our father had slowly nodded, the smirk falling from his mouth, a sadness spreading from his eyes. Then he'd looked over at Scotty and across at me. "But it never kept her from voting the Socialist ticket when she could find one," he'd said. He'd smiled with real pleasure before shaking his head. The smile left, and his head went still. He'd patted his hand against the pocket holding the pillbox, and then he was motionless. So was Scotty, and so was I.

And here was Scotty once more, in the dead man's house, with his new bottle of Green Label and the old devastation to work his way through all over again, and just in order to find a way to start another day of his life. As the raw smell of whiskey cut across the sweetness of reefer like a hint of sewage—what they'd call "the drains" as they bought drinks for Brady in the Bunch of Grapes or the Lamb—I searched for anything I could say to Scotty that wasn't a waste of his time.

He sipped, but this time didn't finish all that he'd poured. Then he asked, "Do you know how much?"

"How much what?"

"Money."

"Money. Well, pretty much. He spent a lot on round-the-clock care, but there's real money left. Sell this place, and we're talking eight or nine hundred thousand bucks."

"That's a fortune," he said.

"I guess it's plenty. Imagine that."

He went toward the bed, and I watched him stare at it, holding his glass, as if all he wanted, just then, was to fall forward and sleep.

"I was wondering," I said, "how come you drink the Green Label. Isn't the Black supposed to be better?"

"Why did you say you wouldn't take the executor's cut of the money?"

I reached for the glass and he let me take it. I sipped a little. It tasted like a medication our family doctor had given me for gastric disorder when I was young, something I'd always thought of as made from tar. I handed the glass back and he studied my expression.

"*There's* a waste of good whiskey," he said. "Why not take the money?"

I shrugged.

"You think I'll need it, right? You're taking care of me, and you think out of my share of close to a million dollars you still have to make sure I get a little extra because I can't be trusted to make my money last? Because I'm the brother is just a little bit wobbly on his legs?"

He was looking at the bed, and I hoped he would crawl onto it and sleep.

I said, "All right. If you think I should, I'll take the extra percentage."

"Ella could use it," he said. "Don't forget the kid has needs."

"You're right," I said.

He said, "That's right."

I backed out of the room, nodding, though he didn't see me go, and I went down the hall and around the curving dark wood of the balustrade to the room in which our mother had died. I took a breath, I turned the knob, and I walked a few steps in, noting that I had first raised my hand as if to knock. I saw a stripped twin bed, a bureau, an open closet, a window shade drawn down behind the open drapes. And I thought of telling her goodbye again—saying the words out onto the air of her room—but I knew that I would be working in the house for many days more, probably over months, before I finally left. Later on, if I had to, I could make speeches.

I backed out of the room and closed the door, and I went downstairs. In the foyer, I saw the dark brown plastic answering machine beside the phone. According to the machine, there were seventeen messages that Scotty or I would have to listen to. We would have to return some calls by telling people he was dead. I knew that I would offer to do that, and I thought he would permit me to. He would sit in the foyer a few feet away from me and, now that he was back on the Green Label, he would sip and waggle his head and make funny faces and imitate my expression as I tried not to gag on the words I felt required to say. He would be keeping me company, he'd think, and I knew that I probably wouldn't mind.

But that would be for another time. Now, I thought, walking back through the living room, passing the rows of books and dusty pottery, turning on lights as I went, it was evening, it was almost dinnertime, it was the high tide of the cocktail hour. In my father's study, I turned on a desk lamp that illuminated the photograph of my father and his Marine Corps boys. On his desk was a picture of my mother from the fifties, in a full skirt that showed her legs. She wore a scarf, and her smile could only be called wicked. I was going to open his desk drawer, but I went instead to the VCR and the little television set, and before I worked at the desk, before I so much as sat down, I forced myself to press the button that played the tape.

I watched it all the way through. I went into my father's bathroom and washed my face and dried myself with a towel he must have used, I thought, for I could smell him against my face—his citric soap, and the slightly sour cooking-oil scent of his skin. I tucked my shirt in and rolled down my sleeves and went toward the side door, near where my car was parked.

Scotty came down the stairs behind me, in something of a rush. He said, "You taking off?"

I kept walking. I said, "I need to tell Ella."

"They were pretty close," he said.

"They were friends."

"Lucky girl."

I didn't want to address her luck, so I turned to tell him, "Scotty, I'll be back late tonight or early tomorrow. I'll sit myself down with the papers and we'll start making some progress."

"The only progress," he said, "is backwards. We make enough progress and there's nothing left in the house."

I couldn't do more than nod.

He looked at me and frowned, stared at me and then took his

money clip from his pocket. He held a finger up, as if to alert me to what he did. He counted off folded bills, straightened them out, counted them again, and put them in my hand—a couple of fives, I'd seen, and some tens and twenties.

"That's a hundred bucks," he said. "Tell her it's for snacks or something. A dinner. I don't know. Tell her I gave it to you for her because I wanted her to have something. We're not that close, her and me, considering I'm her uncle, but you'd know about that. But I wanted to give this. You all right with that?"

"I'm all right with it," I said. "I'll tell her."

"Good luck with that. Their being friends."

It's a pleasant drive from Lakeville to the Vassar campus in Poughkeepsie. It takes about an hour and a half on two-lane roads, and you can look at elegant homes, some you'd call estates, and several grand horse farms. But I was bearing bad news to my child, and I drove with little skill and less caution, thinking of the tape I'd watched while I stood before his pale, stricken face to hear him describe how they had fought their way to the coast and safe sleep and warmth, contending with a huge enemy force as well as frostbite, mortar rounds, the freezing-up of their weapons, and of course the fear. They carried back with them, he said in his ragged voice, their wounded, their dying, and their dead.

SOMETHING ALONG
THOSE LINES

I'm not sure. I think of what I didn't witness at another man's house so many miles from a town I hardly know, and there, inside the building you yourself didn't see clearly or anyway never clearly described to me, there was Rosa. "Your wife," I called her. I still try not to use her name, but in fact I seem to say it often. I try not to talk about the woman I call "my brother's wife." And I do my best not to think about her. We know how well I succeed.

"You forfeited your right to worry about me," she said to you on the phone, and then she laughed, and you figured she was drunk.

Or "You gave up your right to be worried," you said she said—something like that. But, anyway, you knew she was drunk, or that she'd been drinking—maybe that was what you said: "She'd been drinking"—and you worried because she hated being drunk and she did it badly.

"Lack of practice" you told me was the trouble with her and hard liquor.

"I'd have thought you and she did a lot of practicing," I

remember I said. I squinted, and held the phone away from my head and then smacked it lightly against my cheek as punishment. You didn't need to be reminded of the very bad nights and days between you and her at what had seemed to be the end. That was when you dived through the bathroom window over the tub from out in your backyard because Rosa had locked the doors against you. You were so drunk, you said, you didn't know you'd sliced your face and forehead until she shouted and pointed as you lay curled in the tub. She took you to the ER and waited while they sewed you up, and then she convinced the doctor not to call the police. You called the doctor "a Benedict Arnold to your sex," she told you later, and you were proud that you knew about Arnold while the doctor apparently didn't. She got you home and stopped the car at the house that was by that time very unlocked. You got out and stood in the glare of the garage light, and according to Rosa you looked like a serial killer in a TV movie. She backed the car away and escaped to spend the night, she told you later, at the Beau Regard Motel off River Road.

She left her job. She left, as they say, your bed and board. She left the village, the township, the county, and maybe, some of us speculated, even the state. And then, six months later plus one week, she called. She seemed drunk. Or she seemed like she'd been drinking. She told you roughly where she was. You didn't know the man she was with. You had thought of several men to worry about, but no one like this—apparently a pretty rich fellow, and very courteous, she said and, to hear her tell it, someone she hadn't met until a couple of weeks before. This man hadn't broken your marriage up—"I did that on my own, thank you," you said—but there were men waiting. Hadn't some been wait-

ing. And the point was how she had said something about needing your help, or out-and-out needing *you*. That's what you
believed.

Right after that, you and I talked on the phone about it, and I
said what I said about how the two of you were drinking at the
end. You'll remember that I cautioned you to do nothing. "Don't
get your hopes up," I said. "She could even *really* need you, but
not really need you longtime, deep-down, steady-on, for keeps.
Understand? Are *you* drinking?"

"No."

"That's good," I said. "Good. Are you smoking?"

"Please," you said.

I said, "That isn't good."

"It's irrelevant," you said.

"So's her saying the word 'need.'"

"No," you said. "Need's a major thing. In my book, need's
more than love—whatever *that's* supposed to be."

"I don't think so," I said. "Even if she did say it."

"I'm not going to remember my wife Rosa calling me up half
smashed to say she thinks it's possible she *needs* me? En Ee Ee
Dee. That's what she said."

"Still," I said.

"Still what?"

"I'm saying even if she *did* say it."

"Which she did," you said.

And I said, "I'm saying even *though*. Okay? I'm saying *despite*.
Understand? It doesn't mean what it used to."

You got cute. "Are you saying it doesn't mean what it used to
in general," you asked, "or just in the case of Rosa and yours truly
getting his hopes up? Half a hope up is more than I got up for

the last couple of months, by the way. So: the word 'need' doesn't mean *need* anymore? Or just when Rosa calls me up after leaving home and uses it on me."

I waited. I chewed on my lip. I wanted you to sense how hard I was thinking. I was working very hard. I was seeing her half naked with someone. No: I was seeing her naked all the way. I was seeing her flushed and disheveled and terribly . . . *available* to someone not included in our conversation, which I then contin-ued by saying, "Just, when a woman who has left a man calls him up and says the word—"

"God," you said, "you are such a hard-ass."

"Realistic," I said.

"Just don't be smug as well as a prick and a person I hate, all right?"

"Oh," I told you, "I can promise that I'm not smug. That I can promise. The rest is business as usual. Listen. Don't go tracking her down, though. All right?"

"Why not?"

"There are so *many* why nots. I'll tell you some sometime."

It was your turn to hold the receiver away from you, or make a face at it, or just close your eyes and slump your shoulders and stand there, drained, looking an awful lot like me, slowly shaking your head—something along those lines. But here's what you did, as you surely remember. What you did was hang up. And we don't *do* that. We're such talkers. I depend for my living, just like you, on the people we trade words with. We're upstate village men. City people think we walk around like deaf mutes, but what we really do is what these places depend on: we talk. We talk at business, we talk in diners and service stations, we talk at town council meetings, and at squabbles of the board of education, and variance hearings held by the planning commission. You and I live a dozen towns apart, at opposite ends of a narrow county, but our civic problems are the same and our history is pretty much parallel if not exactly identical. One of us married once and one of us didn't and for good and sufficient reasons, I would argue if anybody asked, and both of us are now the children of the same dead parents without any children of our own, living alone in pretty similar ways. But you hung up the phone.

A lot of what followed is clear to me from what you told me later. The rest I figured out. You told Kraus, your paint-and-stain man at the shop, and both your two carpenters, that you were leaving on a trip. You asked Kraus, with his hands and face flecked and dyed, if he could look in at the house every day until you got back. You packed an overnight bag and you took what you call your basic traveling toolbox. You gassed up the truck, equipped it with flashlight and matches and candles for a snow emergency, you took blankets and a five-gallon can of gas and extra wind-shield de-icer, and you left. You knew where to go. Or you guessed right. You never told me which. What you said was, "I got in my truck and I went."

It's pretty much a straight shot north for you once you're off Route 80 and onto Route 12. You went to Utica, then took 28 to 30, and you made for the Adirondacks. Raquette Pond is an awfully large lake, and I don't know how you found his place, one of those millionaires' so-called cottages they built up there in the twenties. I've never understood how a cottage has twelve rooms with a kitchen larger than the house I live in. But I also don't understand how a lake gets named a Pond. Rosa, your not-quite-ex-wife Rosa, was with a man who owned or had access to a big house on a lake that was littered with other so-called cottages as well as smaller houses and old motels, all of them but one shut down for the winter. Maybe you looked for lights. Maybe there was that golden color you get on the blue-looking snow from inside a set of crazed six-over-six antique windows. Maybe the light spilled over the snow and onto the two-lane road where you bucked through drifts in four-wheel drive, the radio off—I'd bet on that—and the cab filled with your cigarette smoke.

And you had also packed a chamois pouch of .22 long rifle cartridges and the old Woodsman handgun, which you carried to finish off deer and never had to use because you never got a deer. It goes in the drawer of the cracked cherry table on your side of the bed in case, you enjoy saying, of an invasion by foreign paratroopers bent on occupying upstate New York.

Maybe you stood outside your truck, taking a leak, and the cold air sucked away the fog of cigarettes and sweat and the hot iron smell of the defroster, and a wind from the lake blew wood smoke from the chimney over your face. Maybe in a manner of speaking you could smell that Rosa was there. But you found her, you said—"I got there pretty damned quick" is how you told it to me—and you parked your car on the side of the road and walked in across what might have been a lawn under all that snow. If there were paths, they weren't shoveled, and the snow was deep. You did find lights, one way or another, because you told me about the mullioned old windows you saw, and the thick, paneled, very old walnut door that you thumped your fist in its mitten against. I guess I was taking out the recycling and locking up my house about that time. I was thinking about you being alone in your house. I was thinking I would call you the next morning, not so much to apologize, though I'd been heavy

with you, clumsy, acting peculiar about what Rosa had said. I
thought of it as our having words.

But the word would be *word*, if I chose to be honest. The actual
word we had or that had us would be *need*. And I knew I ought to
be tough on myself because I had all but demanded that you not
seek out your wife who had called you. She was probably as confused as you were and as buffaloed as I was by what she had let
herself say. There I was, with sliced-up cardboard boxes and
rinsed-out plastic jugs and some emptied wine bottles, and there
you were, five hours north of me and feeling at least two ways.
One: you thought you had every right to be there because Rosa
was your wife who had summoned you. Two: you worried that
you had misunderstood her call and her tone and her motive and
that you'd no right in the world to be there, looming up at night,
late and loud at the door, ready to track your boot prints on
someone's property and more than likely on how someone felt.

You'll recall it was at this point in the telling, in the call you
made after your return, that I said something about violence, and
you slammed your coffee mug down on the table. I could hear it
over the phone. I knew what you'd done and in which room.
Then you laughed the way a person laughs who isn't entirely
confident there's anything really out-and-out funny anymore. This
was either two days or three after you'd got home—three, I think.
But time gets crushed, like some soup can I flatten for recycling.
But I'm guessing it was three. You laughed the bad laugh and you
asked me, "What else would you haul a weapon *for?*"

I tried to say something about what my own feelings might
have been when starting a trip like the one you'd just returned
from. I talked about urgency, emergency. And I remember how I
tried to get hold of a word for the kind of drive you'd made.

"Well," I heard myself say, "on an errand like that one, who can tell?"

"Errand," you said. "Errand? Taking off to get my wife isn't exactly an *errand*, goddamn it. You mean like driving over to the Big M Superette and buying cheese? Errand? Are you aware how much there was to maybe *lose*?"

"No, no, it isn't the thing about cheese. Wrong word."

"Possibly might have been," you said. Now, sometimes when you aim for sarcasm, you aren't sure how much tone of voice to use in cutting under what you've said. Sometimes you use too little, and you end up sounding innocent or mild when you mean to be mean. I'm the one of us who knows with some efficiency how not to say the entire truth.

"I'm sorry," I told you. "I know how important it was."

"No," you said, "but you know that it *was* important."

"Fair enough," I said.

"I don't intend to be shouting at you."

"No," I said, "I know it."

"I don't know who else I could talk to like this," you said. Or: "I don't know if there's anyone else I can talk to." It was lonely-sounding, whatever it was, and I knew what you meant. I know what you mean. We're orphans, we're childless, we live mostly by ourselves though you had just stopped doing that. The women who enter and leave our lives apparently figure us out pretty quickly, and what they figure we amount to doesn't seem to amount to very much. We are physically strong, we're reliable, we are jumpy in our emotions, I guess you would say, and as far as I can tell we both wait too long to say what we need.

I'm remembering Sandra Steinbock, the physical therapist who tried to get me to read poetry. One night in my living room she said, "I'm standing with my back to you." I was lighting a fire in the woodstove. "Catch me," she said.

I turned around and got myself crouched in time to not quite get knocked on my ass by this long, falling woman.

She lies there against me, with those nice, thick eyebrows of hers, looking at me kind of upside down, and she says, "Could you do this?"

"Fall down?" I ask her.

"Trust *me* to catch *you*." And she's got all her weight down on my arms. That's one tall woman to hold.

"Not with your back to me," I told her. "Not if you don't know I'm on my way until I'm halfway down. You could have slammed your head and hurt yourself, Sandra."

She let me stand her up, and then she turned around. She kissed me. She said, "I trusted you not to let me fall. I knew you wouldn't. Right?"

"Well, I guess that's right," I said.

"But you'd be worried *I* couldn't get to *you* in time. Or couldn't hold you up. Something—right? You trust me, you think. But could you *trust* me?"

I shrugged or shook my head, something to show her I was confused. "Of course I trust you," I said. Or: "Naturally." It was something like that.

"Maybe not really," she said. "Maybe only as far as you know, but *you* don't know. This is not your fault. You're trustworthy, but you aren't trusting," Sandra said. It was like a judge in traffic court telling you that you do have to pay the fine. I think that's us. Apparently, that trusting business is a real limitation, according to certain people, and I believe that many of them are women. The trusting business seems to be most of the reason that Sandra's long gone. For all the talking we do at my shop or yours or in general in town, we don't have that many people we can tell *these* things. The things I mean are maybe what you and Rosa from time to time can talk about. But I have to say I doubt it.

Standing at that door in what someone would have to call the dark of night with the cold wind coming off the lake and the truck catching drifted snow and you—with the pistol or without it? Then Rosa let you in. She looked at you and she turned her back to you and walked deeper into the house. She hadn't shut the door, so you knew you were invited to come in, and you followed. It was rustic, you said, with spruce floors and heart-of-pine cabinets and country Hepplewhite tables with those tapered legs. There weren't any overhead lights, just a lot of lamps in this very big room with a fieldstone fireplace a man could stand in, according to you. She was waiting for you at the far end of the room near the fire.

"I knew you'd get here," she said.

"That was why you called."

She nodded. Now, that isn't exactly what she said to you and that wasn't exactly your reply. It's what I have from what you said. I see you standing in the room a fair distance from her because you wouldn't want to crowd her. And I can see her very pale face, kind of square at the jawline but narrow, her hair maybe in a braid, and her looking like a child in a grown-up's thick turtleneck sweater. And you just looked at her, pleased enough to stand there and wait, because you didn't care what happened as long as you got to stay in the room with her. You opened your coat and took out cigarettes and lit one. Rosa, I figure, shook her head. Nurses who don't smoke make faces when people light up. I figure she shook her head and you were happy because that head with its thick hair, blonde-into-gray, maybe a braid moving one way while her face went in the other, was what you'd come that distance to see.

"I shouldn't have called you," she said. I know you went a little closer because you told me you were surprised when you suddenly saw the lines around her mouth and near her eyes. You thought maybe you'd forgotten them. But maybe she'd grown older fast. Maybe it was the separation. You wondered if maybe it was the way you treated her before the separation. "But I remembered your hands," she said.

And you looked down at the one holding the cigarette and were embarrassed by how broad it was, and how long and thick the fingers were, and how they were seamed and scarred and rough. They were a laborer's hands, you said, not a gentleman's.

"Did you think I was drunk?"

You said you shrugged.

"I wasn't. But I was afraid you'd think I was. I thought you'd think I would need to get drunk before I phoned. And I probably sounded incoherent, calling you like that."

"Like what, Rosa?" is what you managed to say.

Apparently she shook *her* head. I am not enjoying this.

You asked her if she was in trouble. She said no. You asked her if she was really all right.

She shook her head again.

You walked past her, hoping to smell her hair or her clothing, her soap or perfume—hell: *her.* I didn't hear you say this. But I don't need to. You threw your cigarette into the fire and lit another one, staying there, one hand up on the foot-thick mantel made from a hand-adzed beam gone dark. You were that much closer to Rosa.

She said, "Yes."

"Yes, what?"

"Yes, I'm in trouble."

"All right," you said. It's what you always say when the news that's on its way is bad.

"I'm his . . . guest here. We work together in the health care satellite office. I'm the RN up there. I'm good. They value me," she told you—something along those lines about how she had settled in and this countryside was becoming her home.

You took your coat off and dropped it on the low coffee table in front of the fireplace. This is the point where Rosa in the room and I on my end of the phone call learned the whereabouts of the gun. It was in the game pocket of your hunting coat and she knew it, I suppose, from the sound. You and she had lived together long enough for her to be able to tell.

"Christ," she said.

"What?"

"Don't tell me what's in your coat pocket."

"I don't mind telling you."

"I don't want to *know*."

"You do know. You were in trouble, I heard it in your voice, and you were asking me for help—"

"I called you. I'm not saying I called you for help."

"No, it's exactly what you did," you told her. It's what I was saying about *need* when you got so frosted off at me. Nothing you do, no matter what somebody tells you in that kind of situation, nothing is going to be right.

"Shit," she said. That's a direct quote. "Shit," she said again. "A man wants to marry me, and I don't know what to do and I keep thinking of *you*. And you come charging up here with a

gun? Are you going to kill me? Are you going to shoot *him?*"
You said she put her hands to her face. The way I see Rosa,
she'd have clutched the back of her neck and rubbed hard
because that's where she seizes up with tension when she's
really pressed. Whatever she did with one hand or both, she got
wild. She was frightened, though we both know that Rosa
tends not to stay scared. And apparently she said, "Oh, Jesus,
don't go shooting anybody."

She went for the coat, she was feeling for the weapon in the
pocket, and you intended to give it to her. You wanted to lift it
out and check on the safety, then eject the clip so she could see
that the piece was disarmed. Though she almost never fell apart,
there she was, with her hands moving jerkily and on their own,
her pale face full of fright.

You wanted to ask her if he was in the house, if that was the
reason for her fear. She couldn't be afraid for herself, she couldn't
fear that you would—well, you couldn't say those words. They
were as far from you on the phone, talking to me, as they were in
that Adirondack living room. That was how he saw you when he
came in: you and Rosa in a tug-of-war at opposite ends of a red
wool hunting coat that was swollen by a large, heavy game
pocket, fighting your way along the sleeves and then along the
shoulders like you were tearing a person apart, to arrive at each
other. I don't need to see or say the rest.

But to tell you the truth, I do see it. I just choose not to say it.
And there was some medical person with silver-rimmed glasses
and short arms and a friendly face with an absolutely bewildered
expression who was standing behind the two of you and blushing
like *he* was the man caught grabbing onto who you'd have to call,
one way or the other, the lady of the house.

This is what you said he said: "Rosa, is that a gun you're kissing him with?"

I hate stories like this. I hate to hear them and I hate to tell them. No matter where they come from, there is some poor goddamned fool who is pretty much innocent, could be a woman or a man, often enough the one who earns the money that pays for the liquor or the drugs, the transportation or other necessaries that the story requires in order to require telling in the first place. And that's the one who says something sorry-sounding like "Is that a gun you're kissing him with?" So that everyone who hears it has to laugh.

Which is why tonight, having driven through the usual March blizzard because an invitation is an invitation, a brother is a brother, and a marriage whether rocky or recovered is something to respect, I am sitting on the green sofa with its red flower patterns over and over and over and I am performing like a man who hears what his brother and his brother's wife have got to say. I'm watching her gray-blonde braid and her square, narrow jaw, and her red cheeks. I'm watching your face that is so much like mine. It's a happy family evening, I suppose you could say.

You look at Rosa and you think you're good together. Rosa, I figure, is afraid you're good apart. She's worried for the man with the glasses and the big house. I think she wants to think that she's relieved to be home. You look at Rosa and I look at you both. It's a family evening, and we smile. What we know we don't tell. What we tell we don't quite know. Everybody talks. Everybody listens. Everybody's wrong.

METAL FATIGUE

What you might notice first is how dirty they are. It probably isn't from not bathing, though you have to wonder how they could have the energy to shower or wash their hair. I think that's what it was, with my daughter and the others. They all had the look, all over their skin, that you see on somebody's hair who doesn't shampoo. There was a dullness to them. They couldn't catch the light.

But coming there to see someone, you still can hope. There are doctors and nurses. There are dirty pink walls and almost-wheat-colored linoleum floors and ash furniture with yellow plastic cushions. There are closed-circuit television cameras in the corners of rooms where pink wall meets bright white ceiling. There is someone in a security office dressed in jeans and a Gold's Gym T-shirt who oversees the little screens of the monitors and supervises as many of the patients as he can. There are bedrooms without interior door locks that can be sealed from the outside and there are several sets of steel doors on each floor that open only with a staff member's card. There is a gray-carpeted room with dark gray chairs and sofas on the street level, inside the locked glass doors, where family members sit until the ward doctor or nurse or psychiatric social worker sends word that they should ride the elevator up. So you can wait there or go up or sit in the ward cafeteria or the television room with its chained cigarette lighter and ceramic red ashtray and the laugh track of the rerun that seems always to be on and, if you want to, you can hope.

Linda and I sat at one of the cafeteria tables and watched a small young woman with matte-finish dark blonde hair writing with a fountain pen in a leatherbound journal. She bent close to the pages and wrote very slowly, pausing to look up, sometimes at us and sometimes at the other patients with their visitors, then leaning to the journal again.

"She's playing tic-tac-toe," Linda said. "Over and over. X and then O, X and then O."

"No," I said.

"Oh, yes. What—you think we're in here because we very sanely write in our journal all day? 'Dear Journal: Today, I took my meds on time. I didn't spit out the mood enhancer or the anti-psychotic. Not once did I try to gnaw through the vein in my wrist with my unbrushed teeth.' Dad, we're nuts. Remember?"

"You're tired. You aren't nuts. God, Linda. If you're nuts, we're all nuts."

"And is that a consolation? No, I mean it was nice of you to tell me. What I'm saying is I can't remember whether I feel good because of it or not."

I got hold of both her hands, which were clasped in front of her, and covered them with mine. The backs of her hands were cold and a little damp. The skin of her face was very dry, and it looked as if she'd been standing in strong winds for days. She was wearing fleece-lined moccasins from which the staff had unlaced the rawhide cords so she couldn't use them to hang herself. They flopped when she walked, but at least she couldn't commit suicide with her shoes.

"What's so funny, Dad? What's the joke?" She pulled her hands away.

I shook my head. "I think I'm getting a little strange, myself," I said.

"They did wonder if it was genetic, the depression."

"Do you think it is?"

"Mom never tried to kill herself and neither did you, right?"

"Well," I said, "no."

She smiled a great, toothy, unfunny smile and said, "Well, there's *time*, you know? There's still time for both of you. Be patient." She furrowed at the skin under her thumbnail. "Mom couldn't handle coming today?"

"She's with Max and Allison, sweetheart."

The wit that made her look lively went out. Her skin looked only wind-scoured again, and sore. Her eyes were as dull as her hair. "The kids are fine," she said. "Yes? The children are fine? They're fine."

"They are. They like it that we're staying with them. They aren't frightened."

"What do they believe?"

"I'm not sure. We told them you were in the hospital and you'd be home in a while."

"Not soon?" she asked. "Not 'imminently'? Well, you wouldn't say 'imminently' to a kid, would you? You would say 'soon,' I think. *I* would. I'd say 'soon.' Could you have told them 'soon,' but remember it as 'in a while'?"

"Yes. Absolutely."

"So you did say 'soon.' 'Mommy will be home soon,' you said."

"Yes."

"Even though you told *me* 'in a while,' you told my children I'd be coming home 'soon.'"

"Yes. Yes, I did."

"And what'd they say back?"

"When I told them 'soon'?"

"Yes. 'Mommy's coming home soon.'"

"Max nodded, you know, like a judge granting a motion. Allison looked at me, squinched her eyes together, and then she smiled."

"Yes," Linda said. "Good. Good." She got hold of soft flesh under her thumbnail and worked it up and out. She put her thumb in her mouth as if it stung, then said something around it.

"I couldn't hear you, Lin."

"I said I was glad to be getting out of here soon. These people are all nuts. Whereas I," she said, "am only tired. Ask my dad. And what should I know about Matthew?"

"He calls and talks to the kids."

"Do they cry afterwards?"

"No. It's always a very short call, and I think he keeps it light. They seem fine with it."

"Do they ask when *he's* coming home?"

"Not so far."

"You're lying, Dad. Lie, lie, lie. You're telling me what you think I should hear. You know, I didn't get terminally stupid to get myself locked away in here. I got crazy is all. I'm still smart enough to tell when you lie to me about the children, et cetera."

"You're not locked away, Lin. You admitted yourself—you

know: you asked them to let you in. You wanted to be safe. You wanted to feel better. Nobody's locking you in here."

"Every door you go inside of, *they* can lock. It's up to *them*."

"That's the paradox of psychiatric hospitals, I guess. People volunteer so they can feel safe. I imagine—"

"What is it that you imagine about me and my overdose and my children and my husband who left me and them and us and everybody else except some *guy*—"

"Oh, Lin, the guy couldn't help it. Matthew couldn't help it. He didn't know who he was when you got married."

"He knew. People know. They're all too goddamned glad to tell you how they always knew and always felt and always wondered and always hoped. And then they met the guy, who was always knowing and feeling and whatevering and praying to meet my absolutely heterosexual husband and *convert* him." She stopped and looked at me the way you would make an apologetic face to a stranger and ask if they knew the time. "Am I making any sense, Dad? Am I being logical?" She smiled a smile I knew from her childhood. "Did I just say it *was* Matthew's fault or it wasn't? I can't remember. Was it he knew or he didn't and the guy converted him? I mean, I know I'm making sense about possibly not making sense, but I'm not sure, at this juncture, whether Matthew volunteered to leave his wife and children and room and board and the meal plan plus activities fee, or whether he had this *attack* of not-heterosexual that kind of set fire to existence. At least as we know that we know it."

She set her face close to the thumb tissue she was tearing. Two lunch tables over, the sad girl with dull blonde hair was leaning over her journal. A smiling man in aqua pajama bottoms, T-shirt, double-breasted blue suit coat, and aquamarine hospital slip-ons came into the room adjusting his dark blue beret. What had looked like a moustache seemed, as he passed our table, to be a double line of scab from deep cuts. Across the room, a very fat woman in a bright red bathrobe was using a hole puncher on the pages of a glossy magazine.

When she saw me watching, she waved. "Don't worry," she called, "I know to clean up after myself. I'm responsible."

I waved back. Linda watched me. I shrugged at her. She said, "You didn't answer."

I almost muffled my sigh. I said, "To tell you the truth, Lin, I can't remember the question."

"Right," she said. "Me, too. It's the meds. They try and keep you stupid with pills here. It makes you more tractable. Was I a tractable child? Do you think I was a tractable wife?"

"I'm sure you were a fine wife."

"And the other category I mentioned?"

"You were my beloved child. You still are."

"Do you think I'd try and kill you, Dad?"

"No."

"Do you think a child would ever try and kill her parents? His parents? You know: general, all-inclusive whoever the parents are the parents of? Do you think *they'd* try?"

My throat closed down and I shook my head.

She said, "Depressives or women whose husbands get converted to gay will often get very, very down on the anniversary of something bad that happened to them. You probably knew that."

"No," I said, "I didn't. But it makes sense."

"Oh, it all makes sense," she said, "if you renounce the logic you're used to and accept either the word of your doctor or the policemen who took you away."

"No one took you away, sweetheart. Remember? I came here with you."

"And who's to say you aren't the cop?"

"Oh."

"'Oh,'" she said, in a deep tone. Then, in her own voice, she said, "Now, what could have happened five years ago to the day I was arrested and locked up?"

"You weren't arrested, sweetheart."

"No. All right. If not five years, then maybe three. Maybe it was only the one-year anniversary of the event. Who's to say? Except your doctor or the cops. But in either case, what was it the anniversary of that flipped me out and I drank all that horrible whiskey—what was it, Dad?"

"Lagavulin."

"Matthew's favorite Scotch. Plus Ambien plus Darvocet plus precious, pure, and dependable Bayer baby aspirin. Puke City, huh? So: what was the question? Ah! Anniversaries. Well, the group and I have been pondering the matter. Did you know that it turns out I *like* group? I bore the asses off of them all, but I talk and talk and talk. And they're so crazy, they'll join in about anything after a while. So they pondered my pondering. And they decided it's you, Dad."

All I could say was, "Me?"

She gave me the toothy, unfelt grin. "I predicted you'd say that. Well, to be fair, I thought you'd say, 'Who? Me?' But that was close enough."

"Linda," I said, "me?"

The man with the beret and the suit coat was bleeding from the upper lip and it had dripped onto his T-shirt and the table he leaned over. A tall, fat nurse in a pink uniform held a little green towel to his face and helped him to stand. She led him out of the room. "Don't you be dripping blood all over *me*," she told him.

Linda came around the table. She sat on the chair beside mine. I could smell her sweat and something salty and sweet at once. I was so tired, then, that I almost put my head on her shoulder. "Dad," she said. "Daddy."

"Sweetheart," I said.

"You looked so bewildered."

I nodded.

"I am, too," she said.

"I know."

"You do know."

"I think I do, Lin. Matthew, and the children, and plain damned fatigue. It tears the wings off airplanes, you know. Metal stress fatigue. The plane looks fine and unless you examine it very, very closely, and often they don't, it takes off and then a piece of the wing tears away."

"The plane comes down," she said.

"Yes."

"And everyone on board is killed."

I didn't answer.

"And they reassemble all the little pieces they collected on the floor of some huge airplane hangar in Queens or Texas. They put it back together."

"But not to fly it. Just to know."

"Like here," she said.

"No. Here they help you get back up in the air."

She leaned in close. Her breath had something like iodine on it, and the phlegm you smell on a sick, small child. "I don't want to fly anymore," she said.

"Sweetheart, they're going to help you do whatever you want."

"Can I still be married to Matthew? And he'll love me," she said.

I said, "I don't know."

"That's not what you told your father."

"What about my father?"

"You know. Shh." She looked behind her, at the girl with the journal. She looked across the table toward the woman with the hole puncher, and the others, at farther tables with their visitors. She whispered, "When they cut off his leg."

"That was diabetes, Lin. It was very bad, and he was old by then. His heart was in awful shape."

She sat back. "And he asked you to help him."

"Yes, he did."

"And you said you thought he should die. He told me," she said in very reasonable tones. "I know about it."

"It was the night before the procedure—the amputation. He was very frightened, very upset. He hadn't much hope. He told me he had already discussed it with his doctor. He'd told his doctor he didn't think he wanted to live like that anymore. 'Like this,' he told me, and he pointed at the leg they were going to take. It caused him terrible pain. He was in pain all the time that we talked. And he had angina very badly, his heart was pretty much shot. He told me his doctor said, 'All you have to do is stop taking the medication. I'll write it up as heart failure.' And he looked at me, Lin."

She said, "Like this?" She stared with a cowlike innocence, and she looked silly. I shook my head. "Then like this?" She looked pointedly at me, just as my father had. I looked away. "Got you," she said.

"So I told him I would help."

"Help what?"

"Help take the medicines away, or pour them out into the sink, or whatever he wanted. I really didn't have much of an idea. I just thought he was asking me for help, and I wanted him to know I would give it. Even if it meant I'd go to jail."

"They'd have put you in jail?"

"If somebody wanted to accuse me of euthanasia, yes. It's murder, or manslaughter, or something terrible. It means years and years in jail."

"I am not staying here for years and years."

"No. But you aren't in jail, Lin. You're in a hospital and you're getting out soon to be with Max and Allison. You never told me you talked to my father about this."

"After they cut off his leg and he didn't stop taking his medicine. When he was alive until he died of old age." Then her face was alight again, and she said, "But maybe he didn't. Maybe he finally died of *you*."

"We never talked about it again. I thought he'd forgotten."

"Yes, but how can anybody really know you didn't talk about it again and then what if you *did* it, Dad? You see?"

"Well, because I didn't do it and he didn't do it and he lived for several more months, almost a year."

"Except he told me."

"Told you what, Lin?"

"He said, 'Harold wants me to die. Harold told me to stop taking my pills. My son Harold said he wants me to die.'"

"No."

"He did. He told me. I was there with him and the nurse went out and he told me. I was his only grandchild, remember. He and I always talked."

"Yes. He loved you plenty. But he couldn't have said I wanted to kill him."

"Wanted him to die, he said."

"Yes. But I mean *no*, Lin. God. Sweetheart, once a person hears something like that about himself and somebody dead, he can't fix it. I can't fix that anymore."

"Well, you heard it, Dad. So I guess it's broken now because that's what he said. And every time you think about Grandpa, you'll think about him telling me how you wanted him to die. Maybe you weren't clear when you and he had that conversation."

"No," I said, "maybe I didn't make myself clear."

The girl with the journal walked past us, reading her pages. She said, "'Bye."

"Bye-bye," I said. "Good luck."

"I guess maybe you wish I didn't tell you about it," Linda said.

"You told your group therapy session about it."

"Oh, sure. We were wondering if it was the anniversary thing that could have flipped me out. Only, I couldn't remember when Grandpa died. Whenever it was you did or didn't kill him."

"So why did you think it might have been some kind of anniversary, since you had no idea when it happened?"

She leaned in closer, until her shoulder fitted under my arm. She pushed up with her shoulder and I put my arm around her and hugged. "It's a simple enough mistake to make," she said. "Don't you think?"

"About me wanting to kill my father."

"Right."

"Right," I said. "But it wasn't an anniversary."

"Good," she said. "It would have been easier, if we could have blamed it on that. But good anyway."

"Good," I said. I looked at the hole puncher punching and the little scattering of glossy dots that lay across the woman's table. She waved and nodded, and I waved back. I said, "I really think it was fatigue, Lin."

"You're saying my wings got tired."

"It's hard, staying up in the air."

"Sometimes you have to come down," she said. She said, "Okay." She sat against me and then moved off to sit in a different chair at our table. She said, "Okay."

"Yes," I said.

"Buy Allison something pretty, Dad. Would you do that? I don't know what. Just so it comes from me."

"Yes," I said, "I'll find something."

"And get Max something about ball. Any kind of ball. If it rolls or bounces, he wants to do it."

"He's a bouncer," I said.

She yawned and shivered. "It's late out, isn't it?"

"Probably it feels like that," I said, "because you're tired."

She closed her eyes and I remembered reading bedtime stories to her. Suddenly, her lids went up. She caught me looking. She said hoarsely, "We'll find out for sure."

"Find out what, Lin?"

"If you're the one who goes to hospitals and visits people, then they die."

"No," I said, "I'm not."

"Well, we'll see," she said.

PATROLS

He kept his eyes closed because if he opened them he would see Murphy's mad, bright stare. Since Marty Mason had been there, the bunchy, gleaming black dog had left his owner's bedroom late each night to patrol the hallway outside the guest room and then the room itself, his claws ticking on the wooden floors while he investigated corners and spaces under furniture, his snuffling inspection punctuated by soft panting, as if he breathed in whispered tones on account of the hour. Then he would settle beside Mason's bed and, head erect or laid on top of his extended paws, he would watch. He was ready, Mason knew, to slap his tail concussively against the bedroom floor if his owner's guest should meet his devoted glare. Closing the guest bedroom door meant only that Murphy would scratch for admittance, whining softly until Mason opened the door so that the dog could check the room, then settle down to watch the guest.

After tonight's long period of stillness, Mason lay between waking and sleep. He'd begun to think of himself as buoyed, like kelp or driftwood or a boat of shallow draft, on top of the waters of the cove. Now, at dawn, the radios of the lobster boats broke the rhythmic night noises—the regular panting of the dog interrupted by its small, strangled squirts of body gas, the rising tide and the slap of ocean on stone, the winds off the sea washing hard against the house—that had carried him out of nighttime and into the day.

He wasn't surprised that he thought he could feel the greasy grit of sand on his fingertips and in the corners of his eyes, over his teeth. He wanted to get to the bathroom and drink from the tap to wash his sandy mouth out, but the dog farted and winked in the brightening room, so he played dead. He thought, of course, about the dead Marines and the dead hajis, as the live Marines called them, and the one Iranian, a bearded man in Western clothes, driving north and west over the Iranian border in a white Toyota long-bed truck into Checkpoint Eight One, established and commanded by Captain Jerome Goldsworthy with whose Alpha Platoon, five light armored reconnaissance vehicles, Mason traveled as journalistic baggage because Major Harvey Fathers, commanding Fox Company, had told Goldsworthy to carry him along for the sake of public relations.

Captain Goldsworthy was a slight, slender man who struck Mason as being made entirely of hard leather. His South Carolina accent was musical, Mason wrote in his notes, and he never raised his voice, even if he swore with conviction. He never chided Mason or complained about having him in tow. In fact, he never addressed him. He referred to Mason exclusively as *he* or *him*, as when, standing before Mason, looking sourly at his Orvis-catalogue traveler's vest and L. L. Bean khakis, he told one of the rifleman scouts to make certain *he* knew how to fasten the rear scout compartment hatches of the captain's vehicle when they needed to swing the turret cannon to the rear. Mason rode in that small scout compartment with three Marine infantry, sweating and sucking warm water from plastic bottles and banging against the walls. "Make sure *he* stays inside the pig until you know for certain we're in a safe environment," the captain told his scouts.

Now, before dawn, at Checkpoint Eight One, Goldsworthy had opened his turret hatch and positioned the vehicles, establishing his firing lanes. Mason heard the hatch go up forward of the turret just after a short, thick PFC, William Pontelecorvo, from Rahway, New Jersey, had pushed their hatches, behind the turret, up and out. About a half an hour later, they heard the driver of the truck gear down, either because he meant to, or to feign stopping. It was apparently a feint, because he began to go up through the gears, gathering speed, and they pinned him with the lights.

The captain said, "This is irksome."

Mason heard the driver say, "Sir."

In his soft, low voice, the captain said, "There's a cure for irksome." He said, "Button the forward hatch." He said, "Gunner. Battle sight. Truck in the open."

The gunner called back, "Identified."

Pontelecorvo said, "He armed with the HE."

The captain gently said, "Fire."

"On the way, sir," the gunner said.

The 25mm turret cannon fired three times. Mason was deafened at once. Pontelecorvo must have been right about the high explosive shells, Mason thought, because although their hatches faced away from the action, he saw the air of the nighttime desert go whiter than their lights had made it, and then he saw bright fragments, blown vertically, raining down around them. He heard voices as if from a distance, and he couldn't hear the fragments strike the ground. When Pontelecorvo permitted him to leave the vehicle, Mason stood with some of the platoon a few dozen yards from the burning truck. The Marines edged closer, he noted, and then closer, as if to prove that they were unafraid of secondary explosions. Then they moved even closer, flinching from the heat but needing the risk, and he joined them because he was afraid to stay behind and seem to be afraid. What was left of the driver lay partway between the truck and the Marines: some beard on some of the cooked face with one wide eye in it, strips of burned gristle, a section of clean, white rib cage, the halved corpse sprinkled with powdered windshield glass that caught their lights and reminded Mason—he faced away from the Marines to write it shakily in his notebook—of ice droplets in the air on a very cold night in St. Paul.

As he thought of the roasted, torn face and its eye, Mason thought of Murphy's ecstatic glare. He remembered the sand in their mouths, and how the night winds carried grit to them as it filled the hairy nostrils of what was left of the driver. Mason raised his fingers to rub at his gums, as if he were still there, watching the corpse's nose fill up. The dog slammed his tail and Mason set his arms down, trying to breathe like someone asleep.

The lobster boats were coming in, some with small outboard motors and some on throbbing, big diesels. He had seen them over the last several days as they drove at a buoy, the lobsterman somehow knowing, out of all those hundreds of bright, bobbing markers, which were his. Then, alongside, he cut his engine and while the boat wallowed on the tide he hauled his trap by hand or by machine, withdrew a lobster if he found one, baited with the chum that drew the prowling gulls to circle the boats, dropped the trap overboard, and took off full-bore for the next nearby buoy. Some of the boats broadcast ship-to-shore CB chatter, while most of them played country music on their radios, nasal complaints about death and passion and diminished prospects.

The cooperatives made money by shipping the lobsters downstate to the resort restaurants and into Boston and New York. The lobstermen, after they bought fuel and paid for repairs, made little profit, he imagined. And he suspected that it was all they knew to do. He wondered if they depended on federal food subsidies during the winter if they couldn't find work repairing vacation houses or salting roads for the highway department. He wondered how many silent, angry children, how many battered wives, that life produced. He wanted Ada Shields, his editor, to tell him about this coast, about saltwater fogs and who ran the lighthouses and how you knew which pound to buy the lobsters from and what the lobstermen's families ate—frozen Salisbury steak, he'd have bet, and artificial gravy on packaged mashed potatoes, all of it washed down with pop poured from plastic two-liter jugs. He knew himself to be a freelance hack with a need to dodge steady work and the habit of asking questions in order to deflect attention from himself. Ada's purpose, which he was coming to regret, was to prod him into studying the self he had tried to omit from what, together, they were working on. She had inherited the house from her parents, and it was where she hid out, she said. According to her assistant, Mason ought to be flattered to be invited for a working week. He knew, as he played dead for Ada's ardent dog, that he wanted their conversations to be local and not about his time with Alpha Platoon because then, he thought, he might not lie under the winking stare of Murphy, unable to sleep because he was selling out, as if by the pound, the Marines live and dead with whom he had patrolled the southeastern deserts of Iraq in order to compile the book he'd once believed it was important to write.

It had begun well enough. The first chapter opened with a character called Mason, who was mostly not him—a vehicle, as he thought, for conveying the strategies of the old men who made this war, and the courage of the young ones taking fire for them—who was on his way, after his time over there, back to the States. This Mason sat in a dark, icy Frankfurt bar, drinking too much and therefore talking too much to Leon Rosenthal, an Israeli businessman who was, of course, not in business. Mason didn't know whether he was a civilian, but he was certainly in some aspect of intelligence. It could have been as high-powered as vetting for assassinations—he was that secret, and that rock-hard confident—or he might have conducted random harvests of raw data from big-mouthed sources, Mason thought, like himself. Rosenthal was a small, muscular man with gold-rimmed glasses that rode over big, dark, angry eyes under a high forehead. He wore a blue blazer with three horn buttons that he kept fastened over an open-necked shirt. He sat straight on his barstool as if a child at school. Mason had recited some of his adventures although he was embarrassed, even as he spoke, because he believed that the little man knew more than enough about wars on his own. In the book, uncleverly exchanging one brand of dinnerware for another, he called the little man Spode.

Mason was telling about Captain Goldsworthy's outrage when his orders were reversed. In Badra, Major Harvey Fathers had spent a night organizing checkpoints and patrols and Cap-

tain Goldsworthy and his Alpha Platoon had run Checkpoint
Eight One, Mason in the compartment of the pig, feeling like a
child in grown-ups' clothing under the heavy flak jacket and the
oversized, chin-strapped battle helmet. At 0400 they had killed
the driver and blown up his truck. The captain had reported the
kill, and Major Fathers had instructed them to patrol to the
north for two hours at a leisurely pace, then descend at high
speed back to the Eight One checkpoint and see if their departure had lulled some bombers, posing as religious pilgrims, into
trying to cross over.

At 0530 new signals came in from the major. Division had
instructed Battalion to instruct Fox that priorities were reversed.
Standing outside their vehicles they listened to Captain
Goldsworthy say, "The situation is now officially a clusterfuck.
You will *not* be looking to capture or kill. We *will* interrogate all
incoming personnel. Those that we have no choice except to
deem true pilgrims, we will respect their faith and permit them
to cross over from Iran"—he said it *Eye*-ran—"in the hope that
the message will go out that U.S. guys are good guys. We will
permit the pilgrims to find whatever it is they are looking for.
Salvation, I believe. Salvation is all right, and they are welcome to
try and find it. You will not fire unless you are fired upon or
deem yourselves in peril. In which case, you will kill with efficiency. You will try to check with me on any peril factor. But
you will stay smart and therefore *live* Marines. And *he* fucking
well had better not be putting any salty language in my mouth
when he writes his tale of Alpha's derring-do."

At that point, watched by the platoon, Mason stowed his notebook away. The captain consulted his own notebook and then he
pulled down on the hem of his flak jacket as Mason had seen him

do a couple of dozen times a day. He made himself remember the gesture to record when he could.

"All right," the captain said. We will carry out the mission. No questions? No answers? Let's get back to the goat rodeo."

Rosenthal, now named Spode, said, "My friend, you enjoy the colorful captain, and he is doubtless a brave man and a bold leader. Goat rodeo: colorful American vernacular. With the occasional fucking this or that. Of course: American. But what you *should* be remembering is the real importance of that particular moment. In two or three years from now, and probably less, you will think of the goats and the fucking and our chance encounter, yours and mine." He poured more Pilsner. "You will know, because I am lecturing you about it, that the captain's address marks the moment when the cancer cells began to grow. And not only inside of the goats. This is the gospel according to Rosenthal, commercial traveler, you ran into him in the Getrunken Pferdchen saloon in Frankfurt in the benign, well-ordered German republic. You'll remember, yes? That they brought the money in, those so-called pilgrims your patrols suddenly permitted to cross. They purchased the information and assistance and of course the weapons that will punch the bloody holes in your soldiers, who will be pinned in place in Iraq, dead Hussein or live Hussein, for a decade. This is minimum, I'm talking about. Boys will grow up expecting that part of their young manhood must be wasted in Iraq. They will become sullen and probably brutal, like our children serving in Palestine in what is finally an occupation, not a war. Those pilgrims from Iran who your President forgot to fight, they assembled the resistance cells, they organized the terrorists. And Iran"—he made a show of pulling back his sleeve to check his watch—"Iran as of this moment has won your little off-the-cuff war."

Thinking of the bottles of Czech beer they drank, and of all the water that Alpha Platoon consumed under orders to hydrate themselves, Mason knew that he would have to dare the dog and get to the bathroom.

"Murphy," he said, "I give up."

The dog's tail banged on the bedroom floor as if a dedicated child were slamming a hunk of hawser rope down, again and again.

The house remained silent. Murphy banged another volley, and Ada, from her upstairs bedroom, called, "Oh, Murphy, you goofy boy." The squat Labrador froze and then, with his nails scrabbling on the slippery floor, he ran out of the bedroom, past the bathroom down the hall, and then up the steps as Mason walked into the shower. He turned his face to receive the warm water in his open mouth. After the early days with Alpha of Fox, when matériel convoys bypassed them in order to get to Baghdad and north of it and there wasn't enough water for showers, when the heat swung between 125 and 135 Fahrenheit, he had vowed never to be ungrateful for water, whether it came in the form of ocean, thunderstorm, or droplets from a leaky pipe. He still felt the grit that had caked the inside of his lips and that sat on his teeth no matter how often he drank to rinse it off.

He had forced himself to make entries in his journal as Alpha fought, patrolled, and bounced between contradictory directives from Battalion. He'd written paragraphs to later be stitched onto what narratives he could generate on his word processor. And he had managed to file several stories, one dictated over a military phone in Badra to an intern at the magazine who patted his every word into a word processor, making him feel as important as one of the real war correspondents. This was the material that he and Ada Shields were turning into a book, she assured him. "It's all here," she said several times a day. "You wrote it. This is just one of those wine racks or bookcases or children's toys you order from a catalogue. 'Some Assembly Required'? I'm the Some-Assembly person. Though I do not know boo about the children's toys part of it."

She was taller than he, very slender, very pale, a little stoop-shouldered, and long of arm and leg. She wore scuffed brown penny loafers over bare feet and usually denim shorts and a work shirt. Twenty times a day, for three days, she had opened the barrette that held her thick, dark hair behind her neck and gathered handfuls to fasten again. The intimacy—the bareness of the back of her bent neck, the opportunity to stare at her unseen because she closed her eyes to fix her hair—had compelled him and embarrassed him. And he had wakened this morning to think not only of the heat, the sand, the eye of the torn, burnt truck driver, and the lunatic eyes of the dog, but also of the tall, slouching editor who read herself to sleep at night by going over what he had said to himself in the intimacies of fright, discomfort, and even despair during six weeks of Operation Enduring Freedom.

They sat now in her breakfast room in the old house that smelled of mildew and salt and resin. A few lobstermen worked their traps farther out, but the gulls had given up on them, stalking instead the broad, flat granite sheets between the back of the house and the sea, while crows made the noises of argument in the evergreens around them. Mason had heard a half of the phone call while he was drying himself after his shower. He hadn't been able to discern her words, but he had listened to her tones, which began sulkily enough and quickly declined into bitter single syllables.

While they chewed English muffins in silence, Ada stood to bring more coffee to the table and, pouring, announced, "I believe that I am starting to smoke again. Would you like to file any objections?"

"It sounds like you'd slug me if I did."

"I might."

"No, then, I think. No objections."

"No, tell me straight. Never mind, don't bother. I know it's stupid and suicidal and obnoxious. But I mean, *aside* from the usual arguments."

"Strikes me as a terrific plan."

"I'll stop again. You aren't, I don't know, allergic to it or something?"

"Just to the cancer part."

She said, "Well, I'll stop again. Before you leave, I'll stop smoking."

"Is it time for me to go?"

"Is this a tolerable process for you? Doing the work like this?"

He nodded.

"It is not time for you to go. We almost have the shape. Structure is the concern for us, because you know how to tell stories. It's—it's like your dead Iranian. He's all over the book. It's like the book's his body. He's all blown up, so how would you put him back together? Same for us with the book. We're reassembling a body of experience. It's going to be different from what happened outside you, in the desert and while they were driving all over, but we have to find the shape it took *inside*. What your memories made it, what your emotions—well, you understand. You know what we're doing. And you know we aren't done."

"You paid me a pretty good penny," he said.

"One hell of a lot more than a penny."

"It doesn't seem entirely fair that I get the more-than-a-penny, and you still have to do all this work."

"That's what I do," she said. "I buy broken, and I fix."

"But meanwhile," he said, "I can't help noticing you've got stuff going on. . . ."

"Stuff."

"Stuff in your life. Private stuff." She left the table to open and close drawers in the pantry. Then she was back, sitting opposite him, looking unhappily at him over the cigarette she lit, sighing. He waited, as if he were the one who drew in the smoke. "It makes you sad," he said. "It makes you smoke."

"Thank you," she said, "but don't worry. The private stuff is just one more—what did your Marine Corps rifleman call it? 'One more shit storm in paradise'?"

Murphy took the half of buttered English muffin she handed down to him, and he fastened his thick black muzzle carefully around it, as if the muffin were alive, and then he carried it off to the doorway of the breakfast room with his head up. He lay and licked it, watching them, then closed his mouth around it, raised his head, and worked at the bread while butter and crumbs leaked down from his leathery lips.

"So I should mind my own business," Mason said.

"I appreciate the attentiveness," she said. "You're a man who has feelings. That's a nice part of the book—your honesty about being afraid, your sweetness about the younger men in combat, and the children you observed in the villages. And—listen. Listen, this is just the killing each other part you're overhearing when I'm on the phone. It's natural, it's part of the cycle, and when you go looking to be happy, if that's what this is about, then you have to do it. There's the smiling part—first shy, then plain damned glad, then the way people smile right after they finish sexing each other tired. There's the happy habit part—you know, how you get to understand each other's arriving early or arriving late, ordering drinks for each other because you know what the other one likes, all of that. Then there's the no longer working smoothly part, and that runs into the let's just shoot each other part. I more or less happen to be in that particular aspect of the human misery sometimes called a relationship. I've been there before. As a matter of fact, it's one of my specialties. Look," she said, "I'm already chain-smoking. See how fast it all comes back? So could you tell me what that was about the Spanish Gate?"

The dog banged his tail against the floorboards and made a sound that was half growl and half yap. Mason knew by now that it signaled his desire to go outside. Ada went to the back porch door and held it for him. She stood at the door, her cigarette in her mouth, while she bent, blinking her eyes against the smoke, and loosened her barrette to gather her hair and fasten it again. Then she held the cigarette and looked out through the screen.

"Do you remember?" she asked.

"Where did that come from?"

"One of your notebooks. Some day in September, October. Just before you went over to Kuwait to join up with the Marines. I could find it. You wrote something about mussels in white wine with brown bread."

"Oh," he said. "I did? I don't remember doing that. But it has to be about Galway, and this little restaurant near the Spanish Gate. We were—I was—there was somebody with me, and we were drinking a lot of white wine and eating mussels, and these thick slices of coarse brown bread. We got pretty drunk, as a matter of fact, and very fast."

"So it wasn't just the wine that did it," Ada said, sitting again now that Murphy had returned.

"It wasn't, no. I was with a friend, as I said."

"A man or a woman? Can I ask? Has to be a woman."

"Woman, yes," he said. "Her name is Marianne Neal. We were in the smiling part of it, according to your breakdown."

"Excellent word," she said, "breakdown."

"I was thinking that something terrific might possibly happen. And of course, a few days later it did. Just, it was terrifically unhappy. We were drinking and eating, we'd just come from some antiquarian fair in a great hall someplace in the city. Terrific city, Galway. Being there made me happy. I'd bought a brass jam pot for her that she thought was beautiful. Marianne's a poet," he said.

"Oh, now, never even approach the outskirts of a poet," Ada said. "Didn't you know that by then in your life? They *love* pain. For you if it can't be helped, but for *them* if they have any say in it. They specialize in the five stages of misery. First, get some love going. Second, find a way to want to kill yourself because of it. Third, polish it and polish it. Fourth, insert it in a vital organ. Anyone else gets snuffed, it's a shame. If the poet, however—this is Number Five—if the poet manages to sustain a dreadful, agonizing, not quite totally fatal wound, then there you have it: a long cycle of poems at the least, and quite possibly a book of them. Never go *near* a poet. Of course, you know that now, don't you?"

They went to work. Each of them took notes, and Ada managed the papers, arranging pages and renumbering them. She indicated with glued memorandum slips where he would have to provide new material or insert old. She asked him, over and over, to tell her the meaning of what he had thought were clear, simple sentences. It was a history of unworthiness, he believed, the story of a man without courage who traveled with young men and their officers who went only toward trouble, whereas he constantly wanted to run away.

"I was always making believe," he told Ada during their lunch break. They ate chicken salad sandwiches and drank rosé under the steady stare of Murphy, whose panting, Mason found, established the rhythm to which he chewed. "I was scared. I was ashamed of being so scared. I made noises like somebody who hadn't ever *heard* of being scared. I kept wishing they would just, goddamn it, turn *around*, go back."

"You suggest it plenty," she said, "but maybe you want to talk about it directly. Give examples—what they did automatically, compared to what you wanted to do or would have done if nobody else was watching. Fear's a great topic. Everybody wants to hear about it. You know: how to fail."

"I'm waiting for you to give me the eleven stages of fearfulness. You have this wonderful habit—"

"Yeah. I know. I break everything down into sequences. I could number the stages of bleeding to death while I was bleeding to death. I'm a comedienne, of course, right?" She drank off her rosé and licked her lips. "Pure amateur."

He said, around the chicken salad, "I find it a little exciting, to tell you the truth."

She moved her head slowly while elongating her neck, and it was as if she were peering down at him from a significant height. "Why would that be?"

"I've always wished I could be chipper and bitter and tough like that, maybe. I don't know. It attracts me."

"I attract you?"

"Yes. It does, and you do."

She nibbled at a piece of chicken protruding from the edge of her sandwich. She poured them more wine. She shook her head. "Well," she said. "And I'm sitting here, telling you how compelling I find your being so scared. Aren't we just a meant-to-be couple? As in, who needs sex when you can have failure?"

He thought that if he said something about sex *and* failure, they might end up in bed. But he was afraid to talk about failure and sex, because then—he was certain—the sex would fail. He wished he could tell her, because it would be a fine joke about his fear, which she seemed to find so valuable.

"Well, well," she said, feeding a piece of sandwich to the dog. She leaned back, removed the barrette, leaned forward to gather her hair, then fastened the clip again. Mason pretended not to watch. "I'm running errands, in town," she said, "mail, and dental floss at the IGA. You take a nap so we can do a session of work before low tide. All right?"

"Why low tide?"

"Because of your pleasure in mussels," she told him. Then she and Murphy left.

Obediently, he took off his shoes and socks, he opened his bedroom window, and he lay under the powerful light off the sea and the winds that waxed and waned as if they were a tide. He sensed a giant shadow passing, but opened his eyes to see nothing except fir trees and the ocean off the rocks below the house. He wondered if a condor or an eagle had flown over. After a while, when he'd closed his eyes again, he saw different structures of rock and in different colors. He knew at once: the strand off the bay in County Sligo. He and Marianne Neal were walking on the coarse tan sand after their time in Galway, where they'd seemed to him so easy with each other. Outside of Sligo town, in Marianne's little stucco house that was several miles northeast of the crowded road to Donegal, he'd felt her grow watchful, as if she had begun to worry about his fragility. And her care made him know that he ought to expect misfortune.

She had driven them in her small, apple-green, misfiring secondhand Ford to a little sandy track that went down to the beach. She pulled up the hand brake and sat, looking out the windshield at other parked cars and the gleam of water farther down. Her lips looked tattered, and he had seen her biting them. When she worried, she nibbled at herself—edges of her lips, her cuticles, a wisp of her frizzy, light hair. His stomach bucked, and he was certain now of unhappiness ahead. There were few people about, perhaps because cool winds had come up. He and Marianne had walked, saying little, along the curve of the bay. A small, white-hulled boat with an orange sail was turning into the wind.

"Can you see her?" Marianne asked.

He shook his head.

"She's got ahold of a rope, she's standing at the mast there."

"Is it a nun?"

"It is, Martin. A nun in her blue robe on a sailboat. She's grand, I think. Martin, there's a man I'm going to see again that I wanted you to know about?"

"Ah."

"Ah. Poor man. What else could you say, then? I'm so sorry. He's the father of my dead child. The infant boy born dead. He's asked to return again to my life. I don't know. I don't. But I don't think I can sustain the two sets of emotions at once. And here you are, off to the deserts over there, and I'm giving you something like the shove."

"This is the shove?"

"I wouldn't feel it inappropriate if you gave expression to some *anger*, Martin."

He knew her powerful poems about the baby. He wanted to say that he would rather cry, just then.

He remembered that he gave her no reply. He looked away from her, at the nun standing against the background of the orange sail on Sligo Bay, and he put his arm around her. She tensed. Then she very slowly relaxed against him for the space of a breath or two. All this time, he thought, and what you carry out of it for certain is how she fought an embrace and then gave in. She would probably write something about that instant of fighting, he thought. Marianne was a revelation about inventing ways to use words, unlike him with his timid notations on how others behaved. He remembered the citrus scent that she wore, and the smell, like crushed ferns, of the Sligo sand that the afternoon's sunlight had warmed before the winds came up—the smell so different from the animal rankness of the tawny sand patrolled by Alpha in its reconnaissance vehicles—and he remembered that her skin was cool to the touch, at the strand at Sligo and in their bed at the Galway Great Southern, or anyplace else. His skin cooked while hers grew cold, and she produced sorrowful poems, and he grew sentimental over mussels steamed with shallots in white wine.

When Ada woke him, she seemed to be wearing sneakers and a long denim shirt and nothing else.

"You slept all afternoon," she said.

"I was running away from work. It's a great tradition of the trade."

"We can work tonight," she said, "or tomorrow. We're doing all right. Listen. Wear some shorts, or a bathing suit if you brought it. I can't lend you one, I'm afraid, unless you're comfortable in a red maillot. And you'd best wear something on your feet."

Ada left, but Murphy stayed, to pant and fart and wink as Mason put on a pair of shorts he wore when he played basketball with his friends, and then tennis shoes and a T-shirt. Murphy went to stand before the back door, his blunt, spade-shaped head leaning on the jamb. Mason let him out and then walked down the narrow path of dark, mossy soil along which Murphy had already run out of sight, past wind-stunted evergreens, then drift-wood crushed against the huge rocks lying on top of the great stone sheets that radiated black and pink-gray layers into the sea. Ada was there, halfway down to the turning of the cove. She carried two plastic buckets, one of which she handed him.

"Your hands will probably get sore," she said. "The more you try and hang on to the rocks, the more you'll get those very pale knees and shins chopped up on the barnacles and all. But it's worth it, because they're so sweet here. It's pretty much a secret place, so far."

"What's the secret about? Did you say?"

"Mussels, for goodness' sakes. That's what I've been telling you. This place, when the tide is low, is a gorgeous mussel bed."

She and Murphy went farther out, climbing over or around immense glacial rocks that lay on top of the pink and gray stone sheets. At low tide, which was now, he imagined, you must be able to reach ten feet or more below the level of the high tide of six hours before. She had disappeared over the edge, and so had Murphy, and he went to find her. She was in ocean to her waist and thighs, and Murphy was swimming away from her, threading his slow, powerful way through the bright plastic buoys of the lobster traps, his head low on the water, breathing in groans that were carried back on the wind.

The rocks seemed steep to Mason, and slippery, and he sensed that, trying to climb down, he would slide along them into the sea, striking his head and shoulders and spine against the sharp white barnacles and—he watched her pry one loose—the hundreds of long black mussels that she faced. The water had painted her shirt against her stomach and groin, and he could see the shadow of a bathing suit beneath the shirt and the movement of her stomach muscles under the suit as she pulled and twisted until a mussel she was harvesting came loose, to be dropped into the white plastic bucket that she held in her other hand.

She looked up with a concentration that struck him as ferocious. Then a pleasure seemed to come over her, and she said, "Come on, all right? Come here."

He held a finger up. It was supposed to say that he would be there soon, though from a different direction. She looked away, as if disappointed, and then she returned to plucking. Mason headed back twenty yards or more, then climbed down a more gradual decline of rocks nearer the house. He made his way along low stone outcroppings that gradually circled toward the curve of the point, where he thought she would be.

He couldn't hear Murphy now. Mason held on to the rock, chopping his fingers on bright white little shells that adhered to it, prodding for the beard hairs of mussels. The pail he held was floating on the tide, and the icy water was soon above his knees as he foraged where the rocks declined. He had worked two small mussels loose, with great effort, and tossed them into the bucket. Now the freezing sea was at his waist. He came around the point to see Ada, tall, spread-legged, and at her ease, with one hand through the wire handle of her pail to hold the rock face, and the other hand working to her right, tearing mussels loose and dumping them. When she saw him, she gave him a look of inspection and then smiled as if all at once, after a time of confusion, she understood him.

He held on to the rock against the bucking of the sea. He was watching the small Labrador attack one of the foamed plastic buoys painted white on top and red on the bottom and fastened to a lobster trap that held to the floor of the sea.

Ada cocked her head as dogs do when they're puzzled. "Murphy!" she called. "Murph! Come here!"

The dog made as if to swim to her, but then he stayed where he was, with his jaws clamped around the buoy. He made paddling motions but didn't come away.

"Get his ass shot up by a pissed-off lobsterman or the conservation patrol," she said, "and nobody would question it. Murphy, damn it!"

"Ada," Mason said.

"Murph!"

"Ada, he's stuck. Isn't he? He can't get his teeth out of it."

"He can't? Oh, he *can't*. Murphy!"

They started at the same time. Ada let go of her bucket and pushed off from the rock face to swim a long-stroked crawl. Mason tried to think of himself as doing the same, though he knew that what he really did was make a little yipping noise, push his head down into the water, and, spitting ocean out, set forward with the only stroke he could swim—if, he thought, you could really call this swimming—a despairing sidestroke that sent him in slants not quite straight at what he alleged to be heading for. He stroked, looked about, corrected his direction, then stroked some more. He had no real breathing rhythm, but he did have strong arms and legs, so he swam in the sea the way a crab scuttles on sand, and he made a little headway. Ada, meanwhile, was almost there. Mason found himself thinking about the great distance that lay between the dark green surface, chopped into patches of white by the wind, and the slithery, teeming ocean floor.

She was trying to support the dog's belly, it appeared, when Mason reached them. The whites of Murphy's eyes seemed enormous. As if to demonstrate his situation, his lips were drawn back so that the pink and black gums and yellow-white teeth were visible, the fangs clamped deep into the soft plastic of the buoy. Murphy twisted his head to release himself, but the teeth were firmly stuck.

"I've got you, little Murph," Ada said, breathing harshly. "I've got his tail and his gut, a little bit," she told Mason. "Can you—"

He tried to say, "Piece of cake." It came out as a wet warble. He did what he considered the treading of water, really a flailing kick—the bottom seemed *so* far below—that shook his torso and head. He didn't try to speak again. He worked his fingers into Murphy's mouth and made the noises, though not the shaped words themselves, of Here we go, boy. Here we go, boy. Here we go. His own head slid beneath the surface several times, but he worked at the teeth and then had them unfastened. He surfaced just as Murphy, in the jaws of panic, clamped his own jaws down again, this time on Mason's left hand. Mason howled shrilly and Murphy, with Mason's fingers in his mouth, turned with great interest toward the noise. Using his right hand, he persuaded the muzzle open and removed his fingers. Ada pushed Murphy off toward shore, and the dog swam eagerly. Mason tried to shift from his flailing into his crooked sidestroke, but he was down to the single hand that would cup against water and he merely rolled a little before his head went under.

He felt her hand in his hair, tugging, and then he was on his back. He tried to protest, but water poured into his mouth, and he could only gurgle. Her hand cupped his chin, pulling back, so that now the ocean stayed out of his mouth and he could breathe whenever he wished. What gifts to give a man, he thought: the fruits of her watchfulness, as well as a choice of when to breathe. She towed him as if he were a blunt, unseaworthy barge and she a gallant tug. She swam what he knew was an actual and very effective sidestroke that resembled his sideways jerk only in the way you said its name.

Although he was kept the length of a bent arm away from her, he was intimately aware of her body. He heard her breath go out on the water. He felt the strength of her fingers as they held his throat and chin. Sometimes her legs, when they scissored, brushed his buttock or the small of his back. His arms trailed, and he sensed that if he moved them up a little he might touch her, and he wanted to, though he kept them at his sides. His eyes were closed. The day had begun that way, he remembered: him on his back with his eyes forced shut. She surged, then relaxed, surged and then relaxed, and he could feel her purpose, the power of her long muscles, and none of the sorrow that bowed her shoulders when she stood on the shore.

Something brushed his trailing forearm, and he squinted to his right to see one of the mussel buckets, right-side up and slowly spinning out toward open sea. He shut his eyes again and thought it possible that, half drowning, his mangled hand a pulse that beat in syncopation to the rhythm of the progress of her stroke, he might actually fall asleep in the waters of this cold Atlantic cove. But she halted them. He could feel her tread water with a different kind of strength from that of her sidestroke. Then she swam him a little farther, paused again, and then began to walk with him still floating on his back, towing him through the shallows. Murphy had made it back, and he lay on a tilted, vast, refrigerator-shaped stone, looking down toward them while he panted at a ferocious pace, his tongue exhaustedly stiffened and stuck straight out. It was time to stand up, Mason knew, and he reluctantly climbed to his feet by holding with his unbitten hand on to Ada, who stood above him with the ocean pouring between her thighs.

"You're all right," she said, "aren't you?" She'd begun to shake.

He let go of her hand and stood before her on his own. He trembled, partly because of the cold. "Thank you," he said.

"No, that was a great rescue," she said. "Thank you from Murphy and thank you from me."

"And you," he said, breathing as fast as if he had pulled someone large through the ocean against currents, gravity, dog bite, and fear. "You saved my *life*, Ada."

"But we won't have mussels for dinner tonight. And I'm sorry. It would have been fun to give you that." He watched her head droop a little as her shoulders bent toward the sea.

Murphy shifted his demented glare from one of them to the other as he panted from above. Mason wanted to examine his hand to see whether the dog had only torn his fingers apart or had also broken a few, but he held it at his side with what he hoped was nonchalance.

"Another night," he said, "please."

"All right," she said. "Yes. But we're freezing here."

"We are," he said. But he was thinking of the nighttime heat in which they gathered at Checkpoint Eight One, the smell of the driver rising through the chemical stink of the rubber and plastic of the burning truck. His legs and loins cooked in the cab while the upper segment lay before them. The driver's remaining eye was wide as if in speculation about these Americans who shuffled closer and closer to the torn torso and its wrecked head.

Ada bent forward, suddenly, and she gathered her hair in a fist, reaching for a barrette that had been torn away by the sea. She stayed bent over, then looked up to see him watch her hair whip backward as she straightened and said, "I'm going up, I'm building a fire in the fireplace, and I'm making tea to pour brandy in. We'll deal with your hand, which looks a little lousy, I'm afraid. And I'm smoking plenty of cigarettes."

She turned from Mason to get herself past pitted, bleached-out boards and hanks of snapped rope that lay among the stones she climbed toward the house. Murphy went slowly ahead of her. Holding his beating right hand in his left, and knowing that he risked a fall on the slippery, yellow-green rockweed and the slimy bottoms of tidal pools, Mason followed them up.

THE BARRENS

He had started to quit his trade when he encountered first-person reports that were not labeled opinion pieces. He noticed them first in his paper's Metro section, long articles about mild curiosities in Staten Island or Passaic that sounded as breathless as dispatches filed under fire from Kosovo. Set squarely at the core of each report was someone called I. He found the same word in what were said to be articles on sports. This I, or an I quite like the others, was now apparently considered important to reporting the situation of the broken-down running back or the bicycle racer who doped his blood.

Now, during the first winter of his retirement, he and Nan were on a road no longer named, though doubtless the locals knew what to call it. Neither of them could remember the name, and the signpost leaned over, empty. Its tar and stone paving, laid down at least a dozen years before, was potholed and ribbed. They had driven it too far from the little village on the bay below them, where the waters of two rivers, dirty from industry and thick with ice, joined to flow past pharmacies, restaurants, car dealerships, and a new supermarket. The road, as they recalled, should have brought them to a road where, turning right, past the corner with its church and broad graveyard, they would bounce downhill perhaps a half a mile on dirt and rocks to the shake-shingled house with its long lawn at which their friends used to wait for them with icy beer that they would drink together in the sun. They had come there in summers before they were parents, and then they had brought their infant, and then the growing boy, and then the couples had visited as a foursome again before they parted from one another for what turned out, he thought, to be nothing less than forever.

"Forever looks so goddamned reduced when you think of it just in terms of people's private lives," he said. They sat in the idling car at the petering-out of the road off which they remembered they should have turned. There were some houses here they couldn't recall, and stretches of evergreen forest had been clear-cut, acres reduced to nothing now but stumps and shadows and patches of snow.

"Wait," she said. "Wait. I think we should drive back past a few of those side roads that go off of this one. Let's try it again."

"I remember passing only two."

"Then go back to the last one we passed, and then, if we need to, go back to the other."

"Because?"

She said, "Because otherwise we'll stay here on this road that just stops, we'll sit here and stare ahead through the windshield and pretend we're going someplace, and we won't be going anywhere and all we'll do is sit."

"But don't forget," he said, "if you're right, then we'll eventually get there to their house. And what happens then?"

"Then," Nan said, squeezing his thigh, "then we have to show our mettle. We have to make good on our decision to drive up here and take back . . . whatever it was we decided to come here to retrieve. Wasn't it your idea?"

"We'll see," he said. "If it's really a bad time, maybe I can shift the credit to you."

"That's my hero," she said, patting his leg.

They drove slowly along the road that ought to have looked familiar, since they had driven it so many times over so many summers for what he thought of as most of his life. "This isn't the road," she said. "It has to be the other. I saw—I just realized: I saw a piece of the church."

His stomach clenched because they might be close. She stopped them at the corner, and he saw that because they were screened behind a new growth of slender trees he had missed the low rows of small, tilted stones and the few large monuments with snow still clinging to their chiseled details: what was left of the congregation. Where the church had stood was a very large, burned-away rectangle that had been, after the fire, raked clear. Weeds grew around the shape of the church and, to its left as they faced it, near a patch of low, gnarled trees, he made out a large, crooked circle of fieldstones. Inside them, painted a glossy black, was a bell with its ox-yolk support that must once have rested on the timbers inside of the steeple of the church. Next to it was a crooked, blackened fragment, two or three feet high, of what might have been a brick chimney.

"That's what's left of the church," Nan said.

"That *is* the church. No wonder we couldn't find them."

She said, "It was starting a long time ago that we couldn't find them. Even when we *found* them we couldn't."

"No," he said. "I mean: I agree."

"I know."

"So the house should be on the other side of these ugly trees."

"Which I don't remember being here," she said.

And when they had driven very slowly down the side road, and had come closer to the small farmhouse that was no more than ten or fifteen feet from the road, she said, "And I don't remember it like this."

"It's the house," he said. "It has to be."

"That's right. You're right. But—"

"I know. It's it, but it isn't."

"It isn't," she said. "Although of course it has to be. Even though it's so small, and shabby, and so close to the road."

"Needs creosoting," he said, and he waited for her to laugh.

"You poor son of a bitch," she said, "all covered with it, and your eyes tearing from it, and there you were, plucky as hell, and Sandy and Leah laughing at you because you were a city guy and they were—what? State-of-Mainers, right?"

"He *was* born in Eastport."

"Right. But that wasn't any excuse. And how about her, with her native Maine sagacity acquired with such depth in deepest Larchmont?"

"I did muck up the creosote job."

"Yes, you did. And I loved you for it."

He said, "As I recall, that's exactly what you did."

"That's right," she said.

"Very creatively."

"What a memory you choose to have."

They sat in the car as if waiting for each to signal the other that it was time to approach the house. Nan opened her window and he heard the wind come up from the cove and through the

stripped, black trees and low hedges. The car grew cold very
quickly, but he was thinking of hot, still days and the long steam
whistle blast from the sardine cannery, how much he had enjoyed
hearing it three times a day because at that time he loved his
work, and it was the sound of people going to their job. Of
course, he wouldn't hear it now, even if it were seven or noon or
four, because the cannery, they had said at the restaurant in town,
had shut down years before. He remembered hearing the whistle
as they sat on the lawn in the sun and told each other silly, familiar stories about the four of them, and traded the news of one
couple for that of the other while Wesley, his and Nan's son,
labored to draw water from the well and then pour it back down,
or collected what Sandy had instructed him to call squaw wood,
fallen limbs from trees across the mostly unused road.

"I'd call it sordid, really," Nan finally said, closing the window.
"Or sad?"

"And sad," she said, a little less angrily.

They had first slept there the summer after Sandy and Leah
came up from New York and bought it for a very low price. It
had been left unoccupied for a long time, and Leah, showing
them the house, had said, "It's like the Goldilocks thing, you
know? You come in here and it's yours, but it still feels like *they're*
coming back any minute. Any minute, somebody comes through
the door and asks you who's been eating their porridge."

"Did you find any porridge?" Nan had asked.

"There are great old Homer Laughlin bowls for it in the
kitchen," Leah said, pointing out metal beds and thick, patterned
quilts that smelled of mildew, white china chamber pots, and a
basket filled with *Collier's* and *Reader's Digest*. She said, "Sandy's a
little nuts on account of there are all these very good tools, all

kinds of clamps and files and levels he has no idea how to use. They're pretty, though—you know, sculptural. And they're trimmed with brass and they have these handles gone amber from somebody's sweat. So he figures he has this artistic legacy responsibility thing to use them."

The house was lighted with kerosene lanterns and food would be cooked in winter on a giant, black wood-burning stove. In the summer they often cooked together outside on a portable two-burner camp stove. They drew their water from the well, and they suffered the dark stink of an outhouse in back. Sandy strode his new property as he had always walked, bouncing on his toes like a boy, but with an evident new satisfaction: he had begun to acquire skills that weren't called for in the filming of current events and documentaries, and he became proficient at cutting and splitting firewood, plucking mussels from rocks in the cove below their property, driving nails true. His light hair, low on his always-wrinkled forehead over blonde eyebrows, gave him his name. But his quicker gait, and his pride in understanding this coastal countryside, his pleasure in denying himself electricity and running water, were new to them and, for a long time, becoming. He seemed to grow broader and taller.

Leah was a still photographer of real skill and reputation, and she appeared, from summer to summer, to grow at Sandy's pace. She usually wore a bikini all of every hot day, sometimes with an open denim shirt against afternoon winds. She was slender and long-faced with dark, glossy hair that she kept in a bun because, Nan told him during their sixth or seventh summer at the place in Maine, it drew attention to Leah's ears which, she had told Nan, came over in the gene pool carried by the *Mayflower* and had stood the women in her family in very good stead. "Unquote," Nan had said after reciting it.

"We're not getting on too well this year?" he'd asked her.

"Sometimes I'm slow in learning my lines again, about being the Cambridge matron come up to Maine for the fresh-caught mackerel and birds and bees. But then, of course, I remember my part, and everything's swell." She had hooked her ankle around his foot, the motion drawing groans from their iron bed in the downstairs front room in which Wesley, in a sleeping bag on the scuffed wooden floor, swam slowly in his deep sleep.

Now, in the car, in the gray-yellow light of December on the coast of Maine, he could see the shingled outside wall of the room. He suspected that the darkness of the shakes was from the creosote he'd applied so sloppily those many years before. Wesley was thirty now and had been six or seven when his father had stripped to the waist and, a little drunk, had slopped the preservative on. Maybe he hadn't done such a miserable job, he thought.

That summer night, in the conversation about Leah's ears which came over on the *Mayflower*, he had whispered back to her, "I would have thought the two of you were on the verge of quarreling."

"She tells me how hard he drove from a shoot in New York City to get up here in June. She tells me how he limped in, just exhausted, but that she needed him to do some carpentry thing in the kitchen."

"She does appreciate what's useful," he'd said.

"That's what I mean," she'd said in a harsh, hissing whisper. "She says, 'All it took was a back rub and a blow job and teeny little nap, and he was ready for his chores.' Jesus. Why should it make me so mad?"

At that time, he didn't know the reason. He said, "It makes me envious." She was running her bare foot up and down his calf. He said, "I did think you were going to slug her when she offered to show you how to clean the mackerel they gave us down at the cannery on account of 'Mackerel sure as shootin' ain't sardines.'"

"It just all of a sudden got a little too full of the hosts' expertise compared to the citified ignorance of their guests. And the utility of the back-rub thing is very annoying."

"I don't know. I wonder if maybe I should start walking on the balls of my feet," he said.

"Dope," she said.

"But this does happen from time to time between couples. Disagreements. Friction. I do think it's all quite fine. I think everything will be fine."

"I suppose," she said.

"And I promise not to walk like Sandy."

And now, in the car as they sat parked before the house they hadn't seen in more than a dozen years, Nan said, "So were we right to come?"

He said, "I think she wrote to Wesley to make sure he'd tell us so we'd know. She was saying goodbye through him."

"That makes it very sad," she said, "telling us goodbye through our kid. That she wanted us to know they were leaving the States for good."

"You're right. It's sad. I think there's a chance they knew, or they were hoping, that we'd end up here."

"You really think so? Because then we did their bidding. They wanted us to sit here in our car and get sentimental."

"I don't know if having sentiments means being sentimental."

"You don't want it to," she said.

"Nobody knows me better than you."

She nodded, looking at the house.

"Or you than me," he said.

She turned quickly, as if his tone had brought her face around. He was remembering the afternoon when he and Sandy took off their clothes after working on Sandy's little one-masted Sunfish down in the cove and they'd stood beneath the outdoor shower bath and hollered as the collected rainwater sprayed them. Leah had come from the house in response to their bellowing, and Nan and Wesley had followed.

"You're all naked," Wesley called.

"Sandy's all *ready*," he heard Nan tell Leah.

"God," Leah said, "Sandy, get *rid* of that thing."

"Now, where am I supposed to *put* it?"

He remembered sitting on the mud beneath the gravity-fed shower and laughing until he lay on his side, weak with what he had always thought of as happiness. The whistle of the sardine cannery signaled the end of the working day. When he was in one of the difficult places he was sent to, he sometimes thought of that sound, and he was aware that he whistled his version of it, over and over, as he wrote the story he would file without saying I. And sometimes his whistling approximation of the real sound would remind him of Sandy erect beneath the shower bath and, in spite of the subject matter he was required to consider, he would feel himself smile as he worked.

"'Now, where am I supposed to *put* it?' Remember?"

Nan let her breath out slowly and she slowly nodded her head, then she leaned back against the window, saying, "They wanted us to remember them in spite of whatever it was that happened to us all. They wanted us to risk the trip."

"Did you think it was a risk?"

"I did. I did."

"I keep remembering Wesley," he said, "looking down the well, dropping pebbles in when he thought Sandy and Leah wouldn't see him. He just wanted to know what in hell was down there on the other end. Maybe that's all we're doing."

"The well's still there," she said. "It looks a lot smaller than I remember."

"All of it does."

"Yes," she said. "I wonder if Leah would look small, or if Sandy would seem, I don't know, ordinary."

"Not Sandy," he said.

"No."

"No," he said.

Once, many summers before, acres of knit, ribbed, dark clouds appeared as they lay on blankets and sunned themselves. They blew in very suddenly and the sun was sealed off, the vegetation grew dark, birdsong paused and then increased in volume, and then rain blew over them for several minutes. Without consulting one another, they remained on their blankets, lying face up, and were soaked. And then the cloud cover blew off, warmth seemed to radiate from the ground, and the arching, immense, almost-vertical leg of a rainbow appeared above the house. He had seen them before, and so had Sandy. They said, almost simultaneously, "Sun dog."

Leah said, "They're having mystical transports again."

"It's how you carry your mysticals around," Sandy said, leaving to return with four small blue glasses in one huge hand and a bottle of Southern Comfort in the other.

They sipped awhile, and then he drank his off and held his

glass out for more. Sandy finished his glass and refilled both of them. They drank and Sandy filled the glasses again. Nan held hers out on the third round and Leah offered hers on the fourth. They went from there as the sun dog faded and then the afternoon itself dissolved into dusk.

Sandy said, "This is very good stuff."

Leah said, "But you could get there on witch hazel, couldn't you, big one?"

Sandy, resting on his elbows, said, "On the occasion itself, the moment of the four friends. And why aren't you bagging us with your Hasselblad?"

Leah said, "Am I the official expedition image bagger? You always do need a still photographer when you run a production. I am *very* sorry I forgot and had a drink with your guests."

Nan said, "We're Sandy's idea?"

Leah didn't answer. Nan stood up and put her shoes on and walked in the direction of the outhouse.

He said, "Leah? What's wrong?"

"Ask Nan," she said.

Sandy, on his back, tried to pour from his blue shot glass held at arm's length above his face into his open mouth. Leah lay back with her eyes closed. And he looked past them at Nan, who stood facing away near the rain-barrel shower bath at the corner of the studio. Finally, he saw, she took a deep breath and seemed to square herself, then turned around to look at the three of them as they lay on the lawn. The sad, composed expression of his wife reminded him of a thin, somber woman he had seen eight or nine years before in Al Fayyum. She had stood outside her Orthodox church, reduced that morning to slivers of wood and lumps of plaster by a bomb for which Egyptian Islamists had taken credit. He had always comforted himself by thinking of the woman as only indirectly a victim—still, anyway, unwounded, alive. But they do receive wounds, he thought, and they feel the shudder of the explosion through the ground and he knew on this winter day that they had not remained the same. He wondered if his son weren't a victim also, for hadn't Leah written to Wesley to say they were emigrating to western Canada? He wondered how many letters or calls they'd exchanged before Wes had told his parents the news.

Nan said, "I want to walk around the outside of the house. Do you think we can?"

"If nobody's home," he said, "why not?"

"How do we find out?"

"Walk around, and get chased or don't get chased."

"You have less fear than I do. Or hesitation. Whatever it's called."

"My manners are bad. I made a vocation out of it," he said. "On the other hand, I got chased plenty and it was always my practice, when chased, to flee. What a vocation all *that* adds up to."

"You went after some stories that people were scared of, and you got a lot of them," she said. "But do stop sounding wintry."

"It's winter, Nan."

"I'm going to trespass. Are you coming with me? Please?"

The wind from the cove was steadier now, and very cold. It was Boxing Day, one day after Christmas, which they had spent in the Blueberry Motel outside of the town where the rivers converged. They had given each other small, simple presents, had spoken by phone with Wesley and his wife, Caroline, and had drunk a bottle of Châteauneuf-du-Pape from good glasses they'd carried in the car from Cambridge. Nan was in her ski parka, but he had come out with only a fleece vest over a turtleneck, and he kept his hands in his pockets against the cold as they stepped from the road to the ice-flecked lawn. She paused at the round well with its wooden cover.

"I was always secretly a little afraid that Wes would fall in," she said. "I didn't want Leah to know."

"So, then, you and she were always suspicious. You were uncertain about each other from the start?"

"No," she said. She said, "Maybe."

"Though she got damned crazy suspicious in the end," he said, "didn't she?"

"Didn't she."

The house was a series of small rooms added on over years, growing sideways from the first broad room in which they and Wesley had slept, the storage attic and master bedroom on the floor above them. Next to their room, separated by a narrow hall, was the kitchen, and beside it, added after the kitchen was built, had come the big shed in which firewood was stacked and tools were stored. Connected to it was a longer, slightly narrower shed that Sandy had converted into a studio for him and Leah. The only electric line on the property had been run into their studio. The roof angles of the little buildings were sharp, and he had always thought of the house as a series of upside-down, beached boats.

They stood at the front door, which he pulled on and which was locked. It was the same wooden frame from their time there, with what seemed to be the same long, narrow oval of sagging metal screen in its center. To the left were the kitchen windows, clouded and curtained. Nan said, "Around here," and they walked to their left, past the room in which they'd stayed with Wes every summer until he was old enough to want to go to camp, although he cried the first year he was away, sobbing over the

phone from the camp nurse's office, while he and Nan stood in a
phone booth and heard that their boy missed Aunt Leah and
Uncle Sandy.

They walked slowly past the four windows in the front, two
on each side of the bedroom's outer door that had always been
locked. He could see the same scuffed floor but with different
braided rugs on it, and a different quilt on the bed they had used.
He remembered a night in that bed, when Leah and Sandy on
their upstairs bed had made drunken love. Their bed rocked and
moaned and it seemed to him that they'd gone on forever. He
hadn't wanted to be stimulated by the sound. Remembering
Leah's back-rub-and-blow-job, he instructed himself that it was
weak and pornographic to surrender to someone else's lust. He
was half asleep, half uncomfortably awake, when Nan's hand
moved on him.

"And I'm embarrassed by it," she said.

"I am, too," he said.

She was moving against him, then, and a sense of illicitness
added to his excitement. "It's not like you aren't somewhat stimulated, big one," she said.

"You don't call me that," he said.

"I don't?"

"Never."

"I'm sorry," she said.

"No," he whispered, "it's just that I'm not the one whose wife
always calls him that."

"No, you're not," she said, moving on him and finally strad-
dling him. "I will never call you that. I'm sorry I did."

"No," he said, rising slowly against her as she rode him, "don't
worry."

"All right," she said. "All right. All right. All right."

Now, behind the house, where there was a chopping block near the back door to the shed, and where shavings and splinters littered the scarred, broad top of the block, they walked slowly over snowy low brush that ran to Leah's small garden which had never produced more than broad, tough beans and rows of lettuce that had always seemed flabby to him but which, like the others, he had eaten with false relish in order to praise her. Behind the garden patch, spreading out toward the church, were blueberry barrens. He had never seen them in the winter, and their glowing, deep orange-tinted maroon seemed to him the coarse pelt of an animal.

"Her and her fucking lettuce," Nan said.

"Worst salads in the whole Northeast."

"She couldn't help it, though," Nan said. "She needed to be praised."

"She was praised plenty," he said. "She exhibited in shows, she got assignments, she got paid. And Sandy spent half of every day raving about her in her bikini, even after she got stringy and subject to the law of gravity."

"No, it was something with her father," Nan said.

"I always wondered about him. He was one of the seven worst men I ever met."

"Worse than Arafat?"

"Worse than Yasir Arafat and Ariel Sharon *and* the Vice President of the United States."

"Somebody should have made *them* eat her salads," Nan said.

"We ate and drank a lot together," he said. "Years and years of decent chow and certainly enough bad food, and I guess you could call it a sufficiency of alcohol."

"It made us laugh," she said, capturing his little finger with hers. "And *we* made us laugh. I hated how it ended up." He shivered against the cold and she put her arm around his waist and pulled him into her as they walked to the corner of the house and headed toward the shed. She was wiry and tense and powerful, a good athlete with a longer stride than his. He had worked for so many years, he thought, at keeping pace with her. The wrinkles at the corners of her eyes and mouth had served, once, as accents. Now, the taut, smooth planes of her girlhood face had lost dominion to the deep engravings in the skin. Her face had become her story. So, of course, had his. And even in bed he panted to keep up with her.

The studio windows were covered with muslin curtains, and of course Sandy and Leah had done their work here before digital processing was widely practiced. It made sense that what they did, based on admitting light, would require that they finish it by keeping light out. The studio was one more building closed to them. They couldn't even look inside. But he knew its layout, the wall of shelves, and the opposite wall with a storage shelf that became a kind of bunk when Sandy and he sat up late like overgrown boys, watching televised prizefights and drinking beer, snacking on hot dogs that Sandy boiled in a little aluminum camping pot over a Primus stove. They folded a slice of pulpy white bread, covered with cheap yellow mustard, around each hot dog. Sandy always finished the night by sweeping the shelf clean and groaning his way up and onto it, collapsing into sleep while he, on an old, re-glued rocking chair, blinked and blinked at the little television set before which they had talked, over the commentary and between rounds, about their professional lives, and of course about their wives.

One of these nights was during the years of Muhammad Ali's

slow defeat by age. He sat and Sandy lay and watched the mature man who still, for half a minute or so of every round, was able to evoke the beauty of his early career. They had drunk a lot of beer, and they were heady, he thought, with the sorrow of Ali, and with the memory of his youth, and with the pleasure they took in one another's company.

He had been complaining about the foreign editor's wish that he participate in the television shows, when he was home between assignments, in which reporters pretended to an expertise he believed that none of them possessed.

"You're becoming an old bear," Sandy said. "You growl and say no, growl and say no. You should watch it, or they'll decide to replace you with a kid."

"Sooner or later, whether I watch it or not, that's just what they'll do. Nan says I ought to go along or, I forget which one, maybe get along. Anyway: she says I should watch it."

"You know her arms are stronger than Leah's?"

Ali lay on the ropes, his elbows at his waist and his forearms aligned on his torso, fending off the looping body blows of a fighter who was perhaps skilled enough to serve as sparring partner to an up-and-coming kid.

"I never thought about it," he said. "I always thought Leah was pretty powerful."

"Oh, she is, she is. No, I—well, I don't know."

"Know what, Sandy?"

The chatter of the TV commentator grew a little baroque as he tried to justify the fight he was hired to extol.

Sandy said, "Listen to this guy talk about Ali. But that's what he makes you want to do. You end up saying nobody gets old and fat and slow. You end up *praying* it."

Ali leaned on the ropes and threw three jabs in a row, and the old piston-power of his left hand was evident again. "What, though? About Nan's arms?"

"They're decent arms," Sandy said, "and loyal and true. Don't you ever think different."

"I promise to try and do that," he said.

"Of course you do," Sandy said, "on account of you are a good man."

"You think?"

"And loyal," Sandy said, "and true."

"The outhouse is gone," Nan said. "I just realized it. I hated having to use it. I thought of it as punishment for overeating and for drinking too much and any other bad deeds."

"They must have put plumbing in for a bathroom. So that means they ran electricity in to the rest of the place. After all that somewhat heroic deprivation."

"Too late for us," she said.

They had come to complete their circle at the well, which was a stone housing with a diameter of perhaps a yard over which a round wooden cover, painted forest green, had been set. He remembered how often Wes had hung over the lip of the uncovered well, sneaking his pebbles down, assaying the depth of all that darkness. Wes wasn't there that year, in the middle of August, when, one afternoon, he sat on the lawn with his back against the well house, reading. He remembered that the book was a musing on the Vietnam War by a *Washington Post* correspondent whose courage and honest writing he had very much admired. Sandy sheltered in the studio, editing, and the fight between their wives erupted in the patch of sickly lettuces.

When the wind came up from the cove, it blew against the

house and toward the garden, so he couldn't hear everything and often he heard nothing but tatters of language. But he did hear a good deal, he did hear enough to know that Leah believed that Nan had betrayed her in a fundamental way, and that the friendship between them, the relationship among the four, had foundered. In truth, he thought, as he and Nan paused before the well on this late December day under a pale yellow disc of sun in a pearly gray sky, he had been able to make out more than enough. During all the years of their discussing it, during the autumn that followed that summer's departure from Maine with Nan's face pale except for a crimson place on each cheek, he had insisted on trying to believe that what he knew was limited to what his wife had told him. But he did know some more. He knew enough, and, in the years of the couples' not communicating with each other, he had never said so to Nan.

"Hang on," he said, and he leaned to wrestle the cover off the well.

"I think we ought to hurry up. What if they come home?" she said.

"They're in Calgary, Canada."

"I mean the new owners, and you know it."

"Someone's been eating my porridge, the father bear said."

"Don't be smart."

"No," he said. "Smart has never been my métier."

When the cover was off, he set it beside him and leaned over the well. He could smell the damp stone, the minerals in the water, the icy earth into which the well was sunk. It was what his son had sniffed, and he thought of him, hundreds of miles away and an interesting man, with pleasure. It was as if he were here in summer again, smelling the warm skin of his small boy.

He squatted to feel in the cold, short grass for stones and, collecting a few, he stood to lean again over the well. He dropped one in and listened. Then he dropped another and listened. He thought of Wes and the others, and he tossed one more, waiting until it hit.

"Okay," he said, first working the wooden cover back on, then taking Nan's arm at the upper bicep, where he liked to grip it so that he felt the muscle but also, with his fingertips, the intimate place between her inner arm and armpit.

They drove from the place where they had been young with each other and their boy and with Sandy and Leah. They went past the relics of the burned-down church and its graveyard and he noticed, beyond them, what he had seen in the fields behind the shake-shingled house: that dark red pelt of wintering berries. And later, after they had descended on the narrow, battered road to the town and then had gone through it toward the motel, he saw how some of the blueberry barrens had been burned off, in a kind of crop rotation, he guessed. They looked like giant bruises, black and brown, alongside the healthy glow of the maroon plants.

"It's sad," Nan said, "and I still feel horrible about you and Sandy losing each other. But I'm glad we went there today."

"What about you and Leah?"

"Well, she was my friend for a long time, but I think less of a friend with me than you and Sandy were together. But we all were friends, and then we lost that. It was very terrible."

"Yes, it was," he said. "I remember Sandy and me, before we left, that year. We stood there swallowing, and looking at each other and then away from each other. I couldn't think of anything to say. We had said it all, or we were just too sad to say any more. Finally, he squinted the way he did and he smiled that half-smile that could be anything from crazy, raging adult to overgrown, goofy boy, and he asked me, 'Are we getting through this?' or something like that. He said he was worried that what Leah said to you was maybe just too tough to get around. He said he was sorry that I had to hear that kind of talk and that, next to Leah, I was the person in the world he sided with the most."

"And of course by then I had told you."

"And I had heard a little from the garden. Very little of it. Just the bare bones of what Leah said about Sandy and you."

"Don't," she said. "All right? Don't say it again. I'll never understand why she said it in the first place." She looked out her window at the barrens, the vast dormant reaches and the burned-off swaths. "She shouted at me and cursed at me in that scrawny goddamned garden—I thought she was going to kill me with a trowel. We sat there under her cute-as-pie fucking scarecrow that was wearing Sandy's jeans and flannel shirt, and she kept bouncing around inside her bikini top while she stabbed the trowel into the ground. 'You and my husband,' she kept saying. 'I give you my house and my allegiance, and you and my husband—' It was the worst time of my life," Nan said.

After a few seconds, he said, "Mine, too."

She turned toward him and he felt her study his face. He looked ahead at the two-lane road.

"Really," she said.

"Oh, sure," he said. "It was like being wounded and bleeding out. It felt like everything went."

She said, "It's just that you never said anything like that."

"Maybe I should have said it like that right away," he said. "But look: even though I thought I would, I did *not* die of it." Then he said, "And neither did you." He felt his lips curl, and he knew it was because he had learned, over a long career of fast rides in the cars of frightened stringers and silent patrols with wide-eyed adolescent soldiers, to always cherish the story and to always distrust its teller.

"So we did survive," she suggested.

They drove past a tractor dealership where two bulldozers sat with their steel buckets raised like the trunks of circus elephants. Passing the Blueberry Motel, he noticed that sheets frozen stiff on a taut white line were the same color blue as the cabins they'd been soiled in.

She was waiting—she had been for years, he understood—to learn exactly what he knew. He steered the car economically, following its hood which seemed to him to follow on its own the road's easy loop among the shining blueberry barrens and the acres of burned-off plants. But then it was as if he were alone in the car, driving on the coastal road in Washington County in Maine, en route to saving his wife, who had been trapped somehow and who waited for him. She needed him to arrive, honking the horn to greet her. She needed him to leave the engine running while he brought her into the warm car and saw to her seat belt and locked the doors and put the car in gear. She needed him, he knew, to make her his passenger.

She asked, "Didn't we?"

He was alone and heading toward his wife. He composed an answer on the way.

SENSE OF DIRECTION

P racticing with no pleasure and little achievement, Alex heard through the wall behind their upright piano the coughing and complaints of his father's patients, and his father's rumbling singsong of counsel, interrogation, and command. He struck the climbing and descending scales of the composition—*I have a lit-tle pup-py dog . . . A lit-tle pup-py dog have I*—in reply to the rise and fall of Dr. Schantz's voice. And now, more than a dozen years later, at the end of his junior year, Alex replied to his father again by traveling on the faded, dusty plush of the Lehigh Valley Railroad, looking out of a clouded window at the spiky brush that grew through the roadbed's chunky brown stones. He smoked a Raleigh and, thinking of his father, he relished it.

In Alex's last year at Midwood High School, his father had delivered a mealtime address. Often, adjusting his tie, and staring at a plate of the dark, middle-European food his mother had cooked—he remembered rich, rubbery chicken gizzards with especial distaste—his father briefly lectured on matters of public health and private hygiene. This evening he had spoken of "Little chest colds, major-league bronchitis, pneumonia with possibly a collapsed lung, you could break a rib coughing, you know, and that's just for starters. Starters, Alex. We haven't begun to discuss emphysema, or cancer that starts in the lung and goes to the brain. But you go ahead and smoke your cigarettes."

Alex was in love with the flare of the match, the bite of the smoke as he drew it in, and the sighed-out stream of oily smoke that curled and drifted in the light. This was the time of his life, he would think, years afterward, when much of what he did was because it felt very good and because there were risks—in the smoke and a good deal of drink, and in the girls against whose sweated skin he lay and into whom he was invited to plunge. His father spoke gravely and walked ceremoniously, slow feet falling heavily, a solemn expression on his raw, square face. Alex thought it possible that he, on the other hand, might swagger like his Uncle Vincent Ostrovsky.

And it was because of what his father said about Uncle Vincent that he had put underwear and a clean shirt into an athletic bag along with his toilet kit and a couple of books he knew he'd fail to study during the weekend ahead, then had taken a cab from campus to the station in Easton, and had sat down to smoke while he traveled the sixty miles to New York.

His mother had grown up on the Lower East Side of Manhattan, and as a young woman she had lived in Greenwich Village. When he was seven and eight, in 1948 and 1949, the names of groups she'd belonged to—Youth Against War and Fascism, Ethical Culture, the Art Students League—came into the air of their kitchen in Brooklyn and, when they did, he knew that she'd soon chivy him into putting on his good corduroys and a clean seersucker shirt and then take him for a trip to what she called New York.

She meant Manhattan, of course, separated from them by the East River and reached by subway. In the 1940s, a woman traveling into Manhattan would put on a good dress, such as his mother wore when teaching high school in Brooklyn, and she would wear uncomfortable, dressy shoes, and she would put on white gloves—cotton if it was summer, leather if autumn—and, often, she would take her eight-year-old son by the hand and walk to the Avenue H station of the line then called the BMT, the Brooklyn-Manhattan Transit, where you paid a nickel apiece to get through the broad, wooden turnstiles and climbed to the elevated tracks.

In a time of many uncles, Uncle Ben was the taller of the two grocers who ran the store near the station, and Uncle Sidney was the shorter one with his hair pasted down. There was another Uncle Ben at the Avenue J butcher shop where he sometimes was sent for lamb shanks or tripe or stewing beef. These uncles were fixtures in a neighborhood where a boy could run errands by bike or browse among comic books which took up an entire wall, and cost a dime, in Uncle Howie's newspaper shop. In Manhattan, they very often visited Uncle Vincent, who lived in a long room in a cobbled courtyard where the iron gates were kept locked. As a boy, Alex created waking dreams about castle keeps and courtyards, about slipping through the gates, as Uncle Vincent unlocked them, just in time to evade the onrushing hordes. He was never certain what constituted a horde, nor what kind of speed onrushing meant, but he did move quickly through the gates as Uncle Vincent opened them.

Alex had seen Vincent at work in this studio, hammering at wood and stone, and he had watched him, often, sketching someone while Aunt Vladja, who wasn't always around, played the piano. She was tall and wore her golden hair in a coil at the back of her head. Her long neck, he would later remember, was arched, as if she were dancing, and her prominent nose rode almost parallel to the keyboard as, with very long fingers on very large hands, powerful enough to rise, arched like her neck, against the weight of many rings, she played something that his father would call Russian and morose. Aunt Vladja was Uncle Vincent's wife, the boy believed, although he wondered why a wife was away from home so much and especially when he and his mother paid a visit in New York.

"Sylvia," Vincent would say at the gate. "My little Reubens, Venus to fit in my pocket, I could carry you about. And Alex! The Prince Regent himself! Please. Come inside, you'll let my day begin."

Alex's mother was short and abundantly curved. His father at one time seemed always to touch her arms and shoulders, and their son, years later, would think he remembered that sometimes his father's fingers brushed the start of the swelling of her breasts, then slid away. They stopped touching each other very much at about the time of these trips to the city. But this was how Uncle Vincent touched Alex's mother when they took the subway to New York.

He was a broad-shouldered man who wore wrinkled white shirts with rolled-up sleeves and dark trousers with stains. He had small feet in brown loafers and very powerful hands. His wavy, white hair was as high as the crown of a hat. He and Vladja lived in the studio, which was a long room with several sculptures on wooden stands, and a broad, black piano. At the other end of the far wall, close to the stove, was a wooden bed that was shaped like an enormous horse-drawn sled. There were a very small refrigerator, two wooden chests with leather straps, a bureau, and some chairs and lamps. Vincent made coffee with brandy poured into it, he opened a heavy, small, green bottle of Coca-Cola for Alex, and he drew pictures of his mother, and sometimes of him, and Alex was permitted to bounce his pink Spalding in the courtyard while they talked. This required excellent aim, for he had to land the ball on the mortar between the courtyard cobbles to keep it from bouncing every way except straight up. Like the courtyard gates, the door to the studio always was locked, and he would need to ring the doorbell and wait and wait until one of them came to let him in.

"And you didn't get lost," Uncle Vincent would call from the far end of the studio, where he poured coffee at the wide, black stove.

"I never get lost in the city," she said.

Vincent laughed. And Alex remembered how she would stand at an unfamiliar street corner, reciting to herself in a breathless whisper, "If this way is downtown, then east is across the street, and Fifth is two blocks over. That's all right. That's fine."

"Nearly never," he said, and Alex smiled for the pleasure on Vincent's face.

"Maybe in the Bronx, I would, I suppose," she said, "but not down here. Well."

"Yes. Well, dear Venus."

She shook her head. "Actually, anyplace else. I still get lost in Brooklyn. But never here. This is home."

"I remember," Vincent said, "you came in for the first time after you moved out to your very grand dacha in Brooklyn. Can you remember so far back?"

"Of course."

"And you were worried about the subway directions? You hadn't ever taken the train from what-you-may-call-it, Midwood, over to the Village. Your Philip was writing you out a set of directions to come and go back. Or is it going and then coming back? He wrote on a pad from his office, I remember. *Philip Schantz, M.D.*, and you held it like a what-you-may-call-it, a prescription—that was it. On his prescription pad, he wrote it. Like medicine. Sylvia, did you take your medicine?"

He looked at her across the long studio, and she looked back. It was quiet, all of a sudden, and Alex bounced the Spalding and headed for the door.

"Be careful," his mother said. But she was looking at Vincent.

Alex said, "I will," and he meant it: he thought of the onrushing hordes outside the gate.

She said to Vincent, "Yes, I did. As you remember."

"I do," he said, walking back toward Alex's mother while the door closed, "I remember very well."

Sometimes his mother made lunch at the studio, sometimes they went out on the town. That was how Vincent referred to it. His favorite restaurant was on a tiny curving street and part of its name was Mill. Alex could never find it when he was a young man taking girls out to eat; each time he tried, he found himself calling it out on the town, but he couldn't get back there because, like his mother, and even in Manhattan, he was able to get lost with remarkable ease.

Usually, she was pale. His father called her anemic and urged her to take iron supplements. But when they went to the city, she always looked shiny and flushed, and especially when they were out on the town or in Uncle Vincent's studio. He would talk about Aunt Vladja's concerts and he would curse the critics.

"They make her crazy," he said, "and then she must of course make *me* crazy. I am saying to these bastards—the Prince Regent will excuse my idiom?—I beg them, 'You give her a decent review, something fair, even, and she doesn't turn my brain into what-you-may-call-it, hamburger meat.'"

"Chopped chuck," Alex told him, remembering his errands to the Uncle Ben of Avenue J.

"Precisely," he said, "and I thank you. Of course, there is a setback, there then has to be on the side an *affaire* of great importance—a tuner? a player of the fiddle? who knows!—and much perspiration, gone for a week, only General MacArthur knows where anybody is."

Alex's mother smiled a smile he rarely saw and Uncle Vincent stopped talking, lay his head nearly on his own shoulder, and said, "Don't move." He turned a page of his drawing pad and pulled a pencil from the pocket of his dirty, white shirt. Alex watched as his mother, transformed, appeared on the page before him.

Uncle Vincent kissed them each goodbye on the cheek, then walked with his shoulders wagging one way as his head moved in the other, like a man who listened to a catchy music, back to his studio to work. "He'll chip at one of those pieces of marble," Alex's mother told him, putting her white gloves back on, "and he will make something where there was nothing. Imagine. Are we walking north?"

During that late summer, Alex was permitted to attend the early hours of a social Friday evening with a couple named the Gelbs and Vincent and Vladja. He was made much of by Mrs. Gelb, whose tendency to think him clever he cultivated, while Mr. Gelb liked to teach him chess moves and then defeat him in game after game. "A-*ha*!" Mr. Gelb would shout as they sat on the bench of the upright piano, the board between them, moving to place him in checkmate. He was a teacher of English in a preparatory school the faculty of which, he often reminded them, included only one Jew besides himself. If Alex were to threaten his king, he would announce, "The further persecution of the Jews."

Alex's father silently made drinks, and he silently carried them in from the kitchen wearing his brown tweed sport coat and maroon woolen necktie, with a striped dish towel hung over one shoulder. Alex sensed that he was uneasy at these gatherings until everyone, including himself, had consumed several drinks. He prepared Rob Roys for Alex's mother, with two maraschino cherries that bobbed in the dark drink, and Alex was pleased that what she drank was named after a warrior. His father drank from squat glasses of a clear liquor that looked like the dreaded mineral oil and was known as *schnaps*. He enjoyed watching him hold the little glass, filled to the brim, conveying it slowly to his mouth, then tipping his head back and pouring the drink, as if into another steady glass vessel, over past his lips. He did this often on such social evenings, remaining quiet while his guests and his wife drank more and grew noisy.

"It's a taxicab!" Alex called into the laughter and talk. "In front of the house! A taxicab!"

His father walked to the heavy, carved front door, his mother stood behind him in the hall. Mr. Gelb asked, "Is it drawn by a lathered horse? Is there a pale, spectral stranger inside? Does he carry a gleaming scythe?"

Mrs. Gelb said, "Don't be jejune."

Mr. Gelb answered, "Don't be provincial."

His father said, "Behold the soul of Russia, brooding, burdened, and giving somebody hell."

There was Vladja, standing outside the open front window of the cab, leaning to berate the driver while Vincent staggered up their walk under what seemed to be the great weight of a package wrapped in brown paper and tied with string. Alex stood behind the bristly green sofa, looking out of the living room window, wondering if Vincent had brought him a marvelous toy. In preparation for the receipt of his gift, he moved toward their small hall.

"Philip," Vincent groaned at the door, "stand back and let me set down this immense obligation I impose by presenting it to you." By the time Alex had reached them, Vincent was using a long-bladed pocketknife to gently cut the string from the paper that covered something he would know, years later, to be four and a half feet high. It rocked slightly and his mother gasped. Vincent said, "No, Sylvia, it will stand. But I will provide for you a block of wood—a what-you-may-call-it. A pedestal. Unless you choose to toss it into the rubbish. Well. Philip couldn't be carrying such weight the way I do. I suppose by rolling it . . . Hello, Dorothy," he said to Mrs. Gelb, "and good evening, Hesch," he called to Mr. Gelb, who remained at the piano bench around the corner in the living room, invisible to them at the door.

Mr. Gelb chanted, "It's the *Russians*, Phil. Count your *silver*ware."

By then, Vladja was in the hallway, taller than anyone there, her long neck arched, her expression majestically grim. "This driver: displaced person formerly of Karlovac, some good distance south of Zagreb. You are knowing it?"

"Displaced," Alex's father asked, "or a fascist on the run, like so many of the Croats?"

"I am not knowing," Vladja said, scorning the question or his father or the driver of the cab. "I *am* knowing what *he* is not knowing. He is not knowing Brooklyn. He is not knowing way to drive across Brooklyn Bridge, and he is not knowing, once we have demonstrated him—'There you turn, then there onto Fulton, then Bedford Avenue here'—is how to count streets, apparently, down from Bedford to Ocean Avenue, Nineteenth Street, Eighteenth, and then so on. This is a man takes money for services? He asks me, 'Lady: how come no tip?' When I instruct him, he debates with me. I tell him, 'Sir, I am not debating with servants. I am artist. These hands—'"

Mr. Gelb called to them, "Those hands have plucked at foreskins in every major city of every great nation in the world."

"Hesch!" Mrs. Gelb said.

"Let me make you another highball," his father said.

"Gelb is addressing me?" Vladja asked.

"Show us," his mother said, her voice low, her fingers touching the brown paper.

"For you, Sylvia," he said, delicately pulling the paper away. It was a life-sized dog or a wolf, its long, tapered muzzle pointing straight up, its eyes halfway closed, the smooth white marble of its neck and face growing from a column of coarse, pebbled stone. "Not far from Houston Street, they are tearing down a bank to make—what else?—a new bank. Capitalism is the national disease, so why would lower Manhattan be immune? This is one of the steps. It used to be. Then? Stolen by the mad sculptor who almost grew himself a hernia, taking, carrying off in what you must call the dead of night to his studio. Then looking. I am looking at it and looking at it. This, you know, is what we do. We look."

"He looked so long, I thought it was naked woman," Vladja said, walking from the hallway to the kitchen where ice then tumbled into glasses. "I thought it was rival for—what is that, Sylvia?"

"I wouldn't know," his mother said.

"Ah!" Vladja said, "I am remembering. Of course. Rival for my affections, I should say. Yes? He looked and he looked."

"It is what we do," Vincent said. "And I let the tools approach the stone, then. Only then. And then I barely touched the chisel to the stone. It was like lovers. Did I dare? I dared, finally, but I was—ah, I was *timid*," he said, smiling large white teeth, his eyes bright, his face ruddy. Alex watched his father tip his empty *schnaps* glass and hold it at his mouth as if he hoped that it had filled again. He heard Mrs. Gelb whisper something to his mother. He saw that his mother only looked at Vincent and the statue he had brought.

"But not for long," Mr. Gelb called. "I'll bet not timid for long."

Vincent said. "Heschie, we are required to work, yes? I approached the stone after long what-you-may-call-it."

"Contemplation," his mother said.

"Exactly," Vincent said.

"Oh, exactly," Vladja said in the kitchen.

"Touching it like it is lover's belly, or her breast. Not to listen, Alex. And the stone was telling me soon enough, now, what was in it. What would appear. This. *Homage to Venus*."

"Mother Macree," Mr. Gelb said.

His father said, pointing at the sculpted animal, "Well, anyway *he* knows which way is up."

"It's primeval," his mother said.

"This is good?" Vincent asked.

"Oh, yes," she said. "Good."

"Philip," Mrs. Gelb said to his father, "drinks. Many more drinks."

Vladja said, "Commands! Like Arturo setting tempi."

Mrs. Gelb said, "You performed with Toscanini?"

Vincent, smiling, said, "There is time, still, for this. For good fortune, always time."

"Until they knock on your door and take you to the cattle cars," Mr. Gelb said.

Mrs. Gelb said, "Vladja, did you tip the poor Croatian or not?"

"He is lucky I am paying fare," she said, entering the hall from the kitchen. "Here," she said to Vincent, "have highball. You are glowing too bright. Cool down."

The ride to New York, which he would think of years later, began with a call from his father, received on the wall phone of his junior-year dorm. "Shchantz! On the hook!" someone shouted up the stairs.

"So," he finally thought to ask his father, "how's everything?"

"Everything is good. Good."

"Mom's good?"

"She's good," his father said.

So everything was wrong. His father didn't call, he sent notes—sometimes with checks, often with newspaper clippings of stories about threats to health, especially sexually transmitted diseases—but he didn't phone.

"Good," Alex said.

"And you?"

"I'm good," he told his father.

"Great. Great. Listen: just in case you were thinking of coming home in the next few weeks—"

"I have assignments up *here*," Alex said.

"I figured. But in case."

"Right."

"Don't."

"Don't come home?"

His father said, in tones that Alex thought of as professional—as if Alex were afflicted and his father were telling him precisely with what—"I would advise you not to come home."

"Don't?"

"Do not. Yes."

"Am I banished, Dad?"

"Never. Don't be ridiculous. It's your mother."

"*She* doesn't want me home?"

"I'm giving you advice. I'm advising you that it's very difficult at home right now."

"Is she sick?"

"Not in the sense you mean, no."

"Are you?"

"I'm a little bored and, as I understand it, often rather boring. But my health is fine, thank you."

"What, then?"

"Alex, Vincent Ostrovsky's the one who's ill."

"I took somebody to his studio to meet him! I mean, recently. Well. A while back. At the end of last year, last spring. I took a girl named Jean."

"And Vincent made much of her?"

"Well, you know, he was very Old World, very courteous, he took her wet raincoat off and hung it up like it was a floor-length mink."

"Palpating her chest along the way," his father said flatly.

"She liked him, I remember. He showed us sketches of Mom."

"Was she asleep in any of them?"

"Asleep? Jesus, Dad. How would—"

"Come on, Alex."

"Yes."

"Yes," his father said. "And he was a little pale, and a little thin."

"Yes, he was. I thought it was, you know, getting old was all."

"Prostate cancer."

"That's . . . down there."

His father snorted. "That's where it is."

"Is he in pain?"

"Not all the time."

"Are you taking care of him?"

"He isn't my patient, no. I've tried to give him advice. I've put him in touch with people. You did know Vladja's long gone."

"He never told me."

"He told us. He told us and told us. He did a very nice bust of her, recently. Some shining, dark-colored stone. *Homage to a Loose Screw*, I called it. Your mother didn't entirely appreciate either my title or the sculpture itself. Are you understanding what I'm telling you?"

"I don't know, Dad."

"I can't make it clearer."

"And I shouldn't come home."

"Not this weekend, my friend. It's a little grim around here."

"Will you call me when it's all right?"

"Don't sound so bereft," his father said. "You're not an orphan. You aren't homeless. And we might yet be a happy family again."

"You think?"

His father said, "There's a chance."

"Jesus, Dad."

"It's a chance," his father said. "Nothing's guaranteed, my friend."

He could afford a round-trip ticket on the Lehigh Valley Railroad through New Jersey into the city, and he smoked his Raleighs and remembered the trips on the BMT to New York. From Penn Station he took the subway and rode in the wrong direction, traveling uptown to Times Square, then changing trains in great haste to travel down past Thirty-fourth to Twenty-eighth to Twenty-third to Union Square, then Eighth. Outside, he walked until he found himself at Christopher Street, then turned to walk back east but went too far, not stopping until he reached Mercer, a street unfamiliar to him, where he realized that he was breathing faster, as if he had been loping. But he was not in a panic. He assured himself that he wasn't, and he breathed deeply, walking back the way he had come until he saw the Eighth Street Book Shop, its window filled with *Catch-22*, and then, a block later, a record shop with its austere window display: one copy of Coltrane's *Africa*. He remembered these stores, so he grew confident, but he turned uptown by mistake, forcing his face into what he thought of as bland self-assurance—he didn't want anyone to think of him as lost—and he stopped at Eleventh Street to turn back. By accident he came to Washington Square Park. It seemed abandoned. He thought he remembered people playing chess and singers with guitars, but he saw mostly old men nodding under layers of torn, dirty overcoats and a limping, dark dog that chased squirrels, barking with a shrill yelp.

He walked each side of the park but he couldn't find the hotel he thought he remembered from his weekend there with Jean. He drifted across the Village and by accident, on East Tenth Street, came to the Hotel Albert, where, pretending to a great confidence that he thought he ought to possess, he took a room that smelled of heated laundry starch and tobacco. It would cost him most of his money, he thought, for this hard chair on which he sat and for the mauve rug, the bed with its matching mauve coverlet, and the window that he looked at but not out of. He tried to explain to himself, so that he could tell his father, if he had to, or his mother, or Vincent himself, why he had come. He looked at the indentations of his shoes on the soft, chalky carpeting and he thought of saying, "You just go where you have to." He stood, suddenly, and left the room, as if fleeing the footprints and the half-cooked thought.

It was close to dusk, and because most of the buildings were low, he could see the New York sky which tonight was a neon cherry on darkest blue. Its brightness made the streets seem grim and gray and unfamiliar as he searched, but with little memory of the Village streets, for Vincent's courtyard gates. He found a set on Greenwich Avenue, but they seemed to lead only to the backs of shops. On Sixth Avenue, he saw several single gates, but they felt wrong, and then, wandering west, he came to Patchin Place, with its wrought-iron fence, but he knew that it was not the one he had crossed through when he was a boy. He wished that he could ask for directions, but he could not imagine how to describe where he wanted to go. So he forced himself to stand still, swallowing in unchewed bites a searing slice of pizza near West Fourth, and watching people walk with a purpose that he coveted. He skirted the park again, walked along Sheridan Square, crossing Seventh Avenue South. He turned to walk on Bleecker Street and stopped to watch as a tall black woman pushing a baby carriage unlocked a set of wide wrought-iron gates on the cobbled courtyard he ached with.

It took Vincent several minutes to come to the gate in response to the buzzer. He moved slowly, and he looked small. "Alex," he said breathily, as if his lungs were weak, "the Prince Regent arrives unannounced."

"Is that all right, Vincent? To kind of drop in?"

Vincent said, "You can kind of drop in whenever you like, Alex. You can kind of come inside. Here. Come. Come upstairs and talk to me. Your mother sent you?"

He turned before Alex could answer and led him to the door to the studio steps, which was closed but not locked. They trudged up, and he could hear Vincent's whistling breath. Once inside the studio, he clapped his large hands and rubbed them vigorously, offering a choice of coffee or what he called overrated Armenian brandy. Alex had been reading Saroyan's *Daring Young Man on the Flying Trapeze*, which made him feel strangely optimistic about being, probably, bound for an early death, so he accepted the brandy. Its dark, acidic power pleased him. This, he felt, was the flavor of a solitary voyage to a vast city in which one wanders, lost. He lit a cigarette and Vincent stood, took a bright red saucer down from a shelf, and placed it on Alex's leg.

They sat in the old leather club chairs near the sleigh bed, with its soiled-looking sheets unmade. It was an intimacy that embarrassed Alex, but he found himself drawn to look at it.

"I didn't hear from you a long time," Vincent said.

"School's been kind of busy," Alex said, flicking ashes into the red saucer.

Vincent pumped an arm and said, "Your parents tell me you are busy representing the Czar's army among the maidens of the college. There are still maidens in colleges?"

"There is still a Czar's army?"

"Ah. Riposte and en garde, young swordsman. You know swordsman? You understand the meaning?" He pumped his arm again. "You were the sweetest boy, Alex. Your mother adored you. She adores you still. But now you are large, you are independent, she wonders what is the use of being the mother. I say to her, there is no choice. Be something, I say, while *also* the mother. She points to Vladja, who is not there to be pointed at, not here, not anywhere, and she says she cannot play piano like that one or be suddenly—what? the woman of science? What would I have her do?

"Here," he said, "more of the awful Armenian. They are famous for their imitation Cognac and for their suffering. The suffering they do better, but drink anyway, yes? And this I must confess to you, you are of an age, as they say. You are what-you-may-call-it, a *burly* fellow. This, maybe, now, you can understand. I say to your mommy, 'Come live with me. Be muse. Be mistress and muse.' I call her Pocket Venus, you knew that. Yes? Remember?"

His gray-white face grew redder as they drank, and he leaned forward in the big chair to touch Alex's knee, to reach farther at one point and pat his cheek—this was while he said "mistress and muse"—and then he sat back, breathing with his mouth open, staring with his bright, small, very dark eyes as Alex tried to formulate a reply.

He was conscious of taking a breath before he said, "You're each other's lovers, right?"

"Were, sonny. We were. Oh, yes." He looked patient, exhausted, and very pleased. "We got older. It wasn't our fault. We were looking up at each other one afternoon, and there we were. Not so young. Old, maybe. I thought it wouldn't make us sorry, but it did."

"Sorry for what you did," Alex said.

Vincent opened his lips and Alex expected to be laughed at. But then he closed his mouth and, although his eyes seemed merry, his expression was sad. "I am sorry we couldn't be sorry, if you are hoping for that. But we were sad because the time was passing. Passed. Not only an afternoon in the bed, Alex." He looked at the sleigh bed and Alex looked away from it. "What I am saying—" Vincent stopped and studied him.

"I shouldn't be hearing this," Alex said. He lit a cigarette. And then, because he knew he still was a kid, he asked, "Should I?"

Vincent said, "Surely, this is why you came to visit Uncle Vincent. Or maybe because of your mother. The story about us: this is not for boys. When you are older—very soon, you will be plenty older—you will maybe want to tell it to somebody else that they would weep for your mother, your father, and me. Or smile. Who knows? I wouldn't know. I strike stones with a chisel. Who knows from telling things? We should drink some more Armenian."

"Are you all right, Vincent?"

"You are a darling boy," he said. "Thank you. Not entirely all right, but not dead. But not entirely in the purple."

"Pink?"

"Yes?"

"I think it's 'in the pink.'"

"So," Vincent said. "I wonder why." He shrugged. "So," he said, filling each glass, "we are now in pink. In *the* pink. A little bit of cancer seems to be the problem. Your father was helping with it. A gentleman, you know. A patient man. And this cancer goes along for years. Then they have to cut you or you die. And when they cut you, still you die. Also, they need to poison you with atomic what-you-may-call-it, and then you die anyway. I told

him, 'Philip, no thank you. But thank you.' He called me gallant
and stupid. I am feeling afterward like a Cossack, gallant and stupid, except of course artists and Jews do not ride a horse. Still.
Your father, though, was good to me. This you should remember.
But you came all the long way to find this out? He could have
told you."

"I needed to see you," Alex said. "I couldn't tell you why."

"You are such a sweet boy, and I repay you with this cruel
liqueur." Alex lit a cigarette, they drank, and Vincent laid his head
against the high, soft back of the chair and closed his eyes. Alex
did the same. They sat in the silence of the studio, removed from
the noise of feet or wheels on the surface of the city, and Alex
soon found himself afraid to look out of the quiet and darkness
into which he leaned. He was certain that he would see Vincent
dead in his chair.

In his late thirties, he would find the pages after his mother's
death, a half a dozen years after his father's. He would be cleaning
out their rooms before selling their house to an Ashkenazi physi-
cist, recently come from Israel to Brooklyn to teach at Midwood
High. In the drawer containing his mother's stockings and her
underwear, he saw, folded in half and secured with a bobby pin,
three sheets torn from his father's prescription pad: instructions
to his mother on how, fresh from Manhattan and afraid of getting
lost, she could travel back to what she thought of as home.

He read his father's cramped, slanted handwriting in blue-
black ink. There was no heading. *Take Brighton Beach local from
Avenue H or Avenue J station on* <u>uptown</u> *side. Stay on this train—it
will be a local. Past Newkirk, Cortelyou., Beverly, Church, etc. Tunnel or
bridge train goes to Manhattan. Pass Whitehall, Rector, Cortlandt, City
Hall, Canal, Prince, then 8th St. If ride past, don't panic. Change for*

downtown train at Union Square, one stop uptown from 8th. If do this, just remember Brighton Beach line—same as when coming home. Leave 8th St. station & walk <u>west</u> to Sixth Ave. Home free. Then in pencil, his father had added, *Can call whenever need to if worried about getting lost.* It was signed with his initial, *P.*

Alex sat in the silence of the studio, frightened that Vincent had died. He felt the heat of his cigarette, and he blindly tamped it on the saucer, then opened his eyes to check on the coal. He saw Vincent watching him. He remembered the night in the forties in Brooklyn, the sculpture made from the savings bank step. *This, you know, is what we do. We look.* Vincent's expression was soft, familiar, and comforting. It was the face of a parent who studies his sleeping child. But it was his mother's face, Alex thought, or at least the set of her mouth and the lift of her brows. He thought about how often, and with what intensity, Vincent had studied his mother's face.

Before he understood that he would do it, he set the red saucer on the floor and took a step to stand beside Vincent's chair. He bent to embrace his shoulders and head, smelling stale skin and talcum powder, and then he kissed the thick, white, wavy hair on top of his head. Vincent sat stiffly, then softened, and then he patted Alex slowly, rhythmically, on the rump until Alex, releasing him and standing back, said, "I have to go."

Vincent looked up with eyes that were his own again. He said, "You know the way?"

"To what?"

"You can find your way back?" Vincent asked.

Alex would remember that he answered, "Oh, sure."